Hunger

Stasia Black

Prologue: The Wedding

My husband-to-be and I have barely talked in the past three weeks, ever since our abrupt engagement was announced. My heart thumps so fast and so loud I can hear it in my ears.

I'm standing behind an archway of hydrangeas and lilies in my beautiful wedding dress, Grandfather at my side. It's a gorgeous ballgown organza white dress with crystal embellished lace on top. It's cut low while still being modest, with off the shoulder cap sleeves.

I feel like a princess. Which I am. Princess to a dynasty of vampires, even if I'm not one myself. No, I'm just a whole other bag of creepy. On a day like today, I feel it more than ever. And all I ever wanted was to be *normal*.

I should be standing here with my father, who should be whispering in my ear how proud he is of me and how much he hopes for my future happiness.

Instead, Grandfather Vlad chortles as he pushes me forward by the small of my back. "Go. Produce me good, strong little babies to grow up and be my soldiers."

With that, I'm shoved unceremoniously down the long aisle towards my groom.

All heads turn towards me. There aren't many in attendance. Only one side of the aisle full of the pale faces of my vampire uncles, alternately bored, hungry, or aggravated looking. The other side at least has Layden's family, but I can't quite bring myself to look their direction because all I can do is stare at the floor as I take measured steps towards *him*.

My husband-to-be.

Layden.

He's still as gorgeous as he ever was. It's been hard to be near him since he called last month, needing my help.

After all this time, to hear his voice again... He only called because he had to. His family was in trouble. He had no other choice.

I can't bring myself to lift my eyes to look up at him even as every step brings me closer. I can't believe I allowed Grandfather to trap us in this ridiculous arranged marriage. It was everything I didn't want.

Does Layden still hate me after how we left things ten years ago?

I would.

I climb the small step onto the elaborately decorated staging area where the priest Vlad arranged—more likely blackmailed or blood-compelled into being here—stands.

Layden's black shoes have been polished to a mirror shine. His legs look nice, too.

"Phoenix," his familiar voice whispers. "Are you all right?"

I nod, still not lifting my eyes or my head. I just can't look at him. Not yet. It's all too much. I'm still fighting the impulse to bolt for the door. If Vlad didn't have a blood oath held over Layden's family, I would.

But no. Vlad's got us both exactly where he wants us. Like always.

The priest begins to chant the service. It's a shortened ceremony, I notice, because he quickly gets to the, "Do you take this woman, Phoenix Dracul Tepes, as your lawfully wedded wife?" part.

"I do," Layden says, loudly and solemnly. After hating his brothers for so long, now Layden would do anything for them. Even marry me.

I'm still staring at the floor, but when the priest puts the question to me, I'm finally startled into looking up.

"Do you take this man, Layden Eques, to be your husband, to have and to hold, from this day forward, for better, for worse, for richer, for poorer, in sickness and in health, to love and to cherish, until death do you part?"

I can't breathe. That's so much to promise. How did Layden just say, "I do," so easily?

When my head finally swings up, I find the priest's face. He's an elderly man who looks kinder than I expect. It helps me squeak out, "I do," with the last of the breath in my lungs.

I ought to be looking at Layden, I know. I just promised to have and hold him until death do us part. Which considering we're both immortal beings... is awhile. I'm being cowardly, and I pride myself on my strength, usually.

I can feel his eyes on me.

Still, I can't look at him, even as we exchange rings. I'm proud when my hand doesn't shake as I lift the ring Sabra hands me to slip on the fourth finger of Layden's left hand. His hands are warm. Mine are like ice. I try to touch him as little as possible as I slide the ring over his knuckle, then withdraw quickly.

He lingers, or maybe I just imagine he does, as his warm hands take my left hand in his.

"With this ring, I thee wed, and pledge my love and fidelity."

He just added the last part. That wasn't part of the priest's script, was it? Everything's moving so fast.

Layden's still holding my hand and I blink up at him, confused. His gray eyes are dark with intensity as he stares down at me. Still, I can't read the severe look on his stunningly attractive face.

"You may now kiss the bride."

His eyes search mine for the briefest moment, and then he swoops down and crushes his lips to mine.

My stomach drops to the floor as his soft lips meet mine for the first time. Gentle but demanding. He's kissing me. Really kissing me.

Holy shit, I'm kissing Layden. My brain can't connect the thought together with how my body is coming alive. My fingertips tingle. My toes. My stomach. Between my thighs.

Is it just for show? To please my grandfather and assure him he'll fulfill his part of the deal?

A second later I can't care, because Layden has dipped me low. My fingers dig into his shoulders when the very tips of our tongues connect and I think—oh god, is this what it would have been like to kiss him all those years ago?

Because this feels like the kiss we never had.

When he finally pulls us back upright, I'm blinking and gasping for breath. I tear my eyes away from him because again, I can't bear to see whatever I might find on his face. Was that kiss for revenge? Or because he actually... could he actually feel something for me after all this time?

It's impossible and besides, none of it matters because I can't allow any of this to continue.

I look back to the priest, still breathing hard. My hands are trembling now so I clench them into fists. I can't believe Vlad actually allowed a man of the cloth into the grounds of his compound. No doubt he wants this to be absolutely legitimate in the eyes of the law, so he can have so-called legal claim to whatever offspring Layden and I might produce.

Layden's an angel and I'm... whatever I am. If we had a child, they would be strong, it's true.

Which is why I can *never* allow that to happen.

Chapter One

Phoenix slams the door shut to our newlywed suite and leans back against it, her eyes closed. My new wife is so beautiful in her wedding dress, with her long black hair pinned back, her full lips pink, and her blue eyes flashing.

"Thank fuck that's done with!" she says, expelling a loud breath.

Not exactly the reaction I might have hoped for on my wedding night, but what the hell do I know? I've never done this before. And my brothers' back slaps, winks, and bawdy jokes about not breaking the bed on the first night weren't exactly helpful.

It's ridiculous—we're grown men, thousands of years old, but just because I was last born, they've always treated me as if I'm a perpetual schoolboy. Even though I was the only one of us courageous enough to stand up to our tyrant

1

of a father two hundred years ago. An act I still pay for to this day. There's not an hour that goes by that the wound on my shoulders doesn't ache from where my father cut off my wings with his burning sword. The molten hell-metal he poured overtop them ensured they'd never grow back.

None of my brothers did a thing to stop it, but they still have the gall to try to play the "big brother" act with me? It pisses me off even on a supposed day of unity like today.

My wedding day.

I look over at my bride, who's yanking the pins out of her hair. Her beauty makes me ache in the way I always do when I'm around her. Deep in my empty belly. With hunger. I want to walk closer. I want to touch her.

But my hunger has always been dangerous, so I stay back and ask, "Can I help?"

"Do I *look* like I need help with anything?"

I'll take that as a no.

Today's "celebration" wasn't anything like an ordinary wedding day. More like a merger between two powerful families, solidifying the blood oath that Phoenix's vampire grandfather tricked one of my brothers into. Although no, I suppose the terms of that won't be contractually fulfilled until Phoenix has a baby by me. She's not a vampire, but she's still a powerful being. Any progeny we produce would be highly coveted.

My mouth goes suddenly dry as my gaze shoots toward the central piece of furniture in a newlywed suite Vlad had set up in a north room of the compound—a giant four-poster bed.

"So," I say, and swallow so she can't hear the craving edge to my voice.

Phoenix's head comes up, and she stares at me before pursing her lips. "We might as well go ahead and get it over with." She walks toward me and sits down on the edge of the suddenly looming bed, leaning over to unbuckle the strap of her white high heels.

"Um." I blink a couple times. I will stay calm. I will not be a ravenous beast. "Right."

I shrug off my suit coat, undo some buttons at the top of my shirt and then tug it off over my head. Except I didn't undo enough buttons so it gets caught, and I have to wrestle with it a bit before finally managing to yank it all the way off.

Only to find Phoenix staring at me wide-eyed as I hold my shirt and undershirt awkwardly in front of me. Her eyes dance briefly down to my abs before she looks back at my face. "What are you doing?" she whispers.

"I—" I feel my face heat a little, fist clenching in my shirt. "Do you want some more champagne first to get in the mood?" I glance back at a little set-up on a table near the en-suite refrigerator.

She reaches over to slap me on the shoulder, whispering, "Now is not the time for jokes. Come on, we've got to make this believable. They'll be listening." My shoulder tingles from her touch.

But it's nothing to the low swoop in my groin when she suddenly lets out a loud moan. At the same time, she grabs the bed poster by the top frame and bangs it against the wall.

"Oh," she groans loudly. "Layden, yes. Just like that. Oh god, yes. Right there. Touch me right there!"

My brain short-circuits with lust even though I'm quick to catch on. It's just that her moans are very believable, a little too believable, and I– I shift so that I'm standing firmly against the tall mattress to cover the front of my suddenly tightening pants.

Phoenix waves a hand at me impatiently. Right. Time to pretend I'm not the big bad wolf that I know I am. I don't devour cities. I'm friendly. Nice. *Safe.*

"Baby," I say, and she rolls her eyes. So I deepen my voice, and really, it's not difficult to make my voice low and lust-filled as I lean in and stare into her eyes. "You like it when I touch you there?"

Now she's the one blinking a little, but then she seems to get her wits back, nodding along with another little moan. "Yes, just like that. You make me so wet."

"I can feel it," I say, giving way to my hunger a little too easily as her breath hitches. "Are you ready for me?"

"I'm ready," she says. "You're so big and hard."

It's not what I imagined tonight would be like. Because yes, I imagined tonight. Over and over again. I've been envisioning how tonight will go ever since her grandfather announced we had to wed and make him an heir.

With all my brothers going off and getting consorts and wives, I thought maybe fate had finally intervened for me. I've craved Phoenix since the first time I met her, but craving is nothing new.

I'd thought about getting close to women in the past. I knew I had a handsome enough face, and back before my big white wings were cut off, women were ready to see me as an angelic being or a god, so they wanted to fuck me for a variety of reasons.

But all it took was barely making skin-to-skin contact once and watching the human woman's cheeks begin to cave in with starvation before I leaped away from her. Turns out you can't lie down with the Horseman of Famine without dire consequences.

So I never dared to ever again and rarely even let myself be around humans.

Phoenix and I, well, it had never been like that between us. I'd never allowed it to be. At first because I didn't know who or what she was. Plus, I was such a broken shell of a monster when we met… and then in later years, it seemed too foolhardy to wonder if she was the one woman I might be able to connect with because of her unique heritage.

I never really let myself linger on the possibility, though. For almost two hundred years, I'd had no one in the world, and I'd suppressed any and all cravings. After our first meeting ten years ago, when she helped bring me back to life, I convinced myself she didn't need me ruining her already complicated existence. So we'd shared knowledge and friendship and parted ways.

Until fate brought us back together… or at least a homicidal, angelic AI did. But when her grandfather decreed the blood oath could only be satisfied by us mating, for a few days, I'd felt a wild joy that maybe, just maybe—

I look into her eyes. For once, I tell her—and myself—the truth. "Making love to you is all I've been able to dream about," I say. "Night after night."

"*Louder*," she mouths, gesturing with her hands, and I'm reminded that this is all a farce. She's not really my wife, not in truth. She doesn't actually want this—or me. She never did.

"Oh god," she cries, "You're so big."

She bangs the headboard.

I get it; I really do. Phoenix knows me better than anyone. Better than my brothers. Sometimes, I think she knows me better than myself. I like to think I'd give her the world and more. But maybe I'd only fill her with an endless void so big, she'd never feel full. Never happy or content, I'd suck her dry exactly like her grandfather does his victims, and she knows it.

So I climb up on the bed, still angled away from her and bounce so that the bedsprings squeak.

"Phoenix," I groan loudly, helping her bang the head-board into the wall rhythmically.

"Oh, oh, *oh!*" she cries, higher pitched with every exclamation. Until finally, she screams out my name, "*Laydeeeeeeeeen,*" and we both collapse on the bed. Unsatisfied.

Chapter Two

I run until it feels like my lungs will burst, and only then do I stop, bending over and putting my hands on my knees. But even then, it's not enough. The rage inside me is still too big. So I stand back up and, finally alone with nothing but forest around for miles, I scream at the top of my lungs.

Nope, still not enough. I scream again, brace my arms out in front of me, and run at top speed toward a towering oak tree. I batter into the tree with tremendous impact, knocking its roots from the ground and toppling it sideways. I leap up the trunk as it begins to really fall, stomping on the bark like a furious toddler in a tantrum as it tears through other trees in the forest, riding it on its way down.

I leap off right before it touches down with a thunderous crash on the forest floor, grabbing onto the branches of the nearest tree to break my fall.

I finally land, sweaty and breathing hard, my hair falling into my face and leaves and twigs caught in the strands. The rage inside me is just barely banked. It seems no matter how much I exert myself or scream, I can't get rid of it.

I scream again anyway for good measure.

Back in my real life, I'm never allowed to lose control. Even talking back with a barely elevated tone could be interpreted as disrespectful.

I collapse onto the ground, head in between my arms.

Maybe it's over now. He's lost his leverage over you.

I can feel my own frown, though. Because I can't imagine ever being truly free of my grandfather's control.

But then I pop back to my feet and spin around. There's another heartbeat out here with me in a place where I'm supposed to be all alone. And it's far larger than that of any animal.

Dammit, how did I miss it? Usually, the human heart-beats are such a loud cacophony in the city that they all blur into a white noise that's always there in the background. But right now, there's just a single one besides my own. Even most of the forest creatures have been scared away by the tree I just knocked down.

It doesn't even take much focus to zero in on exactly where it's coming from. Far too close.

I swing around, at first not seeing anything. But then, eyes blink at me from the tree behind me. Immediately, I leap forward, tearing a man from a tree where he's been completely camouflaged.

"Don't touch me!" he calls weakly as he tumbles down face-first when I let go of him. He's so covered in moss and mud I can barely tell what part is the man and what part is the disguise he's covered himself in.

"Did Vlad send you to track me?" I yell furiously.

He just lays, bent at the waist, face down in the mud.

"Answer me!" I demand, using my foot to nudge him.

"Don't," he jerks back away from me, but he's just like a flopping worm with barely any control over his limbs.

What the hell kind of trick is this? I back warily away from him.

"Hey," I shout. "Who are you? What are you doing here?"

He mumbles something. Frowning, I inch forward, finally able to make out what he says. "Leave me."

Is this just a homeless man from one of the villages who came out into the forests and got lost?

I look around. "Are you with anyone? Someone I can get to help you?"

I start to reach down to help him sit back up again. I grab his shoulder, or what I think is his shoulder, considering how caked with mud and leaves he is, and heft him back to sitting leaned against the tree.

It's shocking when the clear whites of his eyes flash up at me, stunning gray irises so alive. This time, he says, "Leave," and his voice is still wan. I'm even more shocked when he half lifts an arm, and white-blue light sparks erupt from his hand. The ghost of strange shapes form in the air but then dissipate like smoke as the man slumps back against the tree, apparently passed out.

I blink once. Twice.

What the hell?

For once, I don't think this actually has to do with my grandfather. Yes, that looked like magic there at the end, but there was no way Grandfather knew I was going to run away, much less that I'd come this direction and happen upon this tree-man. Is he an elf? Some kind of fae?

Are there other magical creatures out there besides my family? Well, and my best friend Sabra, who's a witch. Sabra and I are always theorizing that other beings or spirits might be able to break into this plane like my ancestors did. Just because we hadn't personally run into any didn't mean they didn't exist. Grandfather Vlad had stories of running into... *things*, not that he ever got specific. But he always tried to have a good witch around in his employ for just such occasions.

I bite my bottom lip.

Maybe I should let whatever creature this is alone. He'll do much better if he never gets entwined with my family.

But as I back away, ready to flee in the opposite direction, I take one last look at him. He looks so weak. How long has he been sitting against that tree? I didn't see him at first because he looked like he'd become *part* of the tree he'd been there so long, an unending bed of moss and ivy covering him, crawling around his chest up the tree trunk.

He doesn't seem to have much energy, either.

Maybe I'm not the only one who's run away to the middle of the forest because I don't have anywhere else to go.

In the end, it's not so much a decision as an impulse. I can't just leave him here.

I step forward, heft him into my arms—he barely weighs anything, and what weight he has feels like it's mostly caked on mud and plant matter—and I start jogging.

On my way in, I ran past a remote cabin maybe twenty kilometers back, so I head in that direction. He's motionless in my arms the entire time.

I hate having to drop him at the doorstep of the cabin once we get there, especially when his eyelids flutter, and I read what I think is distress when he realizes I've brought him to a building. He starts shaking his head and mumbling, "No. No people."

"Hush," I hiss at him as I knock on the door. "I'll get rid of them."

His eyes pop open wide, those shocking translucent gray irises flashing, but at least he shuts up.

A man in country attire opens the door. With a shotgun in his hand. He threatens me in the local dialect and gestures for me to get off his property.

"Is your wife home?" I ask him back. "Bring her to the door. Along with anyone else in the house."

His eyes go blank in the familiar way they always do when I apply blood compulsion on someone, and he immediately drops the shotgun to his side and nods.

"Mariana," he calls.

A woman's voice calls back from the other room, along with a yelled something about how he's a fool and she's not even dressed.

But he demands she come again, and several moments later, a grumpy older woman with a handkerchief around her head and a cigarette hanging out of her mouth appears beside her husband.

"Hello," I smile at the both of them. "Please leave and don't come back for a month. Go take a lovely holiday."

Her angry expression drops, and her eyes zone out. I barely even have to think about applying the compulsion these days; it's such second nature when dealing with outsiders.

I pull out my wallet and give them more money than

they probably see in a year. But it's the pressure I put behind the words that has them both walking directly out of the house at my command as the husband silently accepts the money. They head down a little path toward the road beyond.

I watch tree-man's eyes follow them and come back to me. "How?"

I roll my eyes. "You aren't the only one with magic. Now come on, let's see if they've got a hose somewhere out here."

I scan the side of the house and sigh, seeing the water pump in the little overgrown front of the yard. "No such luck," I tell him. "This is going to be cold."

"If I leave you here, will you be here when I get back?" I ask him.

He only looks at me, unmoving, and I narrow my eyes.

"Stay here," I order, adding compulsion, more focused and stronger than I bothered on the couple. Still, will it work on him? Sabra has learned to shield herself against me, something we practiced, but my grandfather Vlad is the only other person it's useless against. I can even wield it against my many, many uncles.

I hurry inside the small two-room cabin and get what I need, including swiping a plate of still-steaming stew off the table. Good timing. We got here just in time for dinner.

When I get back outside, I take a quick breath when I see tree-man has made it halfway across the yard, dragging himself in a pathetically slow army crawl away from the cabin.

"I told you not to move," I say loudly. He collapses to the ground at my voice, giving up what was a truly pathetic attempt at escape.

I walk over to the water pump and drop the soap, towel, and blanket, then head the next few feet toward where he's collapsed, still holding the plate of food.

"You do realize I'm trying to help you," I say, crouching down and rolling him over. He winces when he lands on his back, and I wonder if he's injured somewhere that's hidden by the layers of mud. It did look like something might be stuck on his upper back. But I won't be able to tell for sure until I've gotten him cleaned up.

First things first, though.

"Come on, let's get some food into you."

His eyes fall on the stew in the bowl I'm holding, and even though most of his face is covered in mud, I can see the hunger there. Still, almost as soon as he looks at it, he stubbornly turns his face away.

"What? Don't like stew? I can tell you're hungry."

I sit down on the bed of mulched leaves, the last of the sunlight glinting down through the tall trees overhead, and lift his head so that it's propped up in my lap.

"Come on, you're going to take some sips for me," I say, gentling my voice.

I lift the spoon to his lips, but they stay stubbornly closed.

"Open your mouth," I order, pouring all the compulsion I can into the command.

Still, he keeps his lips stubbornly closed.

Suddenly, I'm so frustrated I shout at him. "Do you want to die? What's wrong with you!"

His eyes flash up to me, and he nods his head once.

I grit my teeth and glare down at him. "Well, too bad, buddy. You ran into me on the wrong day. I'm not leaving until you eat this goddamned stew, and I don't care if I have to force it down your throat. I'm your fucking angel of mercy, and you're going to let me help you."

A noise comes from his throat. It takes me a moment to realize it's a laugh. "Angel?" he asks, voice croaking. His eyes lift toward me with a look I can't decipher. Probably because his face is covered with god knows what.

"That's right," I say. "I'm your motherfucking angel today." And with that, I grab his jaw, tug it open, and shove a spoonful of stew into his mouth.

I expect him to spit it out, but he keeps his eyes locked on mine as he chews a little and then swallows.

His whole body seems to expand with the breath he takes after swallowing. How long, I wonder, has it been since he's let any food pass his lips?

It's not time to question, though. I mean to press my advantage while I have it. I push another spoonful to his lips and then another after he swallows.

He eats half the bowl before I relent. It was a large portion, and I don't want it to come back up after hitting an empty stomach.

"Good job," I say. Those large gray eyes just watch me silently. I have no idea of his age and really, I've only guessed at gender by the width of his shoulders.

"Now let's get you cleaned up, then we'll go get some rest."

"Aren't you hungry?" he asks, more strength in his low voice. I smile down at him. "I'll eat once you're cleaned up."

His eyes seem to watch me warily as I help him crawl back to the water pump.

"It'll be cold water," I warn. "Not pleasant."

He doesn't say anything as I help position him underneath the spout. I move the supplies out of the way, then stand up to work the iron handle of the old-style pump. As I start to pump up and down, clean well water pours out the bottom.

He shivers but makes no move as the water falls over his head. At first, the water makes no difference to the caking mud. So I lean down and take the bar of soap I grabbed from inside to scrub his face.

He allows me, his body still mostly limp.

I'm shocked as the mud finally begins to loosen and wash away. He's young. Far younger than I thought. He's not some old, toothless beggar. He looks to be in his mid-twenties, though it's hard to tell with his long beard. He's so gaunt and bony, I'm shocked he's alive.

His hair is too long and tangled to be washed. I use the scissors I found inside to clip off his gnarled hair, washing it again and again until the brown washes out and to my astonishment, I find it's blond. I do the same to his gnarled beard. I can't remove it completely, but I trim it to about an inch.

He begins helping me as if enlivened by the bit of stew I fed him, clawing the layers of mud off his torso and legs. If he was wearing clothes at some point, they've long disintegrated from being in the elements.

When he turns, bending to modestly wash between his legs where I can't see, I gasp at his revealed back.

Crouched over, he turns his head to look over his shoulder at me.

We share a long, silent look. He knows what I've just seen.

Protruding from between his shoulder blades are two blackened stumps with some sort of garish, bronze-like *metal* covering them—it looks as if it was poured on them while it was hot because there are still drips of it burned into the flesh of his back. Little white feathers stick out around the metal, as if what was once there before is trying to grow back but can't because of the metallic cap.

"Are those—" I reach out unwittingly to touch them.

He yanks away, standing up with his hands covering his manhood. "Do you have a covering?"

I stand up, too, my knees and shins wet with the pool of water we've created underneath the pump spout. But I hurry to hand him the large gray towel I brought with me.

Wings. It looked like wings on his back. Wings that were somehow brutally shorn off and kept from growing back by hot metal being poured over them, if such a thing were possible to survive.

"Here." I turn my face away, averting my eyes as he takes the towel and wraps it around his waist.

"Thank you," he says quietly.

We face each other again.

"I must leave you now."

I shake my head. "No. You can't. You're not strong enough."

Seeing him now, standing tall and lanky, barely more than bones with skin wrapped around them, he looks painfully young.

"I'm poison to any who are near me," he says, taking a step back from me. "You've seen the truth of what I am."

"And what is that?" I ask, taking a step forward. "I'm not easily scared off."

He comes forward and bares his teeth. "You should be scared of me," he hisses. "I am the hunger in the darkness. I am the monster that separates crying babes from their mothers. I am the slow death, the angel of Famine, a Horseman of the Apocalypse. Run before I steal all the fullness and life you've ever known, little girl."

I laugh in his face, obviously startling him and his attempt at menace.

"Oh, honey, you're adorable." I pat his lean cheek right before he can yank away from me. "I'm a much bigger monster than you. Now come inside. You can barely stand on your feet. Let's both get some more dinner."

Chapter Three

LAYDEN
Present Day

I lay awake most of the night, watching Phoenix sleep beside me in bed. I can go a long time without sleep, and considering she means this marriage to be in name only, I know this may be a rare opportunity. The fact that we're even sharing a bed is only because we're in Vlad's compound.

It's better this way, I try to tell myself. I don't want to lose the best friend I've ever known. It would kill me if I ever did anything to drive Phoenix away again. I lost her once because of my own idiocy. And the loneliness afterwards... I've always known hunger of every kind, but that was an emptiness that almost drove me mad. I lashed out at the whole world and almost destroyed my brothers because of it.

The thing is, when Phoenix first came to me in that

18

forest, pulling me out of my self-appointed exile and bringing me back to life, or really, *to* life for the first time... It was like color bursting into the world. I'd been cold so long, alone so long. Even before I came to the forest, when I was with my brothers. We just *existed*, moving robotically through each day, doing what our Creator-Father demanded like we were mere cogs in his constant war machine.

All I did was destroy and deprive, bringing misery and devastation everywhere I went. No one was more surprised than me when I finally lashed out at the Creator-Father. But I snapped. I'd had *enough*. It wasn't so much courage as the build-up of a lifetime of desperation. I didn't care what happened to me if I failed.

Granted, I regretted the lack of forethought as my wings were cut from my back and the searing hell-metal was poured on the raw stumps.

I close my eyes, chest clenching as it always does with the memory. Then I open my eyes again and look at Phoenix as she sleeps. She huffs out a little breath in her sleep and moves, snuggling in against my chest and throwing one of her legs over mine.

I freeze as the fullness of being close to her makes me feel... so many things. Then I force myself to relax in case going tense makes her wake up. She's so *warm*. So warm and soft, I think I might die even though I'm not capable of it. I look at the ceiling and try to memorize the feeling of everywhere her body presses against mine.

A monster like me doesn't deserve even a night's respite of such heaven, but I'm stealing it all the same. Maybe I'm a thief, just like my Creator-Father after all.

Because when Vlad said I needed to marry his grand-daughter in order to fulfill the blood oath my brother owed him, I didn't protest. The hunger in me rushed to agree. But Phoenix hates the way her grandfather manipulates her, so of course she wouldn't be interested in me last night.

I was a fool, seeing my brothers with their consorts and thinking this was my opportunity for the same. What do I know of comfort or love?

My mind immediately shies away from the word. I don't *love* Phoenix. I just feel affection for her. It's all I'm capable of. We are good companions. A good match. I'm a being of hunger, and she's fed by beings of endless thirst. Plus, she couldn't respect anyone susceptible to her compulsion.

It still doesn't mean she wants you.

I shake off the thought. Wanting doesn't matter anymore. We're married now, for better or worse.

I sigh quietly and close my eyes, going back to memorizing the feel of her. The soft exhale and the feel of her abdomen against the side of my torso as she draws in another breath and then releases it again. Her warm thigh tucked against mine. The way she clings to me in her sleep with complete trust and vulnerability.

In wakefulness, she is all hard lines and cool, unfeeling determination. But here, in the dark of night, she has gone so soft. So, so soft.

My body reacts in the way a man does to a woman being so close, but I ignore it. I may crave her, but I would never disrespect her trust. The torture of having her so close is welcome, and I'm familiar with disciplining myself.

I continue committing the feel of her to memory until morning light begins creeping through the window. I want to deny the light. To message the old charioteer and threaten him until he carries the sun backward and allows the moon to linger a little longer. Just a little longer.

But too soon, Phoenix's eyes flutter awake. Almost

immediately, she realizes how close she's crawled against me and yanks away, wiping at her mouth.

"Sorry," she mutters, sleepy eyes averted from mine. "I'll go get showered."

And just like that, her warmth is gone as she flees the bed for the bathroom. My teeth clench in emptiness as the door slams shut, and I jam my head against the pillow. I scrub a hand down my face. "Fool," I reprimand myself harshly.

Twenty minutes later she comes out wrapped only in a towel. In the time she was away, I've mastered myself. So I avert my eyes from her and her exposed thighs, keeping my distance as I pass by her. "I'll get washed up as well," I say.

She makes a small noise of assent. Fuck, but this is awkward. Our old easiness around each other is gone. Considering the circumstances, I suppose it's to be expected, but I hate it. I take the fastest shower of my life. By the time I get out, Phoenix is already dressed in her usual tight black jeans, long-sleeved black shirt, and busted-up combat boots. Her black hair is up in a ponytail. Princess of darkness. I hide my smile.

She looks up at me, and her cheeks color briefly before she turns her back. I still just have my towel tied around my waist.

"Hurry up," she quips. "There's a lecture I don't want to miss in the city at eleven."

I pause as I tug a shirt over my head. We had a few weeks to prep for the wedding, but I was busy running interference between Vlad's entourage and my family most of the time. The little I did get to spend with Phoenix, Sabra was there too as we monitored global communications to screen the fallout from the bit of magic we did a month earlier to stave off the end of the world.

Mostly, it was just squabbling amongst officials about the various government cover-ups and military solutions, along with rampant conspiracy theories floating about what *actually* happened. So far, we haven't seen anyone except the mages guessing the truth. And even they didn't know the whole of it. That Phoenix, Sabra, and I had called over interdimensional beings from another plane to consume the nuclear energy before an angelic AI launched World War III. It was a near thing. Some missiles were already in the air, but we pulled it off just in time.

The mages from various continents were rumbling about putting together a global council for the first time—something like a magical United Nations—to keep something like this from happening ever again. Or at least to punish any magic movers who got out of control. The human population was supposed to be ignorant of the existence of magic and other planes. Or at least it was a hot topic of debate amongst the mages. Sabra said there were so many factions and divisions she couldn't imagine them ever getting together to agree on a council. But time would tell.

For the moment, things were calm.

"What kind of lecture?" I ask.

I see her shoulders straighten a little. "Are you decent?"

I finish buttoning my pants. "Yes."

She turns around and takes a deep breath. "So we haven't exactly had a lot of time to talk, huh?"

"We were kinda busy dealing with the fallout from the almost end-of-the-world." And we willfully allowed that to distract us from the reality of our upcoming nuptials. But I don't add that part.

"I'm in school. Getting my Ph.D. in Ancient Religions."

I blink several times. "Vlad lets you—?"

"Vlad doesn't *let* me do anything," she bites, and I hold up my hands. "I live my own life."

"I'm..." I tread carefully, "glad. Things were different last time I was here."

She stares at me, almost glaring, before her eyes drop. "Yeah, well. He and I came to an... understanding."

I feel my eyebrows go up. I've never known Vlad to be understanding about anything.

She obviously sees my skepticism. "As in, I made him understand some things after you left."

After I left.

"Phoenix," I start to say. "We never talked about it, but I want to apologize for how I was back then—"

But she holds up a hand before I can finish.

"Please don't," she says with a pained smile. "You were fine."

My chest clenches tight. I wasn't. I know I wasn't. She'd clouded all my senses, and I hadn't been conscience enough of what she was dealing with. "I'm sorry I cut off all contact. Sabra told me you'd asked about me months later. But I just—"

"It's fine," she says, still with that plastic smile she gives the rest of the world. Not the real one that touches her eyes. "If you'd stayed, Vlad would just have found a way to use you against me."

Another shot fired. *Like he did the second I came back.* She doesn't have to say it, but it lands all the same. I get it now. How doomed any of this always was. She'll always resent me. She stood up to Vlad and found a way to break his hold on her. But then I came back and now she's under his thumb again, which she hates more than anything in this world.

I nod, my eyes dropping. I can't look at her right now.

Not with the cold, empty, familiar ache that's seeping into my chest. "I know you always dreamed of going back to school. I'm so proud of you."

When I look back up, she's turned away from me again, her back moving up and down like she's heaving for breath.

"Phoenix?" I take a step forward. "You okay?"

"Fine," she says, but her voice comes out a little strangled. She stomps toward the door. "Let's go. Breakfast will be ready."

Chapter Four

I feel his eyes on me as he crouches, shivering in his towel on the bed while I eat the stew after reheating it on the woodfire stove.

"It's rude to stare," I say.

"You're eating." He sounds surprised.

I just stare back at him. Does he think it's rude of me to eat in front of him? "You said you didn't want any more yet."

He waves a hand warily as if that's not what he meant. "Humans don't."

"What?" I shove another spoonful of stew into my mouth. It's a little bland, but the potatoes, carrots, and bit of gamey meat are still hearty and fill my belly nicely.

"Eat when I'm around."

"I never said I was human."

25

His eyebrows go up. "What are you?"

"Well, that's also rude to ask a girl on a first date, don't you think?"

His eyes narrow, and I roll mine.

"You really need to learn to take a joke. Lighten up, man. You don't have to be so goddamn serious all the time."

He just blinks. Then again, I guess a dude who exiled himself to the forest for god only knows how long might not exactly be brushed up on all the social niceties.

I drop my spoon in my empty bowl. "So what are *you*? 'Cause we both know you aren't human either."

His eyes flick my way, and not for the first time, I'm a little stunned by the piercing, translucent gray of them. Especially now that he's more cleaned up.

Still, so much of his face is hidden behind his bushy blond beard that I feel like I don't have an idea of what he looks like beyond those stunning, deep-set eyes peeking out from beyond the strong bone of his brow. "I told you. I am Famine."

I arch an eyebrow. Is he serious? "You weren't kidding with that whole Horseman of the Apocalypse thing?"

He shakes his head, and I let out a low whistle. I guess the whole staring at me while I eat thing makes a little more sense now.

"Can you control it or just everywhere you go—" I hold out a hand, gesturing vaguely.

"I stay away from people."

Damn. And here I was, all caught up in my own shit, whining about how bad I have it.

"So you've, like, what? Been out in the middle of the forest all alone? For how long?" I blink, reaching to take a sip of the cup of cool spring water I poured myself before coming in. Maybe Horsemen of the Apocalypse are like my supernatural family and a new one gets born every twenty-five years?

"Two hundred years or so."

"What?" I cry, doing a spit-take. "You were out there for two hundred *years*?"

He just shrugs as I swipe my forearm across my mouth and jump up from where I'm sitting at the roughhewn little table. "What about before that?"

Another shrug. "With my family."

"Well, what the hell happened to them?" I cry, moving to sit beside him on the bed. He winces away from me, and I'm not sure if it's because his body aches after moving for the first time in centuries or because he's trying to angle the messed-up stumps on his back away from me so I can't see them.

"Shit," I pop back up to my feet. "Let me get you something to wear. You must be so cold just being in that towel."

"It's fine," he says. "The fire is warm. Much warmer than I've been in a long, long time."

I'm already walking toward the wardrobe of the small, one-room cabin, but I look back at him. Jesus Christ, how many winters did he spend in these mountain woods, covered feet deep in snow? Months every year just covered and waiting for the spring defrost?

How could anybody—any being—live like that?

"Where is your family now?" I ask as I pull open a dresser drawer. I yank out a slightly musty but otherwise clean, thick-knitted sweater. Another drawer produces some men's work pants. They'll probably be too big on him with as emaciated as he is, but we'll find something to use as a belt. "Can they help you?"

"No," he barks. "They're no good to me."

Okaaaaay. Touchy subject, obviously. But I get it; I

really do. Talking about family is one thing that lights up all my buttons, too. I wonder if it's just a supernatural thing or if most people's families are super screwed up. Maybe when you add power into the mix, it just jacks it up to *extra* fucked levels. But I also note he didn't say that he didn't *have* a family. So he's got someone out there, somewhere. Other creatures like him?

I carry the clothing over to him and set it on the bed.

His brow narrows. I try to make out what the expression on his face might mean, but it's difficult with only a little skin beneath his wild hair and beard exposed to show what on earth he might actually be thinking.

So, I decide discretion is the better part of valor and all that. "I'll be in the bathroom while you change." It's the only other room in the place. "Just knock on the door when you're done."

He gives a slight shake of his head that I interpret as a nod and head to the bathroom.

When I open the door to the little room, I find a closet barely big enough to close myself inside. Aha, I should have known. A house like this is really old school—no inside bathrooms. There must be an outhouse out back. Either way, I shut the door behind me as best I can to give my new friend as much privacy as possible while he changes.

I listen in case he tries to make a run for it after he's got his new clothes on. I'm more gratified than I probably should be when I hear his light footsteps on the wood heading toward my little closet. His knock is light, and I all but tumble out on top of him.

He looks surprised but stays silent as I push past him, my elbow brushing his. He yanks his back dramatically, likely out of habit, and I wonder exactly how old he is.

Then again, I'm not sure what it matters. I don't know

how old I am. I mean, on my human birth certificate, it says I was born nineteen years ago, but secretly, I know that's a lie.

I'm much, much older.

"I think I'm ready to eat a little more," he says softly.

I pause, realizing exactly how close I'm standing to him. He pulled far enough away so that we weren't touching, but only just. He still looks far too skinny in the country farmer's clothes. But cleaned up and in fresh clothes, he looks so much better than when I first found him. And it's as if I realize just how tall he is for the first time. And how broad his shoulders are, even if the thick woolen shirt hides how boney they are. It's like a glimpse of how he will be one day once he's been fed enough.

He's younger than I first thought, too. Well, young for having just spent two hundred years in the forest. Do Horsemen or whatever he is not age? Will he look young forever? I think of my grandpa, who's actually my great great great great great great times about eight more *greats* grandpa, and yet still looks like he's just in his mid-thirties.

Another thing this stranger and I have in common. I feel my cheeks flush and force myself to look at the floor. I'm afraid I've been staring.

"Then let's get you some more food." I turn on my heel and head toward the fridge. Apparently, there's electricity in the cabin, just not running water. Not so odd out in the mountain country in this part of the world.

Of course, Grandpa would have a fit seeing me anywhere like this. Only the best for Grandpa Vlad. The way he drowns himself in luxuries makes it obvious to anyone with a pulse that he's overcompensating for something. That's just it. The rest of my uncles surrounding

Grandpa don't have one. A pulse, that is. A fact which only occasionally wigs me out.

I come from a family of the undead. So what? Until me, every one of my relatives on my father's side lived as a human until twenty-five. Then they became overcome by bloodlust and took their first bite to become a vampire, impregnating the next generation at the same time because the bloodlust was accompanied by the good old-fashioned kind of sexual lust. I always thought this was TMI to know about one's own parents, not to mention every other living relative.

Because though I call them "uncles," they're really just a line of about twenty grandfathers and great-great-great grandfathers—you get the picture— who all look twenty-five. Calling them "uncles" seemed less confusing. Especially when most of them have the emotional maturity of a prepubescent boy. Four uncles from the 17th century are barely above feral status.

I always hid whenever I saw them coming down the hallway as a kid. Grandpa Vlad was the oldest and somehow kept them all in check, but I didn't see how. They tended to communicate more in bloodthirsty grunts than anything else. A couple from the 19th century were more bearable but the newer ones were so power-hungry I was careful to never let my guard down around them.

They were each sure Grandfather was going to leave his dynasty to them. Pointless since the old man couldn't be killed and never planned on going anywhere.

Also pointless since if Grandfather ever did appoint a successor, the unspoken acknowledgment was that it would be *me*—the one who broke the chain. I wasn't a vampire but I was more powerful than all who came before. Vlad valued power more than anything, so I was still favored, despite the fact that we rarely saw eye to eye, and at this particular moment, I had theoretically run away from home to escape the hateful bastard.

But he seems to always find a way to get me back. Vlad always gets what Vlad wants.

I sigh and push away the thought as I close the refrigerator, turning instead toward a hunk of bread I see on the counter. I slather it liberally with some butter that's also been left out on the counter, and after pulling open several cupboard doors, I finally find a plate.

I walk back over to the bed where the man's watching me with those cool, eerie gray eyes of his. He reaches out for it, but I pause before handing it off.

"What's your name?"

He hesitates as if this is somehow far more intimate than telling me what sort of creature he is. But he finally inhales deeply and releases the breath, as if he's telling a secret, or maybe just a name that hasn't been spoken aloud for a very, very long time. "Layden."

I say it back, if only so he can hear it again, "Layden. It's nice to meet you."

I hand him his plate of buttered bread, and his eyes show his gratitude as he takes it.

"Why are you being so kind to me? From the world I remember... before," his eyes cloud over as if it's a very long time ago he is trying to remember, "no one was kind to one another."

I frown, thinking of my life, of my parents and wondering where on earth they might be at this moment. Wondering if they're happy. If they've forgotten me as they go about their day-to-day life.

"There's not a lot of kindness in today's world either."

The furrow in his brow deepens. "So why are you—"

I shrug. "We all need somebody every now and then."

"Who was your somebody?" he asks.

My chest clenches tight. "My mother," I say, then withdraw my hand because I can't think about Mom today. It's been too long since I've seen her. "And my best friend, Sabra. There are good people in this world. It just takes a little hunting and patience to find them."

His eyes seem to lighten. "Well, it has taken me a very, very long time for my path to cross with yours. . ." he gestures, obviously waiting for my name.

"Phoenix."

"Phoenix," he says, and it's like his tongue is relishing the syllables. "A perfect name for a perfect being."

I laugh a little at that, feeling an unusual heat rising in my cheeks. I pull away from him. "Eat your bread. I'll go pump more water."

I'm still shaking my head and replaying the way his mouth seemed to caress my name. Phoenix. For the first time in a long time, I feel born anew, and I wonder, is this what hope feels like?

Chapter Five

Breakfast at Vlad's compound means breakfast with my whole family, who are still gathered here. We all came for sanctuary, and they stayed on once Vlad tricked my brother into the blood oath and I had to get married. Might as well stay for the wedding since everyone was already here.

Any time my whole family gathers, it means chaos. We can't help it. We carry it with us, and being at Vlad's compound has everyone more on edge than usual.

A bigger breakfast table had to be brought in, considering usually it's only Phoenix that eats, well, *food*. As soon as the nuptials were announced—or should I say, decreed—Vlad was suddenly more than happy to make accommodations for the rest of us. He had his minions clear out a storage room, one of the few rooms in the compound with rows of windows, as a dining room.

It's not that Vlad and his family *can't* go out in sunlight like all the legends say; they just greatly prefer not to. Something about how it pains their eyes and gives them headaches. They see much better at night, like most nocturnal creatures.

Vlad insists on joining us for breakfast every morning and sits at the head of the table, but he keeps the two windows nearest to him heavily shaded so he can stay comfortable.

He claps his hands together as soon as Phoenix and I appear, standing up with a smile on his face. It is not a pleasant sight when Vlad Tepes smiles. The few times I've seen him flash his teeth at me, his fangs only slightly more apparent than the rest, I always got the impression that he's about a millisecond from attacking and ripping my throat out. A.k.a., I know a savage predator when I see one.

Ksenia and Kharon's baby starts to cry at the other end of the table. Smart kid. I look away from Vlad toward the rest of my family. Apparently, we're late to the show. Everyone else is already seated. Abaddon and his wife, Hannah, sit nearest Vlad with their toddler, Raven, between them. Her black wings flutter behind her, but she remains seated for now as she plays with the silverware in front of her. Then there's Ksenia and Kharon and their baby, Luna.

And finally, my conjoined twin brothers Remus and Romulus—it appears Romulus is awake and in control of their shared head at the moment—with their consort Lauren.

The two seats beside Vlad and across the table from Abaddon remain open. How nice. He's given us pride of place. Or no one else wanted to sit beside him. Likely the latter.

I also don't miss that Vlad has several of my so-called "uncles" stationed around the shadowed corners of the room. He never enters a room without them. They're ostensibly his guards, but he just likes to keep them around as creepy reminders that he's always in control.

Phoenix takes her chair first, closest to Vlad, and I sit between her and my brother Kharon.

Vlad lifts his hand and makes a gesture with his wrist. Women dressed in barely decent thigh-high red robes come in, each carrying a steaming breakfast plate for all the "eaters" at the table and, in a synchronized motion, set them in front of us. I cover my distaste and nod my thanks to the woman who delivered mine. Her eyes are distant, almost void, and she doesn't respond. I wonder if she can even see us.

I feel Hannah's discomfort and anger from across the table. This has been a point of contention since my family arrived and discovered that these women are Vlad's family's blood slaves, which means they're just kept around as regular drinking sources whenever Vlad or his sons need feeding or, I suspect, other *comforts*.

It's distasteful and occasionally puts me off my dinner. Or breakfast, as it were. The food in front of me looks amazing. I suppose one of the women must be a chef? My plate has a fluffy omelet, strawberry crepes dusted with sugar, and strips of thick-cut bacon. I eat in spite of my churning stomach because I heard Vlad yelling at them one night when we didn't eat enough. It won't really satisfy my hunger, but nothing ever does. Doesn't matter if I stuff myself with a feast or just drink broth. I don't mind it, not when it means I can control whether or not I inflict it on others.

I'm glad my brothers and their families will be getting out of here today. I'm just sorry Phoenix had to grow up in this toxic environment. It's only more of a testament to the strong person she is.

I take a bite of my food as Phoenix politely asks her grandfather how his business dealings are going. Likely to fill the awkward silence that has fallen over the table.

Vlad waves a hand impatiently. "The only business I care about at the moment is you. Tell me he rode you thoroughly enough to breed you last night."

Gasps come from the women around the table.

Vlad ignores them, staring pointedly at Phoenix.

She glares back. "Don't be vile. There are children at the table."

Vlad sniffs the air and narrows his eyes. "I don't smell the scent of fucking on you."

Abaddon jams his chair back, standing in fury, but I take my cues from Phoenix. She's quietly furious, and I know she wouldn't want me making a display on her behalf.

"Not that it's any of your business how I conduct myself in my marriage, but I showered this morning."

Vlad leans in, face hard. "You should have been fucking this morning."

All right, I've had enough. But before I can say anything, Phoenix is already there, slamming her knife into the table between her and Vlad.

"You might get to say who and when I marry, but the biology of when I conceive is something beyond either of our control. You will stay the hell out of my sex life." Venom drips from her voice. "Don't push me."

Vlad glares right back at her, and the entire room

holds its breath in the strained silence that follows. Until Vlad finally breaks out in a low chuckle that releases the room's tension. "That's my girl. Fine. I'll stay out of your sex life, but don't think for a moment that I don't expect results. By this time next year, I expect to be a proud grandpapa."

"It hasn't gotten old already?" Phoenix can't help asking snidely, gesturing to the four men in the corners. Because we both know his "sons" are actually grandsons going back untold generations already.

"None so interesting as you, my lovely," Vlad says, reaching out a hand to caress Phoenix's face. She jerks back from his touch, and I feel her shudder.

Vlad just smiles that predator's smile again.

Fuck I wish I could kill this bastard. Phoenix swears he's untouchable, and I understand her reasons, but still...

To my right, little Raven suddenly flies up out of her chair, evading her mother's arms as Hannah tries to reach for her.

"Raven, honey, you know we sit while we eat breakfast," Hannah tries.

Raven's little face is contorted, and she points a finger at Vlad.

"Bad," she pronounces loudly.

Then the small toddler flies up and out of her chair at Vlad like a little bullet.

We're all so shocked that no one moves in time to do anything about it. All of us, that is, except for Vlad's sons, one of whom shoots from the nearest corner and snatches Raven out of the air by her wings a moment before her little snaggle-toothed fangs can connect with Vlad's face.

"Filthy meat-eaters," Vlad's son snarls at her.

Raven's not finished with her surprises for the morning,

apparently. Suddenly, she transforms in Vlad's minion's hands from a cute little toddler into—

We all gasp as she lets out an animal growl and shapeshifts—I can't think of any other word for it—into some sort of monster three times her size. She opens her mouth and has three rows of razor-sharp teeth and a tail with spikes whips out. Her torso is furry and muscled. Instead of being cute and fluffy, her wings have become leathery and veined and stretch out behind her like a huge, mutant bat.

Vlad's minion drops her at the same time that she shoves him back.

When Vlad's minion grabbed her cousin's wings and snatched Raven out of the air, Luna began crying. As the vampire flies back from Raven's shove, a portal opens behind him. He doesn't even have a chance to realize what's happening before he disappears into the shining man-size pool hanging in the air like a liquid mirror before it closes up behind him.

Right after, Raven transforms back into her adorable child self and hovers to the side of Vlad's chair, fluffy wings flapping madly as she looks at where Vlad's son disappeared. There's a moment of silence as the rest of us do the same.

It's broken by Vlad clapping loudly, enjoyment transforming his angular features. "Such delightful allies I have as in-laws." He looks at Phoenix and me and, with a dark, avaricious tone, adds, "I can't wait until we get our own."

"Raven!" Hannah jumps up, holding her arms out to her daughter. "Get away from him."

"Father," another of Vlad's sons objects. "Make them bring Avram back!"

"We're leaving," Abaddon declares as Raven lands back

in her mother's arms, thumb embedded in her mouth, looking for all the world like a normal toddler apart from her wings and the little horns peeking out from the abundant curls on her head. "*Now.*"

The rest of my family stands up from the table.

Beside me, Phoenix shudders, and I understand last night's performance more than ever. She'll never give Vlad what he wants. If I'm really her friend, and I am—friend before hungry monster, always—then I'll do everything in my power to aid her cause.

"That's hardly necessary," Vlad says nonchalantly from his throne-like chair at the head of the table, his tone no more bothered than if a fly had just been swatted in his presence.

"Father," his son says again. "What about Avram?"

Vlad looks annoyed for the first time since breakfast started, turning a stone face toward his son. "We'll have a far-superior replacement for your fool brother soon. If Avram had been quicker-witted, he'd still be with us, wouldn't he?"

His son is astonished and obviously furious, but one look from Vlad has him swallowing it back as he bows his head to the floor. "Yes, Father. Of course, your wisdom prevails." He backs away to the corner.

Abaddon is already shuffling my family out of the room. Good. I'm glad to have them out from under this man's roof and sphere of control. I'm just sorry I can't get Phoenix out with them. I hate that she's under his thumb in any way.

I hurry over to my brother as he ushers the last of my family out, pulling him aside. "Will you go back to the castle?"

I can feel Vlad's eyes on us, and it makes my skin crawl.

I pull Abaddon into the hallway, even though I hate to have Phoenix out of sight for even a moment.

"I'm not sure that's possible now that it's been discovered, even if we tried to hide it again with more runework," Abaddon says, and I hear the regret in his voice.

"I might have a possible fix."

Abaddon rolls his eyes. "Let me guess. Magic."

"You've witnessed Phoenix's mage at work."

Reluctantly, Abaddon nods. "I found us a villa in the city for the time being."

"I'll start working on it with Sabra immediately. She's in the city, too."

He nods and cuffs me on the shoulder, his face softening. "Good night last night?" His eyebrow arches up.

"As if I'd tell you," I glare, and he laughs good-naturedly. I turn away before he can read anything else on my face and almost run straight into Phoenix. We both pull back before colliding, and her eyes widen before she composes her face into its usual mask. "Come on. If we don't hurry, I'll be late."

"Right." I blink. "Your lecture."

We just witnessed the sort of complete control Vlad exercises over his family. I've never seen him willing to sacrifice any members of it before, but then, they're unkillable. All that nonsense about stakes and beheadings is just lore to make humans feel more in control in the face of the unthinkable. Vlad and his sons are immortal in the true sense of the word, like my brothers and I. Slice us and dice us, and still, we continue on.

I learned this the hard way, climbing out of my grave after I'd painfully regenerated.

Vlad has learned more creative means of controlling his family over the centuries. Phoenix told me he locked one son in a pit for three hundred years for disrespecting him. Mostly, his methods involve breaking them from childhood while they were still human, a process he got to repeat every twenty-five years.

He experimented with making blood slaves of his own progeny until they became vampires themselves, but apparently, it made them dullards when they came of age and turned into vampires, not the killing machines he was looking for.

So, I can't imagine how Phoenix possibly "came to an understanding" with him. He's intractable and ruthless.

After learning the lengths he's willing to go, it's nearly impossible to imagine the strength it took Phoenix to become the woman she is today. She survived him with not just a scrap of humanity but an ocean of it.

She's the kind of person who sees a suffering creature in the woods and stops to help it even though she has plenty of her own problems to worry about. Who does that? She helped me believe that goodness was possible anywhere in this or any other plane, and she grew up with an evil to rival my father.

As she strides confidently down the hallway in front of me, I have to fight the surge of emotion in my chest. She's built a life for herself here apart from his control.

And I vow silently to not allow myself to be a means of his manipulation. He's trying to tighten his leash on her and bring her back in; that's obvious to anyone with eyes.

But unlike ten years ago, maybe the solution isn't leaving.

Maybe it's staying and fighting at her side.

Or is that my hunger talking? Look how strong she became without me.

* * *

Phoenix is quiet as she drives us into the city, and I follow her lead, keeping to myself. I hate this awkwardness between us when I once felt closer to her than I ever had to any being in the universe.

And there's the fact that I'm busy gripping the handle on the door with white knuckles. I don't think I'll ever get used to these motorized vehicles, even though we used them all the time when I first lived at Vlad's compound with Phoenix. I have more of an affinity with human transportation devices like planes and helicopters. Probably because flying comes naturally to me as I spent the first two thousand years of my life in the air. The dip and sway of the metal beast in the different air pockets and changing air pressures were familiar since I navigated it with my bare body and wings for so long. It felt like second nature.

But this? Wheeled vehicles flying down the road with so many other vehicles jostling for space? The lines on the road are treated as mere suggestions in this country, and a three-lane highway can be choked four cars abreast. Occasionally, cars even jump on the sidewalks when it gets a little too tight, and honking is the music of the highway.

Phoenix is adept at it, and she leans on the horn as she slips into a pocket that opens up between two other cars before zooming into a parking lot and hauling the car up onto the sidewalk—the usual way of parking here.

"Come on, we've got to hurry."

"Right behind you," I say as she all but leaps out of the car.

She jogs across campus, shouldering a backpack, and I keep at her heels. We don't slow down after sprinting up a mountain of steps to one of the bigger buildings. Phoenix shoves through the doors to a big, circular glass atrium in the center of the open foyer with stairs leading up to each floor. Behind the glass is a model of an early religious temple to scale, about the size of a car.

Phoenix shoulders her way past students as she takes the stairs two at a time. She only seems to take a breath once she slides into a seat at the back of a huge auditorium-like room that is packed with students and faculty alike.

Only minutes later, a man pulls out his earbuds and walks up to the podium, a camera casting his image onto a large screen behind him. He looks to be in his early to mid-thirties. Handsome. I glance over at Phoenix and see her watching the screen with rapt, excited attention.

"That's Professor Rossi," she whispers. "He's at the top of his field and one of the reasons I was so thrilled to study here with him as my advisor. Well," she rolls her eyes, "Vlad did tempt him here with a huge endowment, but for once, I wasn't mad about letting his money and influence actually work for me. Professor Rossi is an absolute *genius* in the field."

There's an odd curdling in my gut as she gushes over this man.

But then she waves at me to shush as Professor Rossi leans over the lectern to speak, even though she's the one who's been talking.

"Signs and wonders used to be a regular part of daily life. It's easy to write off these historical descriptions in the ancient texts as people without scientific explanations simply describing natural phenomena."

He clicks through the slides reflected on a screen behind him to show a demonic mask. "So-called "demons" were merely people with schizophrenia. Sudden storms or volcanos weren't manifestations of the gods' anger; they were simply warmer ocean waters and the moving of tectonic plates." He clicks through to another slide that shows how the flow of warmer ocean waters evaporates to become hurricanes. "But while yes, our ancient forefathers might have had only a proto-understanding of certain scientific phenomena, in other ways, their understanding of mathematics and physics was far more advanced than we give them credit for."

"These are the people who built the great pyramids and the Parthenon!" The screen flashes with slides showing images of the building he describes before coming back to his face. The professor speaks with such passion that it's easy to see why his audience is enrapt.

"They might not have cracked germ theory at the time, for which many in our modern age judge them as barbarians, but they still had an astonishing ability to thrive, invent, nurture artistic talent, and create vast civilizations with astounding communication networks."

Beside me, Phoenix scribbles notes furiously in her notebook. "Since Freud and Jung, it's been commonly accepted among the scientifically minded that religions were created as mere manifestations of mankind's neurosis or shadow selves. Or, to put it in the framework of Marx, religion was merely an opiate of the people meant to keep the masses drugged and unaware of the fact that they were pawns in the machine of the more powerful.

"The thesis I present to you today, however, especially in light of the supposed *hoax*," he uses air quotes for the last word, "that we all collectively witnessed with our own eyes this past month, is that some of the signs and wonders our ancient brethren witnessed were *real*."

I sit up straighter in my chair and realize that I'm not the only one reacting. Some of the other professors in the room stand up and heckle him for buying into conspiracy theories. Just as many students stand up in his defense.

Finally, Professor Rossi holds his hands up, and the shouting dies down. "Is this not a university where we gather to discuss new ideas and theses?" he asks. Students eagerly nod, along with some professors. Others stare stonily ahead.

Professor Rossi leans forward, clutching the sides of the lectern as he continues, his voice intimate as he speaks into the microphone. "There *were* ancient powers that occasionally visited or even inhabited this world for a time during the ancient era. Ladies and gentlemen, I am suggesting that ancient man did not *invent* the gods but merely documented their presence among us with papyrus and ink. Just like we're doing now capturing video on our phones of the phenomena we're witnessing now all around us as these unknown beings visit again."

This time, when the crowd erupts, there is no bringing back order. Factions shout and argue all around the room, and Professor Rossi has to be shuffled off the stage.

"Come on," Phoenix whispers excitedly, grabbing my arm and pulling me toward an exit off to the side, away from the chaos. "I want you to meet him."

Frowning, I follow her. I can't think of anything I want less.

Chapter Six

L ayden stays in bed for several days, shivering underneath the covers even though there's a sheen of sweat on his forehead. He doesn't seem to have a fever, though, and every time I try to talk to him, he just shakes his head and turns away. It's as if, after so long alone, the concept of human interaction and even a warm, soft bed is too much for his mind and body.

The one thing he will accept, however, is food. I spend the days chopping up vegetables and making soup. Funny since, at home, I usually rebel against anything that overly feminizes me or that I consider woman's work. In a compound full of kinsmen who are older than me, I fought from the beginning not to be the one left to do the house-keeping. And I'd certainly always refused to be involved in any sort of food acquisition for my family. I shudder even at the thought.

They all took care of themselves well before I got there, and nothing needed to change, even though the more cavemen-like of my "uncles" sometimes disagreed and tried to push things with me. Compulsion came in handy, and when a couple of them figured out how to fight back against my mind control, it came to proving myself in all-out combat with them. Men with hundreds of pounds on me.

But my might had never come from bulk, and I had more tricks up my sleeve than just the compulsion.

"Here," I say, perching on Layden's bed on day four with some fresh potato, carrot, and onion soup.

He's facing the window, back to me, as he stirs. The stubs of the wings on his back are only small lumps against the heavy blankets as he turns over, and I wonder if they're what makes him wince slightly as they brush against the mattress.

"Are you okay? Does it hurt?" I ask automatically, but my questions make his expression shut down even more. Unlike the first day, his eyes stay down and averted from mine.

He shies away from my touch when he struggles to sit up, and I try to help by stuffing another pillow behind him. "Don't spill the soup," he says.

"He speaks!" I crow, letting go of the pillow when he grabs it and rearranges it himself. At least he's showing a little more life today than he has the past few days. When he's settled in, I hold up a spoonful of broth to his mouth.

He refuses to open, and finally, his eyes lift to mine. I try not to pull back or react in any way, even though my stomach swoops physically at the sudden, powerful eye contact.

"Give it to me; I can feed myself. I'm strong enough."

It's ridiculous that his words make me sad. Feeding him has been the only intimacy he's allowed beyond that initial day when I found him and he opened up to me a little. I don't know why I should care. I barely know him. This is a side trip from my real life that part of me knows I'm focusing on just to help me escape the problems I ran from in the first place. Still, it hurts. And it was stupid to think there was any real connection between me and a random stranger.

"Fine," I snap, shoving the bowl into his hands as he hefts them out from underneath the heavy blanket.

The spoon immediately begins knocking against the side of the bowl, soup sloshing out and down the sides.

"Okay, Romeo," I say, snatching the bowl back. "Try again tomorrow."

He sighs in frustration and leans back against his pillows.

"I'm not used to being so weak," he says.

"What's wrong with a little weakness?" I ask, snatching a towel from the nearby table to swipe up the spilled soup and load up the large spoon to hold up to his lips again. "What makes the strong so superior anyway?"

His eyes look up at me in surprise as he opens his mouth to accept the soup. I smile and slip it between his waiting lips. He swallows, eyes still caught with mine for a long time until he realizes how long he's been staring and jerks his gaze away.

"You're kind," he says.

I shrug. "That's certainly not something I'm usually accused of," I mumble. I look down at the bowl and scoop another spoonful.

When I move it to his lips, I find those thoughtful, too-seeing eyes locked on me again. "That surprises me. You're the kindest person I've ever met."

My stomach swoops at his words, and I'm the one averting my gaze this time, focusing on his lips as I spoon the soup into his mouth. "Well, you don't know me very well."

He swallows, then licks his lips. "Seems like I might be seeing the real you that you don't give others the chance to see."

I can't do anything but chuckle. "Ah, my friend. That's wishful thinking. I know who I am. And it's not a kind person."

"Maybe you aren't surrounded by the right kind of people."

I laugh again and lift my eyebrow, along with another spoonful of soup. "And you're the right kind of people?" Bantering with him like this sends excited thrills spiraling through my stomach.

He shrugs. "I never would have thought so before now. But I know what it's like to be around people"—he swallows another spoonful, eyes laser-focused on me— "maybe family? Who makes for a bad environment. You never know what you could be apart from them until you leave."

I frown, pulling back a little. As I've been leaning in to feed him, my hip has settled into the bed and leans against his. Shockingly, I didn't even realize the physical contact was happening when I'm usually so wary of how close I allow anyone to get to me. "What do you know about it?"

His lips split in a weary grin. "More than you know." The smile disappears from his face as his eyes slide toward the wall. "My family only knew the language of brutality, never warmth or kindness. Still, I was shocked and so betrayed when they buried me alive after my father cut off my wings for rebelling against being the monster he'd created me to be. My brothers, I'd thought might at least..." But he shakes his head.

My mouth has gone dry at his words. I can't relate to everything he's said, but god, if I thought I could connect with him before... His story echoes mine in so many ways.

I drop the spoon into the bowl because I can't think of any words, even though I want to say so much. It's like there are too many thoughts swirling around in my head, and I can't pick any to come out of my mouth. The spoon rattles in the empty bowl.

I look down, surprised. "Oh," I say, blinking. "We're all done."

"Good," he says, pulling the covers up and turning away from me again, the shorn wing on his left shoulder peeking out above the covers for a moment before he tugs them back up angrily.

"Layden," I say, reaching to put a hand on his shoulder, careful not to hit the stump of his once-wing.

He flinches away from my touch, though, and I yank back. "I think I'll rest now," he grumbles into his pillow. I suck in a deep breath and stand up. Is it as difficult for him to allow anyone close as it is for me to? Especially after he was betrayed by his own brothers?

I swallow hard. It hurts the worst when it's family that only sees you as something to use. It's wrong. Family should be like I knew briefly as a child before I had to come live with my Grandfather Vlad. When it was just me and Mom and Dad. We didn't live in a palace or a compound. Just a small apartment.

But they loved me. We decorated a Christmas tree each year and drank hot chocolate, and when I had a bad dream, my mother would rock me back to sleep. My father read me bedtime stories, played soccer with me at the nearby park, and held me when I cried because I didn't fit in with the other little kids.

It was... I turn away so Layden won't see the stupid tears suddenly flooding my cheeks. I breathe in hard, a little shocked. I can't remember the last time I cried. Or let myself think about Mom and Dad.

When I was a kid, so wrapped up in their love, it was easy to believe...

I shake my head and swallow my tears. Foolish.

That time was just a dream. I'm awake now and know the truth, even if it's nice to allow this creature in front of me to believe the lie again for a little while. The lie that I'm an innocent creature, capable of good.

I know better now.

"There's no more meat," I pronounce because I need to be out of this little house with its cozy, friendly softness and the man with the kind eyes. "I'm going hunting and will be back later."

Layden half turns over, and I see concern in his eyes. "Is that safe?"

I laugh. "Believe me, I'm the scariest predator in these woods."

His eyes narrow again, head tilting slightly. I see the question in his eyes and slam out the door before he can ask it.

Half an hour later, I watch the red liquid puddle on the forest floor from the buck I've run down and strung up, bowing my head.

Memories of blood are the oldest ones I possess. Before I truly even understood. When the salty metallic bite was all I had to hold onto in the darkness. I clung to it like a desperate, wild thing. Which was all I was.

I gut the buck ruthlessly, wondering if I'm more animal than this majestic being ever was. I yank out its still warm heart, so recently beating, and wonder if I should leave Layden's side so that I don't become a curse to him like I have been to everyone else in my life.

I am not good. I am not kind.

Sure, in the dark, shadowed beginnings, I didn't understand what all the blood would cost. I wanted the warmth. I wanted life more than anything. But what good are excuses?

I look at the buck, eyes dead and lifeless. Instead, I have become this. I toss the heart to the ground and finish gutting the animal and preparing the meat.

I already know that I'll go back to Layden.

Because I'm as selfish as always. My cold, miserable existence has always felt like a constant punishment for ever dreaming of better.

Yet here I am, still hoping, still dreaming.

Still a fool.

I head back for the cabin, hauling the huge carcass behind me.

Chapter Seven

LAYDEN
Present Day

Phoenix looks down at her phone and makes a girlish noise of delight. "I texted, and Professor Rossi has time for us!"

"Shouldn't he always have time if Vlad bought him for you?" I growl under my breath, eyes flicking all around at the other students flooding out of the lecture hall. I don't know how she can be so excited about this guy shedding light on what we've fought so hard to keep secret.

We always knew the conspiracy theorists would have a field day with the footage of the Devourers that covered the media outlets and internet sites for about six hours straight last month before my brother Remus blasted them out of existence. Governments denied it all as a hoax, but much as I wish they were, people aren't stupid.

Most of the conspiracy nuts are going on and on about

secret government weapons and the like, and frankly, I'm shocked that Phoenix is encouraging anything that, while it might not be the absolute truth, is near enough.

"Don't ever say that to me," Phoenix spins on me, furious. "I don't let Vlad buy anyone for me. That's disgusting. I allowed him to offer an incentivizing package to teach here, but I never expected that to equal special treatment or consideration. I'm just like any other student and will get by on my intellectual and academic merits alone."

Dammit, I really stepped in that one, didn't I? "Look, Phoenix, I didn't mean—" I hold up a hand, but she bats it away, rolls her eyes, and mutters, "Never mind. I don't expect you to treat this seriously."

She strides away from me. I easily keep up. "No, Phoenix, I do."

I reach for her arm, then think better of it and pull back. But at least she stops. I can control my hunger to touch her. I *can*. I lean in, and for once, we're in a mostly shadowed alcove where there aren't a lot of other students around.

"I just don't understand why you're so concerned with what this guy thinks. I mean, sure, he's got his theories, but you *know* what happened."

"*Do* I?" she fires back.

I frown.

"Yes, I know what happened last month. I called a power I couldn't even begin to understand from another realm into this one. But beyond that, what the hell do I know?" She leans in. "You know, one of the last things Sabra's mother foresaw before she died was a fissure in this plane that would allow other spirits in. Professor Rossi found prophecies of a similar fissure—of a time when the gods would *return*.

"*Think*, Layden." She leans in, and I'm briefly blasted

by the scent of her shampoo and can't think about anything except how good she smells. "I know we haven't really ever talked about it. But you've been around far longer than me. Was there a time when gods roamed the earth and then went away? Because while spirits from other realms may have always been breaching this plane, I think they used to do it a lot more often."

She waves her hands as she talks. "But then something happened, and they stopped. Maybe there was even a mass exodus or expulsion."

I blink, thinking about a story my father always told me. "I've felt old my whole life, but you know, I'm still relatively young, too, if you consider the earth's age. Only two or three thousand years old. My father, though…"

I lean back against the side of the stone building, trying to focus on her words instead of her scent. "Many angels from the Great Hall used to walk this plane until one day they left. But my father didn't want to, so he stole the Spark of Life and came back to forge his sons and dominate this world." I look back at Phoenix as it clicks. "Because he was the only one left."

Her eyes light up, realizing the same thing I am. "Because maybe he saw that all his competitors had left, too, and not just the angels."

"But what could have happened to send them all running back to the realms they came from?"

"And how did your father escape the great exile and come back anyway?"

We both stare at each other, stumped.

"Don't you see? That's why I'm studying under Professor Rossi. He might not have all the answers, but he's spent his life studying human texts from that age. He knows what people who lived back then said and thought about what they saw when it was all happening. If the prophecy is right, and more spirits are going to be coming back into the world, don't we need to be prepared?"

"Are you suggesting we need to find a way to send every spirit in this realm back to where they came from? Like some global version of the circle the mage and I cooked up to send my father back to the Great Hall?" Because I can't even fathom... My head shakes in disbelief at the thought. "It took *years* for us to figure that out, and that was just working out the magical coordinates to a *single* realm that I'd already visited once before."

"I don't know! But we have to try and find out, don't we?"

I try to focus on the *we* in her statement and the way she's looking at me so emphatically. I nod and fight the impulse to reach out to take her hands. She's asking for a partner in research; maybe that's all I'll ever be to her, but I'll take whatever I can get if it means being by her side.

She smiles at me, and it makes me feel radiant inside, like the sun after a rainstorm.

But right before I can say anything else or do something stupid like ask if she'd ever want to try this marriage out for real, her phone buzzes loudly in her pocket.

She frowns and pulls it out. Whatever she sees makes her face go absolutely grim.

"What?" I ask, concerned.

"It's Vlad. He's sending us to go investigate." When her eyes come up to me, they've lost all the joy she had when she was texting her professor. "There's been a murder."

Chapter Eight

PHEONIX
10 Years Ago

I dozed off last night in the plump, worn chair that looked like it was covered more in blankets than any of the original upholstery, which had been worn down to bare seams long ago. Not the most comfortable place to sleep, but I wasn't about to climb in beside my patient, and the dirt floor looked a little too hard-packed for my liking.

Something startles me awake and I leap to my feet, all senses on alert. Immediately, I look toward the bed, but Layden's not there.

Then I take in the noise that woke me. Outside the window, there's a rhythmic *thwack, thwack, thwacking* noise.

Frowning, I get low and move in a crouch for the window and then stand full to my feet when I see Layden, shirtless in the morning fog that settles over the dewy ground, chopping wood.

And he's, uh... different, to say the least.

It's as if some magical transformation has taken over him.

He's not skin and bones anymore.

Instead, as he lifts the ax high overhead, large muscles bulge as he swings down with incredible force, splitting a huge log he's got set up on an even bigger stump. My eyes travel down his body. His pecs are round and firm, leading to a six-pack of abs. The muscles in his shoulders ripple in the dancing morning light, but I also catch a glimpse of the stumps still sticking out his back—unchanged amidst the rest of his transformation. His hot skin steams as he stands up after splitting another log into pieces.

I head to the door and push it open, wanting to demand to know what's going on, at the same time realizing that he didn't use his newfound strength to leave when he obviously could have.

But he stayed. He stayed, and he's chopping wood.

I blink when I get to the bottom of the cottage stairs, looking up at him. He's taller than me, I realize for the first time. Before, he was always bent over, as I had to all but carry him.

But now I see that, no, he's tall. He stands about a head over me, in fact. I can only blink at him, my mouth dropping open when it hits me—his new physique isn't the only thing that's changed.

He's shaved his beard and combed his wild hair back.

I can finally see his face.

And he's absolutely stunning. A face like a chiseled god's.

When he sets the ax down and looks at me, I'm

completely dumbfounded. I'd had something on my mind to say to him, to ask him, but I suddenly can't conjure a single thought. I'm completely ridiculous, but I can't help but just stand there.

"I apologize," he says, "but I smelled the meat you had cooking all night and came out earlier. And I, well, I finally felt really hungry, so I ate it all."

I blink out of my momentary stupor and look toward the rudimentary iron smoker beside the cabin where I laid out the deer meat last night and set it smoking. "Oh." And then I really hear his words, and my head snaps back to him. "You ate *all* of it?"

His cheeks are already ruddy from the wood-chopping and cold morning air, but I swear they get a little pinker. "I didn't mean to, I was just *so* hungry—"

"No, no, it's totally fine. We can always get more. It's great that your appetite is back. And it's obviously helped." I gesture vaguely at his chest. "You look... different."

He glances down at himself and, as if only then realizing his bare chest is exposed, reaches for a flannel shirt he tossed near the big stack of chopped wood and tugs it on, quickly stabbing a few buttons through holes. "I heal fast."

I scoff at that as I walk toward him. "Yeah. Understatement. Apparently, you needed meat and a lot of it. Come here; your buttons are all out of whack."

I reach to undo the few he'd managed, line the sides of the shirt up correctly, and start to button it again. I only realize that my knuckles are occasionally brushing against the skin of his abdomen when I hear little hisses of air escape his mouth.

Which makes me suddenly hyperaware of how close we're standing.

And that this man... or whatever he is... is most definitely no longer some convalescing patient I can pretend I'm Florence Nightingale for.

"What now?" I whisper after I have his buttons done correctly all the way up to his collarbone. And why am I still holding onto his shirt? I make myself let go and step back, then force a smile I don't feel. I guess he'll go his way, and I'll go mine, is what I expect him to say.

But instead, he says, "First, I've got to get you another buck to replace the one I just ate."

"Oh." I laugh with surprise. "Well, it was mostly for you."

"But you need to eat." He looks deadly serious as he says this.

I shrug. "I'll just go hunt another deer. It's not a big deal."

He shakes his head. "I ate your deer. I should go hunt the next one."

I laugh at his bravado. "You're barely on your feet again." But I can already see the next protest on his lips.

I'm about to cut him off, but his suggestion surprises me. "Why don't we do it together?"

I blink, a little taken aback. I don't do things *with* people. I'm not a together type of person.

I frown and start striding ahead. "Fine. At least then you'll see why it makes sense for me to do the hunting."

I glance over my shoulder only once to see if he's following and keeping up. His clear, gray eyes are inquisitive, but he nods and starts jogging after me.

For someone I've only seen in bed for days, it's astonishing to see him up and moving again. Half of me hoped that the wood chopping would have laid him out enough that he'd turn back once he saw the pace I was setting. But he easily keeps up with me. I even get the feeling he could go at much greater speeds, which annoys me. I decide to speed up. I was taking it easy on him.

Still, he matches me. So I go even faster, all but flying through the woods now while still being careful to make minimal sound.

He's still right there beside me.

When I finally stop and look at him, I struggle not to drop my jaw in shock. He's told me what he is, but I wasn't quite sure I believed it. I mean, all I saw was a man with stumps at his shoulders and some sparks at his hands, which could have been a magician's trick for all I knew.

But we just moved at supernatural speed, and he didn't even look winded.

Instead, he just motions with his fingers as if *he* thinks we're upwind from the deer and need to position ourselves better.

I want to smack him or tell him that, *duh*, I know. But it doesn't matter. Because I'm a hunter in a far more primal meaning of the word. And now that I've locked onto my prey...

I close my eyes and lock in on the heartbeat of the beast. I can also feel Layden beside me, impatient and sure that I'm doing this all wrong. Oh, ye of little faith. I can't help the small smile from quirking my lips. This surprises me because it's been a long, long time since any of my power brought me much joy at all.

But I think it might actually be fun to watch the look on his face as...

I stretch outwards beyond my body, listening and feeling for the heartbeats hiding in the woods. There are so many, many living things. I even feel the slight pulse of the sap in the ancient trees; everything is so alive out here. It can be overwhelming if I focus on it too long.

Then again, I'm used to hunting in cities, where the chaotic, discordant pounding of human heartbeats all but chokes me.

Here, it's far more harmonious and easier to separate the large beating hearts from the small. For instance, I can feel four beating hearts in the herd of deer nearby and easily pick out the largest.

My eyes fall closed, and silently, I call to it.

Sometimes, I think of myself as a siren of the blood. For when I call, they come. Leaving family and any others behind, willingly, any and all will walk to their doom.

I can feel Layden's astonishment as the buck walks out of the woods, antlers briefly catching on a bush before he shakes free to come to us. He walks right up to us as if he would eat out of our hands and then lays himself at my feet, head bowed.

I bend down beside him and murmur thanks for his sacrifice. "Thank you, my beautiful one."

He snorts in response, a low chuff. I run my fingers through his fur, and he snuggles closer to my thighs. They all love me right before the end.

"That's right," I murmur. "You've done well, my beautiful one. Now you can rest."

Then, I slit his throat with the knife I had hidden up my sleeve. Soundlessly, his head drops to the forest, his wise eyes looking up at me lovingly as the life drains out of them.

Only once the creature goes entirely limp do I sigh and stand, readying myself to dress the meat.

It's then that I remember the other beating heart beside me and look up to see Layden watching me. For the first time since I've met him, his eyes are wide. And wary.

"Does it only work on animals?" he asks.

Ah. So he's not just pretty. He's smart, too.

I stand with my shoulders held high as I tell him the truth. "It works on anything with a beating heart."

I sense he's about to step back, but he stands still. Dammit. He's brave, too. "Did you do that to me when we first met?"

I stare him straight in the eye. "I tried. It didn't work. I told you to stay, and you didn't stay."

Since I'm looking at him, I can see the moment his lips tip up and his whole demeanor lightens. "Good," is all he says, and then he reaches down for the hind legs of the buck to help me string him up and dress him.

* * *

We walk back to the cabin, Layden dragging the buck by the legs. We're walking slow, like we're just out taking a stroll in the woods. If it weren't for the lingering scent of blood that always has my teeth on edge, it might almost be romantic. Blood is such an old smell to me. The first one I ever knew, it feels like. My oldest memory. I try to shake it off and focus on the forest around me, the mid-morning light filtering down through the tall branches above.

"How did you learn how to do that?" Layden asks. "Or is it something you could always do?"

"I could always do it."

"How?"

"I just could."

"I mean. . ." He waves a hand. "What *are* you?"

I sigh. Of course it was going to come to this. But what I am comes with too complicated a history to explain. Right now or maybe ever.

"I have an affinity for blood," I say instead, holding back

some branches so he can walk past. "It calls to me, and like I said, anyone with a beating heart, I can..."

"Control," he says.

"Coerce," I supply instead.

"Can you make people do things they don't want to do?"

I shrug, looking ahead. "They want to do whatever I ask." Quieter, I add, "Because I've asked it."

"Are you a vampire? Do you drink blood?"

"No. And what is this? Twenty questions?"

When I look back at him, he looks a little confused. "Do I only get twenty? Why?"

It's such an absurd question I can only bust out laughing.

He hurries forward. "It's just that I want to know everything about you."

I frown, looking at him over my shoulder. Was I wrong about the compulsion? Did it just take a little while to take effect on him?

"Stay there, and don't follow me anymore," I order.

He pauses, looking confused, and for a second, my heart cinches up in fear. Oh no, it's true. Whatever kind of being he is, it just took longer for it to work, and now he's just as mindless as everyone else I'm surrounded by—

I start to hurry away from him, frustrated and infuriated by the tears suddenly biting at my eyes. What the fuck? I don't cry. I haven't cried in fourteen years, and now twice in a week?

"You didn't actually think that would work, did you?" His voice comes from far closer than I would have thought.

I jump and spin around. Layden is there, somehow able to move even more silently through the woods than I usually do. "How did you—?"

"I don't envy you," he says, his words soft and those damn eyes of his seeing far more than they should. "It must be hard living in a world where you can't trust people's motives for even wanting to be around you."

I swing back away from him. Did he see the almost tears in my eyes? I feel too many things I can't sort out at once, and I don't want him to be able to see my face while I try. And why the hell am I so happy that my compulsion didn't work on him after all?

This man is nothing to me. What the hell am I doing? Playing in the woods and pretending my real life isn't behind me, ready and waiting for the second I leave this forest? This isn't real. This *man* might as well not be real for as much as he could ever fit into my life. A thought which appalls me. Was I really even considering that there could be a place for him? Was I actually fucking stupid enough to start *wanting* something? Wanting *him*?

I swallow hard against all these unfamiliar, conflicting feelings. I saw where wanting got me the first time. So, I force my voice to be strong. "It seems like you're back to full strength. Where will you go after this? What's next for you?"

Silence is his only reply.

I don't look back at him, just keep walking. I can't hear him, but the occasional swish of a leaf or bush behind me tells me he's still following.

"Layden?" I finally ask as the small cabin comes back into view. Still, I don't turn my head. "Did you hear me? What will you do now that you're strong again?"

"I think I still need a few days of rest," he finally says. "To get my feet under me and plan what comes next."

I nod, relieved that he won't leave immediately. Because I'm a hypocrite, wanting what I can't have.

Chapter Nine

LAYDEN
Present Day

"A murder?" My eyebrows lift. "Why is Vlad calling you about a murder?"

But Phoenix is already sprinting back toward the car. I follow and wonder if this is my life now, chasing the beautiful backside of my wife. I blink and try to shake the word out of my head. No. Not my wife. Not in any meaningful way. I'll just torture myself thinking like that. Then again, a little torture can be fun sometimes. After enough time, there's nothing else to do but give in and enjoy the pain. I could enjoy the torture of being near Phoenix, even if it means never touching her.

She only stops once we're back at her car. "Vlad owns the police in the city. Well," she amends. "He owns the city. And the only murders that are allowed here are the ones he orders."

"Still, why call you?

"He doesn't usually. But this one's different. He sent in some forensic photos."

She tosses me her phone before turning the car on.

"What the fuck?" I say, almost dropping the phone as I look down at the bloody images. "How many bodies is that?"

"Just one," she says, and I turn the phone around. There's just so many *pieces*. And blood everywhere.

"It's on campus, so we don't have to go far."

"On campus?" I ask.

"It's a student. That's one of the dorm rooms."

Grimacing, I flip through the images on the phone. Over the past ten years, I made it my mission to not only become familiar with all things involving human technology but to master it. Still, I find their ability to capture moments with a picture or video impressive. I zoom in on various parts of the image as I look around the room. You can barely see the outline of the furniture because of all the blood.

It's not that I haven't seen gruesome things before. After some battles, the bodies were piled three feet deep on the battlefield and stunk in a way that took years to wash off.

I set the phone back down between us, swallowing some of the breakfast that's threatening to come back up as Phoenix parks again. It's just been a while for me.

It was easy to pretend after I first woke in the woods that this civilization had gotten things right and left all the bloodshed behind. Then I did a little traveling and realized they'd mostly just outsourced the suffering to other parts of the world or the neighborhoods they didn't live in.

And here it is, right in Vlad's tidy little kingdom, blood not spilled by him and his kin for once.

Police are putting up perimeter tape as students gather

outside the six-story concrete dormitory, chatter going through the crowd, wondering what's wrong. Phoenix strides confidently forward, and I stay at her side.

When we get up to the perimeter tape, a policeman holds up his hand. "No one gets through."

But Phoenix just smiles at him, and she's never looked more beautiful or alluring as she says, "But you want to let me and my friend through."

The police officer's face immediately turns to one of absolute adoration as he pulls back the cone holding the tape. "Yes, Mistress, anything for you."

It's creepy as fuck. But Phoenix strides through as if nothing is amiss, and I follow her. I mean, I knew about her compulsion power, but seeing it in action is another thing entirely. It makes me even more determined never to fawn over her or let her see my hunger for her. And even more ashamed of the naïve fool I once was.

Police are interviewing students in various pockets in the lobby, but we head straight past them and jog up the stairs since the elevator has been shut down. The scene is on the fifth floor, apparently.

Again, people try to stop us, and again, Phoenix does her thing, gaining us easy passage onto the floor and into the room.

The stink of spilled blood hits me halfway down the hallway, and I can tell it affects Phoenix even more than me. Of course it does.

Phoenix enters first and makes all the policemen and forensic evidence-gathering folks inside file out. Several glance back at her with longing, worshipful gazes. If I think it's uncomfortable, what must it be like for her? I feel doubly determined not to be another fucker longing after her when she's just trying to live her life. She didn't ask for any of this.

I enter the room once it's clear and immediately lift a hand to cover my nose. Because I've looked at the pictures, I assume I'm prepared for what I'll see when we get into the room. But if I thought it was hard to hold back my gag reflex in the car...

The thing is, back in the day, I wasn't as useful in the thick of battle as my brothers were. I was the guy they sent ahead to weaken the enemy by ruining the crops and starving everyone. I was great in a siege. It was the others who had to get up close and knee-deep in the gore.

But this... this is straight-up carnage worthy of any medieval battle. My eyes narrow as I look around, trying to take in everything at once. Yes, there's blood, viscera, and guts everywhere, but it's also so... orderly.

"Did they use some sort of machine?" I ask. "Something that chopped him up all at once and spread him around so... neatly?" It feels like the wrong word to use considering the horrific mess, but at the same time, the chopped-up body parts look very parallel. There's a calf on the left and a calf on the right. Same with his lungs, chopped cleanly in half and laid out like a puzzle ready to be put back together.

"Not a machine," Phoenix says, bending down in the center of the room to examine everything more closely. "Someone would have heard a buzzsaw if that had been used. More like an ax or surgical tools. Although..." she says, parting the entrails with a pen she either pulled from her pocket or got off a policeman to examine something more closely, "these bone fragments don't show any tool marks."

"What do they show then?" I ask, still keeping my distance at the edge of the room. I don't know what help I'll be here. But I'm glad that Phoenix isn't alone in facing such a gory tableau. She's cold and stoic, and if she feels anything as she pokes and prods through the remains of what was once a person, she doesn't show it on her face. The carpet is drenched in blood so thick that her boots squelch with every step.

She crouches down again and prods another bone, making a disconcerted noise.

"What?" I ask.

"No, no machine marks. It's almost as if the bones have been..." She trails off.

"What?"

She looks up at me, a line in between her brows. "Sliced with something that burned as it cut."

"What could do that?"

She stands up, dropping the pen and wiping her hands back and forth across each other. "I don't know."

"Is that a good idea?" I point at the dropped pen. "Could it be used as evidence?"

She waves away my concern. "Vlad owns the police. And it's not as if they'd be of any use in this anyway. No human could have done this."

Shit. That was what I was afraid of. "Because of the bones?"

She points at the center of the room. "The body's been laid out like a ritual sacrifice, and the heart's missing. It's not any of my family trying to fuck with Vlad because the blood's all here. Vlad's sons wouldn't have been able to help themselves from at least having a little taste. And the timing's too coincidental."

I shake my head, not understanding.

Her face is pale as she looks at the floor. "I was afraid of this. Last month with the circle, everything got out of control with it getting so supercharged."

"What does that have to do with any—"

"We obviously let other things through!" she hisses, looking back up at me furiously. "It was *us*. We're the reason for the crack. Sabra's mother's prophecy was about *us*, don't you get it? What we did to stop the Devourers has also let other spirits through."

I start to shake my head but pause to actually think about it. Because a lot of the conspiracy sites I've been tracking online *have* been mentioning other disturbances. Strange things, like monsters made out of rock who disappear into the shadows at night. Or evil women who seduce men's soul out of their bodies and leave them as shriveled husks. But I just assumed it was woman-hating incel shit taken to the next level with people's heightened paranoia since the Devourers came.

I look around the room at the uncanny precision of the dismembering. I can't imagine anything human strong enough to pull a body apart with such disturbing exactitude. "What does the missing heart mean? Is there anything you know of from another plane that would do that?"

"The mages have barely mapped *any* of the other planes, much less used their instruments to look through to the other side to see what lives there. You know that."

I nod, but I'd hoped... I don't know what I hoped. I just hate seeing Phoenix so distressed, and I hate even more that she's blaming herself. "You were trying to stop the end of the world," I say, reaching out a hand to help her as she tiptoes among the body parts back to the doorway. She ignores my outstretched hand.

"I should have found a better way."

"There was no time. And it wasn't all up to you, if you'll remember. The danger came from the angels. If anyone's at fault, it's someone from my plane."

"Well," she hunches her shoulders, "then I went and got a hero complex about it and fucked things up even worse."

I scoff, holding my arms out. "The planet's still here. How is that worse?"

Her eyes squint shut, and briefly, I see emotion cross her face. Pain and self-judgment and a thousand other things she never usually lets me see. I want to pull her in my arms and let her know that, for once, someone else is here to help shoulder her burdens. Dangerous to want, but I don't like seeing her pain all the same. I try words instead.

"You aren't alone," I whisper.

But that only makes her eyes flash open, burning with a fury I can't understand. "You have no idea what I am." She shoulders her way past me. "I have to fix this."

I follow her. "How exactly are you going to do that?"

"I'm going to find whatever did this."

"Did you find some clue?"

Our feet squelch red tracks on the tile hallway, not that Phoenix notices until one of the adoring policemen she used her compulsion on earlier offers to exchange shoes with her. Irritated, Phoenix wipes her feet off on a student's welcome mat outside their dorm room and orders the policeman to clean it and the hallway up.

"Besides the fact it was a non-human who did it? No." She looks away. "The scent of blood was too overpowering."

I nod. While not a vampire herself, she is still a being of blood magic. "All the blood itself was a clue, too," she says as we keep walking. "Blood is not only symbolic of human life..." She lets out a long sigh. "For some spirits on the other side, it can be a tether. Like a source of energy that also ties them to this plane."

I frown. "Is that what Sabra and her mage friends told you?"

She waves a frustrated hand. "Let's just call it a bit of family lore."

I want to ask more questions but don't. Instead, I focus on the case at hand. "So you think the blood helped give the spirit passage through?"

Phoenix bites her lip, giving the briefest nod. "It's a possibility. In the other planes, they don't always understand what this realm is. But human blood and the energy of bloodletting—and the soul that ebbs from the body at death—provides a huge amplification of spirit energy. It's why blood sacrifice was so popular in ancient religions."

"Ah," I say. "One of the reasons you think your professor might be onto something."

"He's not *my* professor," she says irritably. "But yes. I think there was a reason that so many ancient religions had the common element of blood sacrifice. There was power in the blood, as they used to say, and it was more than metaphoric. It fed the spirits who'd come from other realms, strengthening their ties to this one. It fed their power. The more worshippers they had, the more temples, the more blood sacrifices."

I nod. "That's dark. Getting humans to do your dirty work."

"Yeah, well." She huffs out a breath as she starts down the stairs. "The spirits didn't exactly have a conception of the worth of human life, did they? Just like humans don't consider much about the lives of the cows they slaughter to eat."

"Touché."

"Most spirits previously spent their lives in intangible darkness on other planes. Matter often works differently in those places. They became wild and greedy once they got to here and were able to manifest physical bodies."

"Sounds to me like you're the one who could give the Professor a lecture."

We're at the bottom of the stairs when Phoenix spins on me. "What is with you? You keep bringing him up. I thought you'd be excited to hear his theories."

Dammit, I don't want to look like a jealous bastard. Or to feel like I'm putting any more pressure on Phoenix and this pretense of a marriage.

"Nothing," I smile in an attempt at appeasement, holding up my hands. "I'm just wary of outsiders knowing our business."

The hard line of her mouth doesn't budge. "Well, I suggest you get over it because I think we should call him."

"What?" Okay, this does surprise me. "You can't."

It's apparent she doesn't like that.

I gesture back up the stairs. "You just said no human could have done that."

"He doesn't have to know details," she says. "But he's more familiar with all the various factions of ancient religions that were active back in the day. And the spirits who once populated this plane and were kicked out may be the first ones back through if there is some sort of weakening or opening in the planes."

"Maybe, I guess. But isn't it equally possible it could be a completely new spirit? We should call Sabra and see if she sees anything we missed."

Phoenix bites her lip. "Maybe."

I frown. Is it just me, or does she *really* want to bring her —I mean *the* Professor—in on this.

"Look, I've seen it before," she says. "My mother was possessed by an ancient goddess while she was pregnant with me, okay? One who was trying to break back into this world. She was pissed she'd been kicked out of this plane and killed a lot of people on her quest to get back in."

"What?" I'm shocked. "You never told me that." No wonder she knows so much about spirits in the dark and what they want.

"Yeah. Well. It's another reason I wanted to study with Professor Rossi. I think I finally identified who it was, and I want to make sure we're all on guard in case she tries again."

"Fuck, Phoenix, why didn't you tell me that sooner? Is that why you're... different? From Vlad, I mean?"

"What?" She looks surprised by my question. "Oh. No. That was just a coincidence. Sort of. The other goddess could sense there was spirit activity going on with my family and got interested in us. Anyway." She waves a hand and looks away, then starts walking again, a firm stride out of the building as she pulls out her phone, no doubt to text the Professor again.

"You don't think this is her, do you?" I point upstairs.

"No," she says. "That goddess preferred to explode people's heads from the inside out, but she left the rest of the body alone."

Again, I'm left chasing after Phoenix's retreating back.

* * *

We meet Professor Dickhead for lunch.

I glower at him as we approach.

"John Paul!" Phoenix says warmly when we get to the table, and he stands, grasping her hands and pulling her in to air-kiss each of her cheeks. My eyes narrow.

His eyes only come to me when he finally pulls back. "And who is *this*?" He looks me up and down with clear distaste on his face.

Phoenix waves a hand dismissively. "Just a family friend who's staying with us for a while. I told Grandpapa I'd let him shadow me and see what university life was all about."

Family *friend*. I grit my teeth. Can he not see the ring on her finger? But she has the strap of her purse coiled around her left hand. Purposely so he won't see the ring?

Just how far does her interest in her dear professor go?

"We *adored* your lecture. I'm so sorry about the disruption at the end."

"Alas," the Professor says with a long-suffering sigh. "That is the way of things wherever you go with progressive ideas lately. The world is so on edge they are unwilling to listen to the truth." He reaches across the table and grasps Phoenix's hand. And she *allows* it.

"Shouldn't we be ordering drinks or something?" I say loudly. Phoenix finally pulls her hand away and nods, starting to stand. But Professor Fuckface just waves a hand. "I already ordered for you, bellezza. I remembered your favorite."

They smile at each other.

Then, the Professor looks back at me. "But feel free to go to the counter and order yourself something."

And leave the two of them alone? Fuck this shit.

I lean forward, causing the feet of the table to screech on the tile. "You're her advisor, are you not? Is it *advisable* to be so casual with a student?"

"Layden," Phoenix hisses, smacking my leg under the table. But I ignore her, keeping my eyes on the Professor.

His eyes finally meet mine as if truly acknowledging my existence for the first time. "You are a cousin, no?"

"No."

"Ah," he says, smiling a patronizing smile that makes me want to smash his face with a blast of runes. "It is true, I am la signorina's Ph.D. advisor, but her dissertation is almost complete. At this point I consider her more of a peer than a student anymore. She is the brightest student I ever taught and will go on to surpass me in academia, I am sure of it."

"Nonsense!" Phoenix cries.

"I mean it, bella. You are going to produce such amazing work." His eyes turn to hers now with an intensity I recognize. It's the intensity of devotion. But I doubt it's because she ever used her compulsion on him. My stomach turns over as I turn to look at her. Does she feel the same way about him?

Her eyes shine at his praise, but even though she's a little less on guard in this setting, it only means she has different walls up. She plays a part when she's with this man. She's never able to be her true self. This might be the life she wants, but with him, it would always be partially fiction.

Still, seeing the smile on her face as they discuss his new research and the looseness in her limbs, I wonder if she dreams about it anyway. She hates the blood magic part of her life. She always has. Little wonder, considering the way Vlad raised her. Half-granddaughter, half-slave to do his dirty work for him. Of course she dreams of a normal life.

"So, Professor, there's actually a reason I wanted to call this meeting, in addition to wanting to congratulate you on your excellent lecture."

"My busy schedule is always open to you, bella, you know that."

"Well," Phoenix bites her bottom lip. "I know we've been talking so much about all that's been happening last month and how it might relate to ancient worship practices. I came across something this week and wanted to know what you think about it and if you had any insight. Could you look at some crime scene photos?"

He only blinked once with surprise before saying, "Of course."

"I got these pictures from a source I have who's familiar with the deep web." Phoenix pulls out her phone, and the Professor tugs his glasses from his front pocket before reaching for it. Phoenix pulls the phone back at the last minute. "I'll warn you, they're gruesome."

The Professor nods gravely. "I understood they might be from what you asked."

Phoenix nods and relinquishes the phone to him. Even though he was apparently ready for it, I still see his face react to the horrific images Phoenix snapped while we were on the scene.

"*Madonna Santa!*" he whispers, crossing himself briefly before flipping to another image.

He pushes the bagel he ordered away right as Phoenix's coffee and pastry arrive. I peek at the coffee. It's some swirly, milky-colored concoction with whipped cream on top. *Whipped cream.*

I've endured late-night coding sessions with this woman, and all I ever saw her down was entire pots of black coffee. Thick as tar, too.

The Professor puts the phone down and crosses himself again.

"So what do you think? Is it anything you've seen before?"

He takes a moment before answering but then finally does. "Heaven help us, but yes, I have, only once before."

Phoenix almost leaps over the table, I can tell she's so excited. "Where? What was it?"

"During my work with Ancient Egyptian scrolls. They spoke of an evil goddess who would enchant a man with her sexual pull. She would get him alone, mate him, and then demand his life as a sacrifice. After the mating, she'd tear his body apart. 'Rend him limb from limb and joint from joint in a circle bathed in blood' was how the texts described it. And then she would eat his heart."

"Like a black widow," I murmur.

"The heart wasn't there," Phoenix says. "You really think it could be her? Come back after all this time?" She sounds incredulous but also focused. "How do we find her? Stop her?"

The Professor's mouth drops open. "You'll do no such thing. Phoenix! Did you not see these photos? These are powers for us to observe from afar! Not interfere with."

"Of course, of course. I just want to study her more," Phoenix recovers quickly. "To include in my dissertation. What's her name?"

"Ammit, the man-eater."

"Oh, of course. I read about her in *The Egyptian Book of the Dead*."

"That's the best place to start."

Phoenix jumps up from her seat.

"You haven't even touched your latte," the Professor objects.

"I hate to dash, but time's running out on the dissertation if I want to put in this new addition," Phoenix apologizes. "Thank you so much for your time, John Paul."

"Of course, of course, I understand. Your devotion to your studies is what makes you such an excellent protégé."

He stands up as well and holds his hand out to me. "It was wonderful to meet you, Signore...?"

Phoenix's eyes widen like she's appalled at herself for never *actually* introducing us. Or maybe because she hoped to make an escape without him ever learning my name.

"Layden," I say, grasping his hand in a bone-crushing handshake. To his credit, he only winces a little.

"Signore Layden," he says before letting go and shaking his hand out. "Quite a grip you've got there."

Phoenix glares at me. "Well, time to be off. I'll see you later this week after office hours to go over my most recent revisions on my chapters?"

The Professor grins far too wide. "Wouldn't miss it." After Phoenix turns away, he winks at me.

I barely keep back my snarl, and it takes even more restraint not to put my hand behind Phoenix's back in a show of protection and intention to guide her away from Fuckface.

"You really think Vlad's gonna like you getting close to that guy?" I mutter as we finally walk away.

"What's that supposed to mean?" She turns on me, fire in her eyes.

"Nothing," I say. "Just that we're supposed to look married. On our honeymoon. All that. What's he gonna say if he catches you carrying on in your professor's office?"

"We're not—" She cuts herself off when her voice hits another octave. "*Carrying on.* Jesus, why do you have to make it sound so sordid? He's just my advisor and a man I respect."

I scoff. Respect.

"You know what?" She spins on me. "Fuck you."

"Me? What did I do?"

She glares at me like she wants to murder me. "You

came back. I was perfectly happy here. I had a life." She gestures so hard at the university behind her that it looks like she all but dislocates her shoulder socket. "I have friends."

At my stare, she stomps her foot. "I have Sabra anyway. And I have a future. One that doesn't involve blood and my grandfather determining my every move. I'm doing what *I* want to do."

"Looks like it still involves blood to me."

She gets right up in my face. "Studying it, not spilling it. Or having it spilled on my behalf. Or putting compulsions on people so they lose their fucking minds in order to please me. I was doing just fine until you called and dragged me back into all this shit."

The pain of regret pierces, but she's got me too frustrated to make sense of it, and all I can do is get back in her face. "Well, you started it. Maybe you should have left me alone that day in the woods. But you didn't, did you? And actions have consequences."

"Oh, I get that, buddy," she says low, shoving me in the chest so I move out of her way. "You're a fucking idiot if you don't think I get that by now." She stomps all the way back to the car.

I want to keep arguing with her. So I do. Because I hate the despair in her voice.

"Where are you going now?"

She only spins back to me once she's at her car, and I'm happy that at least the fire is still there in her eyes. "Where do you think? I'm going to find this man-eater. Ammit."

"How the hell are you going to do that? Are we going to a library?"

She glares at me like she doesn't actually want to say but

then finally huffs out a breath. "Fine. I'll tell you. But only because you're useful as bait."

That surprises a laugh out of me. "Bait?"

"It's Friday night, and there's one place most of the college kids here hit up on a Friday night. It'd be an excellent hunting ground for Ammit." Then she smirks at me. "You'll feel right at home."

"What's that supposed to mean?"

"It's called the Fallen Angels Club."

Chapter Ten

PHEONIX
10 Years Ago

Layden helps me arrange the meat on the smoker like I did yesterday, and we take turns priming the pump while the other washes off. I try—and fail—not to sneak peeks at Layden as he tugs his shirt off over his head. It's a good thing the farmer happened to be large-shouldered because Layden's arms seem to all but split the seams with his muscles.

How has he gained so much mass back in a single day? It's as if this is his true form, and he simply needed to absorb enough calories to return to it.

"I'm hungry," he says as he finishes buttoning another straining shirt. "Is there anything else to eat while we wait for the meat to finish cooking?"

I nod. "I checked this morning, and there's some eggs

from the chickens. And some unmarked cans in the cupboard we can try opening."

"I'll try the cans. You eat the eggs."

"There's four eggs," I say. "We can split them."

But he shakes his head no. "You need to eat. I should have saved some of the meat for you. It's unforgivable."

Seeing the guilt on his face about eating all the meat, I give in. I know he's especially stubborn about the fact that I continue eating while he's around, and I can only imagine how much he needed the meat if he wolfed it all down like that this morning.

He heads to the pantry and starts opening cans, tipping the contents into his mouth and swallowing what's inside, usually in one go. Green beans. Plums. Corn.

"Oh my god, do you even have a gag reflex?"

He looks my way, wipes his mouth with his forearm, and burps. "What's that?"

I shake my head and laugh. "Never mind."

I head to the big brick stove in the corner that's used for both warming the cabin and cooking. Fresh logs are stacked up to one side, thanks to Layden's morning efforts. The logs go in the bottom, and the burners for cooking are on the sides. Before this week, I hadn't used one of these old village stoves in a long time. Well, *I* never used it, but I saw my mom use them sometimes when I was young.

Some of my best memories are from places like this, with just Mom, Dad and me hidden away in little cabins in nowhere nooks of the world. Hiding away where my Grandfather couldn't find us. It even worked for a while, too.

"Phoenix?" Layden's voice brings me back to the present, and my head jerks his way.

"What?"

"Where were you just then?"

I scowl and reach for the cast iron pan to cook the eggs I brought in earlier. "Nowhere."

Wisely, he doesn't keep asking.

I cook my eggs while Layden continues opening and downing cans from the cupboard. He finally stops and turns back to me right as I'm plating my eggs. "The couple whose cabin this was. You used your compulsion on them."

I shrug. Duh. Obviously.

"What did you tell them?'"

"To leave immediately and go to a relative's house for two months."

His face brightens. "So we have two months?"

I drop the iron skillet hard back onto the brick stove and eat my eggs from the pan while standing. "You looked pretty bad, and I didn't know how fast you'd magically mend. But I guess now that you're better, you're welcome to squat here until they get back."

He squints at me. "And you? Will you leave now?"

My eyes drop to the smooth, packed earthen floor.

"Where would you go to?" he asks, voice softer. "Where are you from, wild Phoenix? Or did you just burst forth from the air? Maybe I've hallucinated all this," he finishes, murmuring to himself. "Maybe this is what happens when I finally snap and lose my mind. Not an altogether unpleasant madness." He looks around the cabin, his translucent gray eyes finally settling on me.

I roll mine. "I'm not a figment of your imagination."

"I don't know, dream girl," he smiles softly. "I can't imagine how you could possibly be real."

His words and too-handsome face make something swoop in my belly. If anything, he's the dream. I want to whisper it. I want to be a dumb, impulsive girl. This feels like something out of those novels Sabra's always trying to get me to read.

But I know better. I know better than to believe in a dream. Dreams don't come true for girls like me. Or maybe they do, but they're double-edged and slice like a knife.

Layden suddenly stands up and comes toward me. "Who are you, Phoenix?"

I hold up a hand to stop him, and he does stop, but only when my outstretched hand is pushing against his chest.

"Where do you come from? Who are your people? Why were you alone in the forest the day we met?"

My mouth stays stubbornly shut. Finally, feeling his eyes bore into me, I answer. "You'll never see me again, so none of that matters."

I start to pull away, but he reaches down to grasp my hand.

"It does too matter. You might not have been sitting alone in the woods for two hundred years, but I can tell we are alike. You are alone like me."

His words pierce me.

"It doesn't *matter*," I insist.

"It does! Because you aren't alone now. You are here, with me. You were running away from something, just like I was. What's the point of bringing me back to life and making me hope if you're just going to disappear into the fog again?"

My eyes flash up at him angrily, heat and emotions I don't understand searing through my chest. "I don't owe you anything."

"No. Of course you don't." He steps into me, and the hand not holding mine lifts to my face to caress down my cheek. "But what if we both stayed right here? Even if for just two months? What if we ran away from the rest of the world *together*?"

His face inches closer to mine and I blink, rational thought blanking at the nearness of him and his lips and his overwhelming scent. I can hear both our hearts beating like a drum line in my head, and mine is the one that's going faster. His is a cool, low-base beat, sure and strong, while I'm the captured, terrified rabbit. Does that mean I'm the prey? Do I care?

Because for only the second time in my seemingly endless existence, everything else drops away and it all seems so clear. I am pure, impulsive *want*.

I want to kiss this man. I want to devour him and be devoured. Our lips inch closer, and the tension between us snaps taut like a rubber band, each of us savoring the moment before connection. Offering a chance for the other to pull away. Neither of us does.

I suck in a breath, giddy for my first kiss but with a terrible, awesome feeling that this is about to change everything. A kiss from a fallen angel.

But just as our lips make the barest contact and Layden's chest begins to glow with a blinding light—

A loud banging knock comes from the door.

We leap apart, eyes wide, as both our heads swing toward it.

Layden tries to beat me to answer the door, which is cute. Obviously, I'm the one who should face any possible threats.

I shove him aside and open the door before he can make a counter move, ready to use my compulsion on whoever's on the other side.

But my eyes go wide. "Sabra!" I grab her arm and yank her through the door, slamming it shut behind her. "What are you doing here?" I ask, staring at her in shock. She shouldn't be here. She looks just like she did when I last saw her. Frizzy brown hair held back by a long braid down her back. Glasses too large for her face. Baggy clothes that are always *just* a little too big for her frame, even though she could afford better. Then again, the money would have come from Vlad, and I knew she hated accepting anything from him, even if she was working for it.

"Warmest greetings to you, too, bestie," she says, pushing her glasses up her nose. It's such a familiar gesture it breaks my heart.

I wave a hand and pull her into a hug. "You know I love you, but what the hell are you doing here? You're supposed to be on the other side of the world by now."

We had an agreement when we both ran away from my grandfather a week ago. Run and don't stop running. It was an imperfect plan. I had to stay within five hundred kilometers of Grandfather in order not to keel over because of my blood connection with him, so I planned to run in a concentric circle—something I knew would only work for so long before he found me. But Sabra should have been *long* gone by now. Safe. Away from me and the nightmare that is my family.

She pulls back from the hug, and by the wary way she's eyeing me, I can tell I won't like whatever she's going to say next. "I made a deal with your grandfather."

I feel my legs drop out from underneath me. "No!" It barely comes out as a whisper. Layden catches me from behind, and Sabra's eyes finally land on him.

"Who's he?"

"Sabra," I cry, "tell me you didn't!"

"I didn't," she says hurriedly, leaning down to help me back up. "I didn't make a blood oath. I'm not stupid enough to make the same mistake my mom did. Come on, who do you think I am?" She rolls her eyes, and finally, I'm able to take a breath.

"Then what—?"

"He knows I'm powerful, and I decided I didn't want to be on the run for the rest of my life. And this has always been my home. So I contacted him and told him I'd work for him but only on *my* terms this time."

"Sabra. . ." My head tilts to the side. She can't be that naïve. "You know what he's like. If you give an inch, he'll steal your whole soul."

But she shakes her head. "This way, I'll be able to study with other powerful mages around the world like I always wanted to. Which I'll have a much better chance of being able to do being bankrolled by Vlad's resources than as a runaway." Her eyes go hard. "He *owes* me. I'm just finally demanding what I deserve out of the bargain."

I can't help the despair in my gut. She knows my grandfather Vlad almost as well as I do. She knows how conniving and *evil* he is. "In return for what?" And then it clicks. I stiffen. "Dragging me back?"

Her eyes soften, and I see our long, shared sisterhood of brokenness being raised in the house of Vlad Dracul. "We both know you'll have to go back eventually. It was only a matter of time before his minions tracked me down."

I shake my head vehemently. "He never found my parents."

"But unlike them, I don't plan on hiding in some hole and keeping my head down for the rest of time." She grasps my hands. "I'm a *mage*. One of the most powerful of my age. I'm meant to do important work. I can't do that if I'm always afraid the ripples of magic I make in the world will be detected by him. Better a long leash than to live my life in a hole."

Her hands squeeze mine. "Come with me? We're always better together."

My whole chest seizes so tight I'm not sure I can breathe.

"Who the hell is Vlad?" Layden's powerful voice suddenly startles us apart, reminding me that he's standing right behind me. "Is he your grandfather? He sounds like a real asshole."

My eyes fall shut for a long moment, our closeness and what I almost let happen between us before Sabra showed up flashing through my eyes. I breathe out and open my eyes as Sabra asks, "Again, who the hell is this?"

"No one," I say at the same time he says, "Someone who's good at dealing with assholes."

A laugh barks out of me at that as I turn to him. "Not this one. Look, we knew we'd both have to go back to our real lives at some point. Well, my real life just showed up on the doorstep. This is where I leave you."

"What?" He immediately looks alarmed. "You saved my life. And it sounds dangerous wherever you're going back to. I can't let you—"

"You don't *let* me do anything," I hiss. "This isn't where you're from, and I assure you, chivalry is long dead."

"I'm hungry," Sabra suddenly says. "Is anybody else hungry?" She bypasses me to the kitchen, where she starts pulling open covers.

Layden's eyes narrow on me. "Then what about your debt to me?"

"What?" I ask, bewildered.

"You drag me out of the forest where I was perfectly happy to molder, forgotten forever, and bring me back to life, for what? To bring back humanity's most ancient nightmare?" He gestures to Sabra. I watch as her eyes light up as she reaches for the end of a loaf of bread, but as soon as her fingers touch it, it turns black and moldy in her hands. She drops it and steps back.

"Whoa. Weird. Did you guys see that?"

"You should've left me alone in the forest if you were just going to leave me the second I got accustomed to company again. I'm a curse upon this earth." He points to the bread.

My mouth has dropped open, both at seeing his particular power in effect and at the logic of what he's saying. Dammit, I never thought about—

"What about your brothers?"

He barks out a bitter laugh. "The ones who buried me alive?"

I wince.

"*You* did that?" Sabra asks from the kitchen counter, nudging at the bread with a knife. It turns to dust in front of her eyes. "Whoa."

Layden looks at her. "I apologize. I am cursed. You should get away from me quickly."

"Whoa," she repeats.

I breathe out hard again, my chest tight. "Look, I didn't mean—"

"What?" Layden turns on me. "For any of this to happen? You were just trying to be a Good Samaritan? Well, next time, keep your charity." He starts to head toward the door, and my hand lifts to stop him, but I force myself to hold it down. He's right. I'm no good to him. I'm no good to anyone. Even in this, the one good thing I've tried to do, I've completely fucked it up.

"Wait," Sabra calls when he's almost reached the door.

My heart leaps even though I don't know what she's going to say, but because he stops and turns around. I look to Sabra with a wild hope she'll say something that stops him in spite of the fact that I know better. He should go. I should let him go and not screw up his complex existence more than I already have. More than anybody, I know there are no happy endings in this life.

"What?" Layden asks, voice low, hand on the doorknob.

Sabra steps forward until she's standing right beside me. "I'm a powerful mage. Maybe we can fix you."

Layden laughs bitterly again, his hard eyes so different from the openness I've seen from him the last week. I hate that, but at the same time, he's better off away from me. I'm a poison to anyone I've ever been near.

"I've been like this for thousands of years," he grates out. "This curse was woven into my very being as soon as I was born, so forgive me if I don't think some human barely out of childhood can do anything for me."

Sabra's eyebrows lift, and she cocks a hand on one hip. "I might not be a crusty thousand-year-old, buddy, but I come from a powerful line of witches. You're a magical being, and I move magic. Have you ever even *tried* anything for your magical disability?"

Layden looks momentarily stunned by her comeback. "I —Well... no." He frowns. "But I guess if I really think about it... my brothers were able to walk around without *always* inflicting their curse on whoever was around them. They could direct theirs. It was just me who couldn't." His eyes flick back toward Sabra. "You think it's a disability?"

"There's more of you?" Sabra perks up, and I bump her shoulder with mine. "Look," she glances back to Layden. "Come back with us, and let us help you."

Immediately, Layden and I lock gazes. Did hope just

leap in his chest like it did in mine? But dear god, hope for what?

"Only if you want me to come," he says.

"Of course we want you to come," Sabra pipes up. "The chance to work with a magical being like you is a once-in-a-lifetime chance! That is, unless you think any of your brothers would be interested in volunteering to work with me, too?"

Layden ignores her, his gaze still holding mine. We both know he was only asking *me* the question. My breath catches in my chest. What does he mean? If I say no, will he just go back and sit down in the forest for another two hundred years? Will there even *be* a forest for that long? He doesn't know it, but the world has sped up around him. Cities and roads and human activity of all kinds encroach further and further into the wild every year.

But if he comes with us, Grandfather will try to use him. He's powerful, and Grandfather loves power more than anything else on earth. Certainly more than he loves me if he was ever capable of such a thing.

Then again, Layden might be powerful, too. Those wings... He was once an *angel*. Maybe he's the one person in the world who Vlad can't use as a pawn.

"Yes, I want you to come," I whisper before I think better of it.

The most beautiful smile breaks out over Layden's handsome face. "Then let's go."

Chapter Eleven

The Fallen Angels Club is right between the university and the edge of downtown, which is probably why it's so popular. It's huge, right off a main subway stop, and at the center of everything.

We stop off at Phoenix's city apartment so she can change. For a second, I think she'll make me wait downstairs, but she finally rolls her eyes and says I can come up.

Before we start climbing the stairs to her apartment, she stops me. "Can we actually not say anything about this to Sabra?"

"Why?" I ask, surprised. "She's always such a help."

Phoenix breathes out, sounding frustrated. "Things have just been..." Her eyes glance up the stairs. "She hasn't been totally happy with me since everything went down with the Destroyers."

"It wasn't your fault that went off the rails. It was Vlad's."

Phoenix shakes her head. "Look, it doesn't matter. I'm just trying not to"—she waves her hands in a flurry—"put any of my bullshit on her for a while. Okay? You and me can handle Ammit without her."

I don't like it, but I still say, "Fine."

She nods and starts up the stairs. After using her key to get in, she heads straight for her bedroom, not saying anything to Sabra, who's working some spell in the center of the living room.

"Hey," I say, sitting on the small loveseat that's been pulled back out of the way so Sabra can work her chalk circle in the center of the wood floor. I look around. It's a nice place, but small. Certainly not the kind of place Vlad would be putting them up in. Are they paying for it themselves?

Sabra barely looks up to acknowledge me. "Oh. Hey."

"What are you working on?"

She uses the side of her hand to swipe off some chalk and then starts rewriting arcane glyphs over the smudged chalk. The flyaway hairs from her braid are worse than normal. Which usually means she's been working at the circle for long hours already.

"Sab?" I question again, knowing she might well not have heard me the first time.

She finally looks up at me, really looks, and blinks. "What are you doing here?"

I jab a thumb toward where Phoenix is changing in her bedroom. "We're going out clubbing."

She frowns. "Why on earth would you do that?"

I don't want to lie to her, especially knowing that in spite of what Phoenix thinks, we could use her help. But I

95

respect Phoenix's wishes and whatever's going on between them. I might not know much, but from the little Phoenix has told me, being best friends for as long as they have isn't always a smooth road.

"Haven't you heard?" I smile. "We're on our honeymoon."

Sabra rolls her eyes and goes back to her chalking. "It's about time. You two have been eye-fucking each other since the first day I found you two shacked up in that cabin together."

"What?" I cough out. "I don't know what you're—"

Thankfully Phoenix opens her door then, saving me from having to reply to Sabra's completely off-base comment.

But then I really get a good look at Phoenix and all but swallow my tongue for a completely different reason. Her hair is sleeked back, and she's wearing a slinky black and silver dress with smoky eye makeup... The hunger inside me roars.

"Told you so," Sabra sing-songs.

I hop up off the couch and ask, "Ready?" about an octave higher than my normal voice as I hold out an arm for her to take. *Touch.* I want to touch her so badly. Phoenix ignores my arm and stomps in front of me out the door and down the stairs, which has Sabra chuckling. "Oh my god, tell me she's not still blue-balling you?"

That doesn't dignify a reply, so I ignore her and head after Phoenix. I want to talk to her and maybe make a game plan before we get to the club, but she just throws a leg over her motorcycle and gestures for me to get on behind her.

It's hard not to look at the acre of exposed thigh as I climb on. But I can still feel her warmth as the smooth denim of my jeans nestles against her outer thighs, and I wrap my arms around her waist. *Touuuuuuch.* The hungering beast inside me rumbles in satisfaction at the pressure of her in my arms, but only for a moment before a craving for *more* is like a drumbeat inside my head. I grind my teeth against it. It feels too good to be wrapped around her like this.

If she thinks anything similar, I have no idea because she just immediately takes off. If I thought the car was bad, it's nothing to the way the bike zips and zooms through traffic. At least it's both an excuse to hold as tight to her as I like and a distraction from the monster in my belly that craves more.

Still, by the time we get to the club, I leap off the damn death trap. "Why the fuck do you ride this thing?"

She laughs in my face. "What does it matter? We're immortal. It's exhilarating to have the wind in my hair."

I get now why she slicked it back so much. She ruffles her fingers through it. With it wild and wind-swept like that, it looks like she just had sex. Dammit, I don't need to be having thoughts like that.

"You look good," I say in a gruff tone.

"Oh?" Her eyebrows rise like I've genuinely surprised her, one hand still in her hair. It catches on one of her rings, and pink colors her cheeks as she tries to yank it out, only getting it caught more.

"Here," I say, reaching over and helping her untangle it.

Her big blue eyes come my way, and it's like she's holding her breath, which is when I realize how close I'm standing to her. I try not to let it—or her dizzying perfume and tight dress—affect me. "There," I say as I get her hand free, my voice suddenly deeper.

"Thanks," she says and then spins away. "Come on, we don't want to miss her if she's here."

Oh right. We're here on a mission, not a date. Besides, we're married already. No need to date if you're already married. Not that it's *that* kind of marriage. I shake my head, trying to make all the stupid thoughts shake loose.

Time to get in the game, jackhole.

"So what are we looking for, exactly?" I whisper to Phoenix as we approach the bouncer. There's only a small line outside the club, and we take our spot at the back.

"Anything out of the ordinary. Any woman who looks like she's on the prowl or leading a guy out of there."

I look around. Most folks are already paired up. "Night like this, that might be hard to tell."

"I don't know," she says. "I'm sure we'll know it when we see it."

Skeptical, I nod anyway. I can't be mad about getting to spend my Friday night dressed up with Phoenix at a swanky downtown club. Even if we are spirit-hunting.

"You go in and flirt with anything that moves," she says, "and we'll see if we can get any hooks on the line."

"What does that mean?"

She rolls her eyes exaggeratedly. "You know, seduction recon. Don't tell me you've never done that before."

I look upwards, shrugging and staying quiet.

"Oh, come on, Lay," she rolls her eyes even harder. "What have you been up to the last ten years?"

I just turn my eyes on her. "Studying with the best techs and mages in the world to find out how to get revenge on my family. And when that didn't work, or, well, when I forgave them instead, I just sort of... Well, you know the rest since I got back in touch with Sabra last year. I never had time for women."

"Oh." She frowns. "I just assumed..." Then she looks me up and down, reaches over, undoes the top two buttons of my shirt, and fusses with the collar. My beast leaps at the brush of her fingertips against my skin. "Look aloof. Turn down anyone who asks you to dance unless you see me signal."

"Oh yeah? And how will *you* know who it is?"

"I'll know."

"How? Is there something about spirits—"

She rolls her eyes. "Look, you'll be the hottest guy in there, and I know women. Human women will approach you differently than a goddess would. They won't have the same confidence and will play dumb games. She won't. Just watch me for the signal."

Does she know that from experience? What has *she* been up to for the last ten years? I know better than to ask. She was confident when I first met her, but now she's... incandescent with this surety in everything she does.

Except around the dickhead professor. I frown.

"That's perfect," Phoenix grins at me. "Just keep looking broody like that. Women eat that shit up."

I roll my eyes, and she claps me on the shoulder as we get to the front of the line of the club. "Here we go, champ."

The bouncer asks for the cover charge, but Phoenix just leans in. "You want to let us in."

He stumbles over himself as he leans over to pull back the velvet rope.

"Remember," she breathes in my ear as we pass through the door.

"I know, I know, the signal. Wait, what exactly is the signal?"

But we're already through and into the club, and she walks away as if she's never met me before.

I get it; we're going incognito. Still, I don't like losing sight of her in the sea of writhing bodies and strobing lights.

I head for the bar, trying to keep track of Phoenix amid the crowd of people. If I can't find her, how the hell am I supposed to know what this mysterious *signal* is? Oh well. Now that she's told me what to watch out for, maybe I can suss Ammit out myself anyway. Plus, I know that even if I can't see her, Phoenix will be watching me.

A couple moves away from the bar right as I approach, and I slide onto one of the stools. Unlike Remus, I never found much point in human alcohol, so I don't know what to order when the bartender yells and asks what I want.

I just repeat the last order I heard. "Whiskey and coke."

He nods and disappears again. Before it arrives, a woman smoothly seats herself beside me.

She chatters at me in Romanian, angling her barely covered chest toward me before eventually asking me to dance. I've always been good with languages, and this is just another variation of an old one I knew long ago.

I gently tell her, no, I'm not interested. She looks offended and flings her hair extensions in my face as she swings off the stool to walk away.

My drink finally comes and I sip it slowly. It burns my throat a little. I look around. My eyes have adjusted to the darkness of the club. Lights swirl from several points in the ceiling, and I can feel the bass of the speakers thumping up through the floor.

As I'm doing a slow scan of the room, I spot eyes on me from across the huge, square bartop. Phoenix gives me a quick wave before looking like a completely disinterested stranger again. Ah, so that's the plan. The bar is in the center of the club, with people packing on all sides around us.

The night stretches on, and the club gets wilder and more crowded with each passing hour. The lines stretching out from the bartop get longer and longer, more people shouting for the six bartenders' attention.

I keep sipping my first drink and turn down woman after woman who asks with varying levels of confidence to dance with them. The ones with giggling packs of friends around them are easy to turn down. I don't even have to glance across the bartop at Phoenix for those or for the women who are all but shaking with nerves.

There are only a few, really, that I need to sneak a peek at Phoenix to double-check, such as a woman with dyed blonde hair and a blinding white smile. "Come dance with me," she all but orders as she reaches out and puts a hand on my bicep. She certainly isn't lacking in confidence.

But when I glance across the bartop at Phoenix, she just gives a nonchalant shake of her head.

I frown but tell the woman no.

As I watch her spin and walk away, I wonder if we've just let the dangerous spirit slip out of our hands. But then I hear a voice in slightly accented English from my left.

"Well, aren't you the heartbreak king tonight?"

I spin on my stool to look at the speaker with the sultry voice.

A tiny, delicate, dark-haired woman sits there, blinking at me from behind dark lashes.

"What do you mean?" I have to speak loudly to be heard above the music.

The song finishes right then, so I can hear her sultry voice clearly as she says, "All night, I have watched you turn down woman after woman. Tell me, do you have a sweetheart waiting for you at home?"

If she's watching me so closely, I don't dare even glance at Phoenix now. There's something different about this woman. I can't quite put my finger on it, but she has a different... energy about her. An aura of power. I *want* to do what she says. It's not quite on the level of compulsion, but I still want to. Is this just the power of a beautiful woman on a man? Because she is beautiful. Even I have to admit it. My hungry beast wakens even though it knows this isn't to its particular taste.

I smile as I turn my full attention to her. "No. No one waiting at home. Just no one who's caught my eye until now."

Her lips tilt up, and she swirls her tiny cocktail straw in her drink. "Until now, huh?"

"You must know you are mesmerizing," I say, leaning slightly in. My monster yawns. "But perhaps flattery isn't the way to your heart."

"My heart," she scoffs, grabbing her drink from the bar and tossing her head back, downing it. I take the opportunity to look back at Phoenix whose features look slightly strained. But she nods, and I know I'm right. This is her. The bloodthirsty goddess.

I turn my attention back to her right as her head tips back down. "Let's not worry about my heart just yet. Let's have some fun. What do you say?"

"Fair," I manage.

"Excellent." The woman grabs my hand in a firm grip and whisks us away from the bar, through the thick crowd, and onto the tightly packed dance floor.

The music seems more... *alive* somehow as she swings back around to face me. As she grins at me and puts my hands on her waist, I feel overcome with happiness and the certainty that I'm right where I need to be and just stand there dopily in front of her. For once, I don't feel my hunger; I'm just... floating.

"Like this," she says, leaning in.

I nod because she's so pretty, and I can't think of a thing to say. She laughs throatily, dark eyes flashing at me. "Oh, my, you are a delicious snack, aren't you?"

I nod again, because I suddenly find myself very agreeable to anything she says.

She lifts her arms around my neck, and we dance to the slow song that's just come over the speakers. It still has a thumping beat underneath our feet that I feel in my calves, up through my thighs, and in my—

I yank away from her as I feel my cock stiffening.

She just laughs again, then reaches down and loops two fingers in my belt loops before leaning in. "It's okay, cowboy. You're a real gentleman, aren't you? Just getting over someone?"

"Something like that," I manage to choke out.

"That's okay. I'm not feeling too picky tonight." She leans in and flashes her eyelashes at me. "Wanna get outta here? Go somewhere quieter?"

I nod, my senses swimming. Somewhere in the back of my head, I remember this woman is dangerous. But really, what can she do to me? I'm indestructible.

She lets go of my belt loops, linking her hand with mine again and tugging me toward the back of the club. I go willingly, curious and lusty as a tomcat. When she pushes through a door into a quiet back alley, I follow like a lemming.

"I'm just parked this way," she says.

"Mmm hmm," I think I mumble. My feet stumble over themselves in order to keep up with her. Her hand is so warm in mine.

We're almost to the darkest part of the alley when suddenly a voice calls out from behind us, "Hey bitch. Let go of the idiot."

I both feel and see the woman's surprise as she turns to look at where the voice is coming from. I spin, too, smiling when I see Phoenix.

"Phoenix," I greet warmly. "This is—" I turn in confusion to the dark-eyed woman. "I never did get your name."

She's glaring at me, pissed. "I thought you said you didn't have a sweetheart."

"Oh, her?" I point a thumb over my shoulder at Phoenix. "She's not my sweetheart," I explain helpfully. "She's just my wife."

"Why are you assholes all the same?" the woman says, rolling her eyes. She shoves me away from her. I stumble back, still feeling a little dizzy.

"Hey," Phoenix sprints toward us. "Don't touch him."

The dark-eyed woman lifts her hands. "You can have him, lady."

Phoenix strides right up toward her, eyes narrowed. "Really? Just like that?"

"I'm out of here."

But before she can turn to leave, Phoenix gets up in her face. "Stand on one leg." My mind clears a little more, enough to see that Phoenix is trying to use her compulsion on her. A test to see if she's just some human woman after all.

"Fuck off," the woman starts to shove her aside, the compulsion obviously not effective. When Phoenix lifts a hand, the woman freezes in place.

"What the fu—" Her words cut off, and then her panicked eyes flick back and forth as Phoenix pins her in place. It's a creepy trick Phoenix can do to any creature with blood in its veins.

A squeak comes from the woman's throat, but that's all. Her eyes shoot to me as if begging me to help her. I feel suddenly uncomfortable. What if we got the wrong... creature? What if it's not Ammit, after all?

But then her dark eyes shut like she's concentrating on something.

Phoenix drops her hand and turns to me. She looks at me like she wants to jump me and tear off all my clothes. I swear I've seen this look in her eye a time or two before, but while I always imagined it was wishful thinking, for the first time, I see the intent that tells me she's about to do something about it.

"Phoenix," I start, holding a hand up.

But then it's like a wave hits me, too. The sleepy beast inside me is suddenly fully awake. Awake and starving. I'm fucking lust-struck. The cock that started stiffening a bit in the club suddenly goes hard as a rock as I stare at Phoenix.

She walks toward me, grabbing the hem of her dress and yanking it up and off. Now she's just in a bra that pushes her plump breasts up nearly to her collarbone and the slinkiest pair of black lace underwear.

Behind her, I hear steps sprinting away, but I can't care about anything except Phoenix. Phoenix and me. Finally alone. My Phoenix. Finally, with nothing between us. Well, nothing between us except my clothes. Why am I wearing so many stupid clothes? Why have we ever worn clothes around each other at all?

I'm ravenous. *Touch her*. Why aren't we naked and touching? All the fucking time? I stumble toward her, then stop. No. No touching. I'm not supposed to touch her. Can't give into the hunger.

Phoenix tugs off the little scrap of lace underwear, baring herself to me completely from the waist down.

I've got my jeans unzipped and shoved down the next

moment, then I'm tugging my long, hard cock out. I'm engorged for her. Starving for her tight, hot little pussy.

And then she's leaping into my arms, bare legs wrapping around my waist. We both let out an indecent grunt of satisfaction.

Stuff yourself. Feast on her. Devour.

I spin and pin her back against the wall of the club and do what I've wanted to since that day at the cabin all those years ago when she found me chopping wood.

Finally, finally, I press my open mouth to hers.

She welcomes it, kissing me back ravenously and reaching down with her right hand for my cock. She squeezes in a way that has my eyes bulging with need. Oh god, how have I gone this long in my life without fucking? Without fucking *her*?

I need between her thighs. I need to stuff her full and thrust—

"Need you to fuck me," she breaks away from my mouth to cry. "Never needed anything so much in my life."

I nod, knowing exactly what she means. She guides my long cock toward where she's already drenched. Still, she tortures us both, dragging my tip up and down her wet center. She shudders against the wall.

"Feels," she shakes, "so," she shakes some more, "*good.*"

I grow thicker, throbbing in her sweet little hand.

"Honey. Phoenix," is all I can whine, shaking with devastating need. It's as if every moment of discipline in my whole life is balanced in this moment, about to be satiated with my first taste...

She guides me to her entrance. We both groan in satisfaction when I finally push in. This is the touch I've been starving for.

"Don't be gentle," she gasps.

It's my first time ever being inside a woman.

And this isn't just any woman. It's *her*. Phoenix. I want to go slow. I want to be gentle in spite of her demands. But the craving that has hold of us was never going to allow that.

I push in slow once but quickly understand slow isn't an option here. She's tight and wet and so, so hot. And tight? God, did I say tight? She clings to me like the tightest glove. A perfect fit.

"Move," she cries. "Fuck me. I need to feel you deep. I need it hard."

Pleasure lights up my spine, and I pull out and drive into her again. Her softness meets my hardness, but she pushes her hips back against me so it's a wet slap of flesh.

"Harder, Layden. *Harder,*" she groans, rotating her hips restlessly against me. Her arms around my shoulders cling tighter, fingernails digging in.

I draw my long cock out of her, feeling the cool breeze rushing down the alley on my flesh before plunging back inside her. She groans needily when I do. For once, I've found someone as hungry as I am.

She grabs one of my hands. "Here," she whines, showing me how to rub her groin above where I'm penetrating her.

I thrust a few more times, but she moans as if she's not getting the satisfaction she needs, twisting on my cock. I can't have that. I need her right here on the edge of this furious pleasure with me.

So I pull out and flip her body so she's facing the wall. She bends over and thrusts her backside toward me. Seeing her round little ass extended out in invitation almost makes me spill my load right there. I feel it in my balls, ready to burst, but this is too good.

"So fucking perfect," I growl, grab her hips, and kick her

feet lightly to spread her legs wider. She bends over further, and I can see her wet pussy. She's so wet for me that she's dripping down her inner thigh. I shove my cock back in and reach a hand around her front, a much easier angle to strum the nub she had me reaching for earlier.

If I thought she was groaning before, it's nothing to the way she moans and hisses like a wildcat now as I strum her while I fuck her. She puts both hands against the wall so she can shove her hips back against me harder to meet my every thrust.

"Oh fuck!" she cries. "Fuck me, Layden. Fuck me harder! Fuck me dirty. *Harder!*"

So I do. I fuck her like I never dreamed I could. I saw my cock in and out of her, holding her hip and rubbing the top of her cunny with my other forefingers.

She howls at the moon as she loses it, creaming all around my cock and squeezing on me so motherfucking tight I can't hold it another second even though all I want is to fuck her forever. The hunger is here and not here at the same time. I'm finally feeding the craving, giving in, and I never want to stop. *Never fucking stop.* But it's a ludicrous wish. No one can hold back this freight train. I feel it at the bottom of my spine, and my balls are tingling like they're being lit up by fucking sparkle firecrackers of pleasure—

Right before I lose my shit and come in the most perfect pussy, though, Phoenix slips off my cock and spins, falling to her knees right there on the asphalt.

I try to pull her up—I don't want her hurting her knees. She's too precious to—

But before I can help her to her feet, she has hold of my pulsating cock, pulling it toward her mouth.

"I have to know what you taste like."

And then she's swallowing me down, using her teeth

along the edge of my cock. Her fingernails scratch my balls, and I can't help it. I thought I knew pleasure. I thought I knew—

I throw my head back and cum down her sweet little throat.

Then I collapse on the ground with her, pulling her to my chest. "Phoenix, baby. I never thought we'd get to this place. I've dreamed of this—of you—forever. You feel so good in my arms. All I want from here on out is—"

But suddenly, she yanks away from me and leaps to her feet.

"What?" I sit up, my cock still out and stiff.

Phoenix looks around, her hands moving down her bare mid-drift, then down to her sex. I never did get that bra off. We'll have to rectify that next time. She shakes her head, her hands going to her hair.

"What's wrong, baby?"

She jogs over to where she threw off her dress, which is when I really take in our surroundings. Shit, did I really just take her for the first time in a back alley? That's not right. My honey deserves silk sheets and the softest mattress.

I scrub a hand down my face, still shocked by the feeling of... being satiated. For once, I'm full.

"Layden," Phoenix snaps.

I look up at her.

"Make yourself decent."

I glance down at myself, cock still out. "Oh."

She turns her back on me as she yanks her dress on over her head.

I chuckle. "Well, that was one way to consummate the marriage."

Phoenix swears, sounding decidedly less happy than

she should, considering the way I just had her shuddering. "What's wrong, baby?"

"I'm not your baby, you fucking idiot."

That has me snapping to attention. I get to my feet. "What do you mean?"

"Are you decent?"

"If you mean is the cock you were just riding put away, yes. Yes, it is."

She swings around, glaring daggers at me. "Don't remind me of that."

I can only stare at her, totally bewildered. I gesture toward the wall. "Were you or were you not just the woman crying out my name as I brought you to a blistering hot orgasm?"

She stomps toward me, and even in the dim streetlamp a block away, I can see her cheeks flush. She waves a hand furiously. "None of that matters, don't you get it?"

Uh, how does none of that matter? Pretty sure doing a thing I've never done in my whole life matters a whole fuck of a lot.

Then again, maybe this is just another Friday night to her. Maybe she does this all the time. Maybe I'm just another dick to her. I start to close down. "Yeah, so what am I supposed to be getting?" I ask, voice more gruff. The happy, satiated feeling is already fading.

She rolls her eyes. "Why the hell were we in this alley in the first place?" she asks, her voice going up an octave. "It was *her*. Ammit. She did something to us. Like infested us with lust or something. To distract us so she could get away!"

Ammit. Fuck. My head whips to look down the alleyway. I completely forgot about her. Which I guess is Phoenix's point. How else would we both have forgotten about what we were doing and jumped each other? The last thing I remember before we...

Phoenix did that freeze-Ammit-in-place thing, but then she just turned and launched herself at me. Then my little head started doing all the thinking, which, yeah, is unusual.

"Fuck."

"Fuck is right," Phoenix says, pacing back and forth. Absently she licks at her bottom lip, then swallows. "At least you didn't—" She looks my way. "You know. You didn't finish—" She gestures limply. "At least we didn't finish in a way that would give Vlad what he wants. That would have been an unbearable ending to this shitshow." She tosses her hands up, indicating around her. Me. Everything.

Well. At least now, there's no ambiguity about how she feels about what just happened.

"Let's go," I bark.

Her head snaps my way. "What's crawled up your ass? You got a free fuck out of this. I'd think you'd be in a *great* mood."

I grit my teeth so I don't lose my shit on her. "There's a dangerous goddess still on the loose. And now she knows who you are. So get your ass back on your bike."

Phoenix's mouth drops open. "No one speaks to me like that."

I spread my arms out. "Well, Princess, wake up and smell the coffee. We're stuck together for the time being. You think I like it any better than you?"

She looks offended and, beyond that, maybe a little hurt. But what the actual fuck? There's no pleasing her. Well... thinking about pleasing her just flashes images of her lying like a pussy cat against my chest, very, *very* pleased. But that's no use to either of us.

111

So I stomp down the side alley to the front of the club where her bike is parked.

As Phoenix walks up to the bike behind me, I hear her on the phone. "Lock down the city. The murderer got away. No, I'm not slipping. She just did, okay?"

By the irritation in her voice, I assume she's on the phone with her grandfather. "Yes, he's here."

She spins to hold out the phone to me, looking pissed. "He wants to talk to you."

I take the phone from her and hit the "speaker phone" button. Even though I'm still pissed about what just happened, I want to keep things completely transparent. I know Phoenix hates it when Vlad tries to use the people in her life against her.

"Hello?" I growl.

"Have you put a baby in her yet?" he asks crudely.

I can see Phoenix fuming as she stomps away from the phone, but still within hearing distance.

"We're after a dangerous threat at the moment. That's not really the priority." Even as I say it, my mind flashes back to the alley.

"Fucking my granddaughter should be your *only* priority!" Vlad's angry voice comes over the phone speaker as if he can read my mind.

My eyes pop back open to see Phoenix's livid face.

Phoenix snatches the phone away from me again. "We're losing time. Did you lock down the city? If this monster gets away, that's on us."

"How did you let it slip through your fingers the first time?"

"My compulsion didn't work. And it had..." Phoenix's eyes flit briefly in my direction, her cheeks coloring, "Other

112

skills that distracted us while it got away. But we won't fail twice."

"You better not," comes Vlad's voice. "It's time to start focusing on your honeymoon."

I can see Phoenix working to control her anger. "I'm having the honeymoon I choose. He's here with me. We're..." Her eyes unwittingly flash toward the back alley of the club, "... bonding."

"The only bonding I care about is the kind that gives me more children to my name. Don't forget, I hold a life debt over his family."

"We'll be in to check city surveillance," Phoenix snaps. "Text me when the streets are locked down." She ends the call, then glares at me as she fits the phone into the snug back pocket of her dress. "What?"

I hold my hands up. "I didn't say anything."

She lets out a furious huff that I assume is intended more for Vlad than me as she swings a leg over her bike and gestures angrily for me to get on. I shut my eyes to try to block out memories of the last time our bodies were wrapped together, but that only makes it more vivid. My teeth grit as I climb on the bike and try to ignore the way my cock stiffens at being near her again.

The monster inside me roars back to life with a staggering hunger unlike any I've ever known before. Because now I'll carry the memories of what it felt like to have her gasping and squeezing on my cock. Like a starving man given a feast only once before being sent back into the cold. I have a feeling this is the type of shit to drive a man mad.

But then again, what's a little more madness and torment to a monster?

Chapter Twelve

Sabra chatters the whole way back to the city as I sit up front in her little Dacia with Layden stuffed in the back. He barely fits in the little European car. He's so tall and now that he's filled out after eating the deer, broad. I sneak a couple looks back at him, and each time, he's shifting to awkwardly fold his long limbs a different way while also holding onto the ceiling, watching with wide eyes out the front window as Sabra swerves in and out of traffic.

I realize, holy shit, this has got to be his first time in a car. If he had been in the woods for two hundred years, he doesn't know anything about the modern world. Which is when I also remember where I'm taking him.

I turn around to give him my full attention. "Look, you

kept asking where I come from, and I should have told you about everything you're about to walk into before you decided to come along."

"It won't matter." He sounds absolutely confident.

"Fine, but you still need to know so you aren't walking in blind. I'm not a vampire, but my grandfather Vlad is. So are the rest of my family, so you're whole," I wave a hand, "*Famine* thing shouldn't be a problem. They don't get hungry or eat food."

"But never forget the most important rule." I wave a finger in his face. "Never let him bite you or accept an offer of a blood oath from him."

He nods, not looking a bit phased. "Got it. Vampires. Don't accept blood oaths. Anything else I should know?"

"I'm serious. No blood oaths. Even if he tries to phrase it in friendly terms, like it's just an easy exchange. He'll try to trap you so he can enslave you forever."

He nods again. "No oaths or promises of any kind."

I breathe out. "Vlad and all of my uncles are serious dicks. Don't trust any of them or tell them where you come from."

He nods, and again, I'm a little taken aback at how easily he's taking in all this information. I've spent my whole life terrified to open up to anyone or bring them into my dangerous life, but to this guy, it feels like it's just another walk in the park on a sunny afternoon.

His confidence and lack of fear make me feel a little less terrified as Sabra pulls onto the long stretch of driveway leading into Vlad's estate.

I ran away, and I've never known Vlad to be lenient when somebody breaks his rules. He was born in the Middle Ages. His namesake, the historic Vlad Dracul

Tepes, got his reputation from spearing his enemy's bodies on spikes while they were still alive so they died gruesome deaths and drenched the fields in the blood of the armies he conquered.

"Let's go around back," I tell Sabra, my chest tight with tension as we come up to the front gate.

Sabra nods, but as she starts to turn, the front gate opens, and Vlad is standing right there waiting for us.

"Shit," I hiss out.

Layden reaches forward from the back seat and squeezes my shoulder. "He cannot hurt you. I am here."

His gentle assurance makes my chest squeeze for an entirely different reason. I never should have brought him to this shark pool. He's too kind. Too good.

But I'm not. I'm bad and selfish, and I always have been. I reach out for what feels good in the moment and don't think about consequences until it's far too late.

I spin around, wanting to shove Layden out the back door and tell him to run, but Sabra's already pulling to a stop in front of Vlad.

Layden reaches for his door but fumbles around, not knowing where the handle is. I take the opportunity to jump out of the car so I can try to calm Vlad's temper before he explodes and takes it out on the stranger who's appeared at his gate.

Sabra steps out with me and walks around to help Layden out while I brace myself in front of my grandfather. I want to turn around and tell her to stop. To wait.

But to my surprise, Vlad smiles at me and holds out his arms. "The prodigal granddaughter has returned. I trust you enjoyed sowing your wild oats, child?"

"I—Uh, I—" I stutter, not knowing what to make of this reception.

He pulls me in for an embrace. "And who is this you've brought back to me? Two little mice run away, and three come back?" His voice sends a chill down my spine.

Sabra opens the door for Layden, and I watch Vlad's hungry eyes fall on him. His nostrils flare as he inhales, and a crease appears on his forehead. Can he smell that Layden isn't human? Does he know what he is? Has he run into Layden's kind before?

Nothing else shows on Vlad's face as he shoots a welcoming, only slightly creepy grin Layden's way. "And who might we have the honor of welcoming into our home? My sweet granddaughter does not bring home strays often."

I'm suddenly very glad that Layden is wearing the farmer's bulky jacket, even though I see Vlad eyeing his wardrobe distastefully. Vlad once told me you can tell everything about a person's wealth in the first five seconds of meeting them—from the tailoring of their clothes and how worn their shoes are to the cut of their hair and the scent of their cologne.

Layden might look like a peasant relation, but I'm just glad his wing stumps only bulge slightly and might be seen as merely an odd lay of the jacket's construction. I make a note to buy him a lot of bulky outerwear. At least it's winter. But what about summer? What will we do to hide his stumps, then?

Then I realize how presumptuous it is to imagine that he'll still be here in summer.

"I'm happy to be here, sir," Layden says, eyeing Vlad warily. "Thank you for your hospitality."

"How did you and my dear Phoenix come to know one another? Sabra told me some, but I love to hear it from the horse's mouth."

My gaze shoots to Sabra, but she's busy thumbing

through something on her phone. I frown. Just how much did she tell him about what she found when she got to the cabin? I feel guilty the moment I second-guess her intentions. She would never sell me out. She's been my best friend forever and the only person I trust in the world... At the same time, I don't think I'm going to share any more of what Layden's told me about where he's from if I can help it. She just knows he's cursed. She and I might love one another like sisters, but he's nothing to her.

"Phoenix came upon me in the Carpathian Mountains and saw the curse that had been laid upon me," Layden says smoothly, looking Vlad in the eye. "She said she had friends she thought could help me."

"A curse," Vlad muses, "how interesting. What kind? Who set it?"

"I'm a curse to all people I walk among," Layden says. "I have been given immortality yet am cursed never to be around anyone else without their food turning to dust before it can get to their mouths."

Vlad's eyebrows raise a notch. "A lonely existence."

"Phoenix is the first person I've met in many years who is immune to my curse."

Vlad's eyes slide to Phoenix. "And your gifts...?"

I feel my face go flat. He's talking about compulsion, and the only reason he can be asking is that he wants to know if he can somehow use Layden as a weapon. "It doesn't work on him."

"Ah," Vlad sighs. The disappointment on his face flashes briefly before he smiles again.

"Sabra thinks she can find a way to help him control it," I say quickly.

"Perhaps you will find your home here," Vlad says with

a sweep of his arm. "There's no need to be lonely anymore. I have many sons who could become brothers to you. You might find it's a shame to leash such power."

Layden's face hardens. "No thanks. I am not in need of *brothers*," he all but spits the last word, and I remember what he told me of his brothers burying him alive. "All I want is this curse removed from me."

Vlad's eyes narrow. He doesn't like resistance to his plans, and I can already see schemes shaping and reforming in his head. Anyone with power is another weapon to add to his collection. We're all just little marionettes to be dragged around according to his twisted and exacting expectations.

Time to cut this little meet and greet short. "I'll show him to his room." I grab Layden by his forearm and tug him forward. Away from my grandfather and many of my uncles, who are always near him like a little swarm.

I look over my shoulder at Sabra.

"I've gotta go get something to eat," she says, "but I'll be back tomorrow so we can start getting to work?"

I nod, wanting to run and give her a hug. I need to sit down with her and have a proper chat. When we made up our minds to run away in opposite directions of each other to try to throw Vlad and his minions off, I didn't think there was anything that would ever bring her back here. Vlad held her mother prisoner in the state mental hospital for decades until she *died*.

There has to be more to her decision. I glance back at my grandfather. Did he find her after all and threaten her to make her come back?

But as she waves and starts walking back to her car, she doesn't look scared at all. There's no tension in her shoulders. Does the difference of being here voluntarily instead of essentially being held prisoner really make all the difference?

"Phoenix?" comes Layden's soft voice. Nothing to do but turn to the burning problem at hand. Namely getting Layden out of my grandfather's presence as quickly as possible. God, what was I thinking, bringing him here?

I tug him through the courtyard as my eyes flick around at the four walls of my grandfather's compound. I can't help the panicky feeling creeping up my throat. This was the best place to come. There was no other choice. Maybe I'm just the one overreacting because Grandfather can be manipulative. Sabra obviously thinks there's a way to work *with* him.

And considering my need to be close to him in order to stay healthy, maybe there really is no other choice. Still, it's like I can feel Vlad's eyes on me as I walk Layden toward the nearest entrance. Grandfather let me have a wing of the compound when I moved in a decade ago because I never felt safe around my uncles. They creeped me out. I don't know how else you're supposed to feel about men who kidnap you away from your parents in the middle of the night.

We enter the compound, and I drop Layden's arm, even though the warmth of his skin is comforting. Instead, I stomp down the hallway under the LED lights that run in tracks along the ceiling. There aren't any windows in the compound, just this cold, unnatural white light.

Contrary to the myths about vampires, my grandfather and uncles *can* stand to be out in the sunlight—they just find it irritating and usually avoid it at all costs. Still, when meeting newcomers, Vlad makes a point of meeting them in the sun to help dispel any rumors.

"What is this place?" Layden asks as we walk down one

empty hallway, then down a set of stairs to yet another empty hallway.

"What my grandfather thinks of as a perfect palace," I reply, my voice hollow.

"You hate it here."

"It's that obvious?"

"Yes."

"We can leave."

I sigh. "It's not that simple. There are things I didn't tell you."

"Such as?"

I sigh again. We're here now. I might as well tell him. I push through the double doors to my wing and see Layden's eyes widen as the dark halls are exchanged for pink ones.

"I wanted to piss Vlad off, so I redecorated."

He nods, eyes watching me, patient.

I look away from him. "So I told you my family are vampires, but that I'm not. That's not entirely true. I mean, I don't have to bite anybody or anything," I say quickly. "But it's like..." I wave my hands in frustration at having to explain it. "When Vlad feeds because he's the eldest or the patriarch or whatever... it feeds me."

"Feeds you?"

I wave my hands again. "Gives me strength. Energy. I can eat as much human food as I want, but if I'm not close enough to Vlad while he's feeding, it doesn't matter. I just sort of start... wasting away."

I finally glance back at Layden. His eyes are only a little wider, but he doesn't look freaked out or anything. Of course he doesn't. He's an angelic being who let himself starve in the forest for two hundred years. There's probably nothing I could tell him he wouldn't take in stride.

Which suddenly feels freeing. I've never been able to

talk to anyone about this stuff. Even Sabra. She always had her own shit to carry with her mom and everything. So there was no one to really unburden myself to.

"I imagine you found this out the hard way," Layden says.

I nod. "I was born here. Vlad had captured my mom right before she had me because he wanted to retrieve his latest vampire progeny. He was extra excited when I came out as... *more.* But my dad came and busted us out when I was still small, maybe four? I was okay for a few years, but then I got really, really sick. My parents didn't know what was happening. We were always on the run and hiding from Vlad, but he found us when I was in the hospital, so weak I could barely move."

Layden's translucent eyes are locked on me as we walk down the hall. Somehow, it feels easier to tell this while we're walking. I can't get as lost in the memories. Still, I have to swallow hard, remembering the worry in my mother's eyes as she looked down at me in the hospital bed that turned to panic as soon as Vlad shoved through the door.

"Right when my grandfather came in, I sat up, feeling stronger all of a sudden after years of being sick. I didn't know then that it was because he'd drained the nurse outside who'd been so kind to me. I was just confused because I felt better, but my mom was so scared. My dad wasn't there because they took shifts staying with me while the other one worked. Then there was this stranger claiming to be my grandfather and saying he needed to take me with him or else I'd just keep getting sick like this."

Vlad had crouched down over my bed and asked me if I wanted to keep getting sick. I shook my head. But then I told him to leave my mother alone.

He smiled and said if I came with him, he wouldn't hurt my mother, *and* I wouldn't be sick anymore.

I saw how scared Mom was, and I believed him. He could hurt her. And I knew this was the bad man that Mom and Dad always talked about. They got quiet whenever I came into the room and they were talking about him, so I learned to listen from just outside.

It seemed like such a simple solution, and I knew what I'd sometimes suspected was true: I was the source of all my parents' problems. If I wasn't there, they wouldn't have to be scared all the time. They wouldn't have to worry about the bad man anymore, and they wouldn't have to worry about me being sick. They could be happy.

As if he saw exactly what I was thinking, Vlad asked, "Are you a selfish little girl or not?"

Other men had come in by then, restraining my mom while Vlad talked to me.

I shook my head no. I would not be a selfish girl. If I went with him, the men would let my mother go. My parents would be safe. From this man. And from *me*.

"I told him I'd go with him but that if he hurt my mother, I'd make him sorry. He laughed in my face, but I was powerful again since he'd just fed, and I forced all of my uncles to crawl on the floor."

I had to hold my mother frozen in place, too so she didn't try to wrestle me away from Vlad. It was something I didn't even know I could do until that moment. But I felt all the blood humming beneath their skin. It felt different in my uncles than in my mother, but I was able to control them all. Cruder than compulsion, I just physically forced their limbs where I wanted them.

My grandfather smiled down at me when he saw his sons crawling on the floor. "What a clever girl you are. All

123

right. I'll leave your mother here, unharmed. As long as you come with me."

I nodded, pulled the IV out of my arm, and followed him out of the hospital, keeping my mother pinned to the wall the whole while. It made me feel bad in my belly, but I did it anyway.

"You were very young when this happened?" Layden asks softly.

"I was eight. I've lived here with my grandfather ever since." I stop in front of the door of one of the guest bedrooms. "You can sleep in here."

I reach for the doorknob, but Layden holds out a hand to stop me. "How old are you now?"

I glare up at him. "Nineteen."

He pulls his hand away, a line appearing on his brow. "Still so young."

I laugh at that and shove open the door. He has no idea. "I've never been young."

I walk into a room that is less pink than mine but still has pink accents here and there. I never particularly loved pink, but I always liked anything that made my grandfather wince. The walls in this room are a bright sea-foam green, and I bought colorful print art to put on the wall. A couple tasteful vases with high-end fake flowers perch on end tables here and in the foyer. All the rooms in my wing are like this. Sabra and I went through a decorating phase when we were fifteen.

An overstuffed couch and a bed with a thick white duvet finish out the room.

"It's nice in here," Layden says, looking around.

I nod, satisfied. No one else has been here besides Sabra and me.

"Did you ever see your mother again? Or your father?"

Any happy feelings the colorful space briefly inspires quickly sour at his question.

"No." I walk over to the little half-kitchenette that's really just a sink, a half-fridge, and a microwave and wash my hands. "But I imagine them out there happy wherever they are."

"They were good to you when you lived with them."

"Yes." I scrub at my hands even though they're not really that dirty. Washing my hands at the hand pump with a rough little bar of soap back at the cabin might have been annoying, but it had done the job.

"Do you miss them?"

I dry my hands on the little hanging towel more vigorously than might be strictly necessary before swinging around to look at Layden. "Does it matter? They're out there, wherever they are, and I'm here. They're safe; that's what matters."

Layden just stares at me.

"Don't do that."

"Do what?" he asks.

"Look at me like that."

"Like what?"

"I don't know. Like you're sorry for me."

"That is not what I was thinking at all."

"Then what are you thinking?"

"That it must have been wonderful to have a mother and father that you cared for and who cared for you. You love them. They love you. And I'm sure they are not happy wherever they are because you are not there."

He says all this, so matter of fact. I love them, and they love me. I hadn't thought about all these things in so long, but being back here after I briefly hoped I might be free of it, even briefly—

I burst into stupid tears.

Layden immediately comes closer, and I turn away from him. I never cry.

"What is happening? Are you hurt? Did I do something wrong?"

I cry harder and wrench away from him when he puts a hand on my shoulder. I don't cry. Why the fuck am I crying?

"Phoenix," he says, and I hear his pain and confusion in the word.

I spin and throw myself against his chest. He just stands frozen for a long moment. But then his arms come around me. I melt against him, sobbing, and he holds me tighter.

How long has it been since anyone held me like this? I mean, sometimes Sabra and I hug hello, but it's not like this. This absolute enveloping clench of safety while I just totally lose my shit. I continue sobbing, and Layden's arms are so strong and sure as he holds me close, his chin notching over my head until I feel all but swallowed up in his embrace.

For the first time in forever, I feel safe. I realize the last time I felt this way was when I was a child and my mother hugged me when I was sick. Which only makes me sob harder.

Layden rubs my back and makes soothing noises until finally, hiccupping, my crying calms down.

I'm appalled at myself, but still, I don't pull away from him.

We just stand there like that, me in his arms, my face sideways against his chest. I can hear his heartbeat, so sure and steady. The extra-sensory part of me can feel his blood pumping through the four chambers of his heart and rushing out through all his veins through his body, filling him with life. He's so strong and alive.

I've never felt so safe. It's a dangerous high because I could chase this feeling forever.

Finally, I pull away and wipe at my eyes. "I'm sorry." I look down. "I don't know why I did that."

"I have cried before," Layden says. "When my brothers and Creator-Father were not looking. Sometimes, I felt better afterward."

His admission makes more tears want to bubble up. How is he so... *perfect* is the word my mind conjures, but I know that's not true. Then again, he is the closest thing I've ever met to an angel. It's probably a girlish fancy to think an angel has come to save me. Though I wasn't lying when I said I've never been young. No matter how much pink I put on the walls. If I ever was a girl, I'm certainly not one anymore.

"Thank you," I say, stepping back from him. I make a useless gesture, still feeling embarrassed. "For listening. And... understanding."

He just watches me with those ancient, accepting eyes. No wonder he thinks me a child.

"I'll let you get settled in. Tomorrow, we can order some clothes and stuff for you on the Internet."

"What is the Internet?" he asks.

I laugh, feeling a little bit more grounded.

"You've got a lot to learn, my friend. Welcome to the twenty-first century."

* * *

The next morning, Layden and I eat breakfast together in his room, which feels far more normal than it should. He's astounded by how good Lucky Charms cereal tastes and eats three bowls. Remembering how much he likes meat, I microwave him some bacon, which he also freaks out over.

It's fun to introduce him to things. So next, I take him to my computer lab.

I drag another chair into the setup I have in front of multiple screens. Sabra was never interested in tech much beyond social media stuff, following celebrity gossip, and connecting with fellow mages, i.e., she was a mostly normal teenage girl despite usually being locked behind these walls with me.

Vlad brought her to live in the compound with us a year after I got here when her mother first went into the psych facility. It was lonely for both of us at first. She was suspicious of me, being Vlad's granddaughter. He'd put her family through hell, so she didn't want anything to do with me at first. And even though she grew up with a mage mother, who was on the brink of losing it completely, Sabra had always been more... normal than me. She'd gone to school with other kids and liked to be outside.

Even once we became friends after a couple years, when I'd disappear into this room of monitors, she had no interest in joining me.

But as soon as Layden sits down in the chair beside me, his eyes light up. Especially when I turn on the screens and introduce him to the Internet.

"So you mean the whole world is connected now—everyone, everywhere—and you can see them and communicate with them through this single screen?" He sounds so excited as he asks the question. "Without ever leaving this room?"

I laugh as I nod. "It takes a little practice to learn how to navigate everything, but yes. You can play any game you can think of with people, take classes and earn a degree from a university, run an entire business, sell things, meet people and just chat..."

I show him Google and how to use it. The basics of where and how to buy things.

"Or," I say, pulling up an anonymizing web browser, "you can use something like Tor to head to the dark web, which is where things get really interesting."

"The dark web?"

I nod. "It's where a lot of the hackers hang out."

"You are one of these? A hack?"

"A hacker," I correct. "I like to keep an eye on things."

I glance over at him as I navigate around to show him what phishing scams are and how to watch out for bots, and then I take him deeper to show him what I do on a daily basis: watching out for what's going on in the world as far as espionage, players who might be looking to threaten Vlad's little kingdom of control or any dangers that could compromise us on a national or global scale.

Layden stares determinately at the screen, eyes bouncing between it and the keyboard I'm navigating with confidence. "I want to learn everything."

I grin at him. "Let's hope you're a fast learner, old man."

"I want it." He's so earnest. "More than anything."

"More than breaking the curse on you?"

He shrugs. "If I can navigate this Inter-net and be here with you, what do I care about that world out there? Everything I need is here."

It's more than a little short-sighted, but I still feel stupidly warm inside to hear him say shit like that. Being here in this room, just him and me, I feel the safety I did yesterday when I was in his arms.

Are you a selfish little girl, or not?

It's selfish to keep him here all to myself when I should be focused on helping him get rid of the curse. But still, he's so enthusiastic about learning Linex and the basics of Python that I text Sabra and ask if she can come tomorrow instead since Layden is still settling in today.

Hours later, I order take-out from my favorite burger joint and enjoy every face Layden makes as he eats a greasy burger and fries for the first time.

"What have they done to *food* since I've been away?" he asks as he devours his third burger. I made sure to order extras for him, knowing his appetite. "How did they learn to make it so much more... flavorful?" He shoves a handful of fries in his mouth.

"I don't know. We learned how to do processed foods and add MSG to everything?" I laugh at the ecstatic expression on his face. "And how to fry things."

He nods. "Yes, the frying. The frying is very good."

He shoves the last of the fries in his mouth and wipes his hands on the stack of napkins at the bottom of the bag. "But we need to get back to learning."

With the hand he just cleaned, he looks back at the tablet I let him borrow, which has a bunch of books on Python we downloaded. He taps through the pages so quickly I don't see how he could possibly be reading them, but by the time I'm done eating, he's finished two books.

And when he sits in front of the computer console, it's clear he absorbed what he read about the computer language because he's already got the basics down. We've only been at this for one day, and he's ready for more advanced things that would take years for a normal person to learn.

"How are you so good at this?" I ask, awed as he builds a

practice machine learning model to predict weather patterns.

He shrugs but pauses, turning to look at me. "Human math follows the same logic as angelic runes." He lifts his hand, and shining blue-white hieroglyphs appear in the air.

I gasp. "You did that before. When I first found you."

He laughs as he swipes the runes away. They dissipate as quickly as they appeared. "I tried. I didn't have enough energy to make a proper rune, or I would have blasted you."

"Blasted me?" My eyebrows lift.

"You have your defenses; I have mine."

"Wow, you really weren't good at accepting help, were you?"

He looks at me, those eyes of his piercing. "No one had offered me help before. So I assumed you were a threat."

He goes back to working on the computer while I'm left staring at him. *No one had ever offered him help before.* For at least eight years, I had a mother. I knew what it was to be loved. To have someone pick me up and coo over me when I fell down. From everything he's told me, he had no mother. Only a cruel father and heartless brothers.

So, how is there any kindness in his heart at all?

Sometimes, I think it's all been beaten out of me by my life with Vlad, but meeting Layden gives me hope.

My phone buzzes in my pocket, and I pull it out. It's a text from Vlad. Automatically, I get a sinking feeling in my stomach.

I turn away from Layden as I click on the text.

VLAD: Now that you're home, I expect you to continue working. Especially since you've brought a guest. If you want him to stay, go make this little problem compliant.

Attached is a photo and a location.

I sigh, which makes Layden look away from the computer. "What?"

"Nothing," I say quickly. "I just need to go out for a bit."

"I'll come with you." He starts to stand up, but I shove him back down by his shoulder.

"No. You won't." My voice is hard.

"What was that noise? And you just looked at something in your hand. A miniature tablet. What happened?"

"It's called a phone, and it's just some business I have to take care of. I have a life and can't just babysit you all the time."

He withdraws like I've stung him. "Of course. I would not expect you to. I am a grown man. Go do what you must."

I cut off anything I'm feeling at having hurt him. This is my world. I am my grandfather's pawn, and I always will be. I just explained to Layden how weak I am if I'm not in proximity to my grandfather while he feeds. I was pushing the distance I could be away from him at the cabin, and even there, I was starting to feel a little weak.

There's no escaping Vlad, which means I will forever be under his power. This was the bargain I struck with the darkness.

I don't see anybody in the hallways as I leave the compound, which is a good thing. Right as I swing a leg over my motorcycle, I text my grandfather back: ON IT.

I'm tempted to say something about leaving Layden alone, but knowing him, that might just goad him into action. Layden's strong now, and seeing his runes again today, I trust him to be able to take care of himself if he needs to. He's the one person in the world I think might actually stand a chance against Grandfather. If only I could survive with Vlad dead.

Even the fact that I'm letting myself think about killing him chills me. It's a useless wish that doesn't do anything except torment me.

I jam the kickstand loose with my foot and take off. The gates open at my approach, and then, finally, I'm free on the open road. Free but always at the end of my grandfather's long tether. At least, though, when I come back tonight, Layden will be here.

Chapter Thirteen

LAYDEN
Present Day

When we pull into Vlad's compound and Phoenix leads me downstairs to her wing, I can't help but feel déjà vu. During the month we stayed leading up to the wedding, I kept to the guest wing with my family.

She even has another computer lab there. I'm pretty sure Vlad had it installed there for her to show anything to visiting dignitaries; he wouldn't have to put up with leading them down her pink-walled part of the compound.

As we push through the double doors to her wing, though, I see things have changed since I was last here. "The walls aren't pink anymore." Instead, they're a pleasant beige.

"I grew up," she says shortly, all but stomping down the

hall. When she shoves open the door, I'm glad to see at least the lab is still much the same.

"Hey," I ask, reaching out a hand but not quite daring to touch her shoulder. I withdraw it. "Are we okay? After what... happened back there?"

"We're fine," she snaps. "Why wouldn't we be fine?"

"Uh..." I just stare at her as she adamantly stares at the floor, then sits down and starts booting up the computer. "Because we just had sex."

"That wasn't us," she bites out.

"Um. It sure felt like it. I remember everything."

She swings around in the chair, all but kicking me with how fast she moves. "It wasn't us," she says again adamantly.

"If it wasn't you that I was having sex with, who was it?" I demand. "Ammit? Because it was my first time."

Her angry eyes soften, half in disbelief. "What? That was your fir—" She cuts herself off and looks at the ground again. "It just—"

"It just, what?"

"It can't be like that between us."

"So what happened earlier was nothing to you?" I don't know why I'm pushing this. But I never could hide my cards with her.

If the sex truly meant nothing to her, fine. I'm not the man that pushes anything a woman, especially this one, doesn't want. I'd throw myself in the sea first. I just need to know now before I get pulled any deeper into this. The way she looked at me while we— I just have to know.

"It *can't* be," she says.

"Because of your professor?"

"What?" She looks up at me, startled. "Don't be an ass. He's just my advisor."

"Are you sure he knows that?"

She stands up and shoves me in the chest. "Don't be an ass. I mean it."

I want to repeat it so she'll shove me again. So I'll have some form of physical contact with her. Even standing as close as we are, I can feel the heat and intensity from back in the alley rising up again between us.

"*Was* it only Ammit?" I ask, taking another step into her so she can feel the heat from my chest.

Her eyes flip from my eyes to my lips, back to my eyes.

Back to my lips.

And then she shakes her head. Hope rises in my chest before she steps back.

"She could already be fleeing the city. We have to search the feeds." She sits back down and starts flipping through surveillance footage without saying another word.

I'm frustrated. But I won't push it. More than anyone, I know how many pressures Phoenix has closing in on her from all sides. But I won't let it go without her knowing, "It meant something to me. Ammit might have pushed me to do things faster than I would have otherwise, but I was still me. Were you *you*?"

Her hand on the mouse pauses, and I think I see her swallow as her cheeks go pink. But then she continues clicking through screen after screen.

"I checked my phone log, and I called Vlad at eleven twenty-three." She zeroes in on the location and accesses camera feeds.

I sit down beside her as the alley comes into view from several angles and don't miss her gasp as she rolls the fast-reversing cameras back enough so that the empty alleyway has several figures on it. She tries to drag the bar forward again, but not before both of us get an eyeful of us having sex in several positions, fucking comically fast.

"Wait, you have to go back," I say. "Ammit fled at the beginning."

"Dammit," Phoenix curses. She starts to reverse again but pauses on a frame of her on her knees, hands on my ass, as she stuffs my cock balls-deep into her mouth. The beast inside me growls at seeing the erotic image of us lost in each other's bodies. I go hard just looking at it and remember how her mouth felt on me. The suction. Oh god, the suction.

"Jesus," she hisses, finally dragging the bar in reverse again before us having sex, stopping right when we leap on each other and start ripping off our clothes.

Because there she is in the corner. Ammit. There's just one frame of her face looking freaked out before she tears off down the alleyway.

"South!" Phoenix announces triumphantly. "She's heading south."

Phoenix zooms in on Ammit's face, takes a screenshot, and emails it off to her contacts at the police, who are watching the perimeter of the locked-down city.

Phoenix seems more than relieved to close out of the window with our sex tape and move on to a camera feed further down the alley. She must have noted the time stamp on the previous camera because this time, she drags the rolling bar directly to where it picks up Ammit running.

I was a little too distracted by the previous footage, but I try to get my head in the game and look at the time in the bottom left-hand corner. 10:47:02. Well damn. We were going at it for almost half an hour. It felt like just the blink of an eye.

Phoenix pushes play, and we watch Ammit run down a

darker part of the alley, then turn left when she comes to a larger street. Phoenix clicks on another camera feed. "Got you now, bitch," she whispers.

Phoenix keeps chasing camera to camera until she gets to a river that cuts through the middle of the city, where there's no coverage.

"Dammit!" Phoenix slams a fist on the table beside the keyboard. I jump a little.

"It's okay," I say. "Vlad shut down the city by eleven-thirty, and look," I say and point to the last timestamp we have Ammit on video. 11:38. "She's still here, somewhere. It'll just take a little longer to find her. Why don't I take over for a little bit?"

Phoenix nods and shoves away from the desk. "I need to take a shower."

Ah. I bet. Does she still feel me on her? Of course she does, and she wants to shower it off. I can still smell it—the scent of sex between us—but all of my brothers and I were cursed with an overactive sense of smell.

She shoves the door as she leaves, but it doesn't close fully behind her, and I listen to each of her steps as she strides to her room. That door she slams.

Chapter Fourteen

I want to ask Layden to hold me again when I get back from the job Vlad had for me. But I don't. I can't. That would feel like I was asking for—Like I was expecting or thinking we could be—

Anyway, even though Layden's still up when I get back, still noodling in the computer lab, probably ready to hack into the Pentagon, considering how quickly he picks things up, I just tell him I'm tired and need to go to bed.

He stops me with a hand on my bicep. He doesn't grab or yank or any of the other forms of physical intimidation I'm used to from my grandfather. His touch is light, and he immediately pulls away. Never taking without asking.

"Are you all right?" he asks, his speech so formal and his eyes so honest and open. Good. He's so *good*.

God, all I want is his arms around me again.

But tonight, I went into the office of another good man and compelled him to ignore all his good intentions and allow the corruption he was about to expose. Because if he did that, it would upset the systemic hold my grandfather has on this city, this country. Vlad controls the entire network of police, government officials, important CEOs, and the media—everyone who's anyone. The man tried to resist me at first. Some of the stronger ones do. But within moments, he was bowing and all but worshipping at my feet. He would have if I stuck around long enough.

It makes me feel disgusting. Ugh.

So, as much as I want to throw myself into Layden's arms, I can't. Because it would feel like I was... tainting him. I need to go take a shower.

"Knock off whenever you want. I'm tired, so I'm heading to bed."

He nods, but I can still see the concern in his eyes. "Do you want a hug?"

My throat burns with tears I refuse to shed. I shake my head. "Thanks. Not tonight," I manage to get out, afraid I'll crack. All but running, I finally make it to the shower and crank it as hot as it will go.

I step in and scrub myself clean of the night. But as the suds wash out of my hair and down my body, my mind starts to stray. What if, in another world, I *had* let Layden hug me again?

I wrap my arms around myself in the hot water and pretend they're his. In the shower, I can pretend the water running down my face isn't tears. I close my eyes and try to remember the safety I felt in his arms. I pretend I can hear the rumble of his voice in my ear, telling me everything will be fine. That I'm safe now. I feel his chest against my cheek.

Everything in my body relaxes and unclenches. The

tension and fear of the night release. He makes me feel so good.

I could make you feel even better, the ghost of his voice whispers in my head.

With my eyes closed, in the safety of my shower, I let myself dream what can never be dreamed outside these four steaming glass and marble walls.

My hand slips down my belly. I hiss as my fingers dip lower. Again, I imagine his voice. *I will make everything better. Shhh, forget everything except my touch.*

Eyes closed, I obey.

I forget everything except his imagined touch. And then it becomes his fingers tentatively seeking my sex. Those strong hands that held the ax, chopping wood outside the cabin, would be curious but still somehow knowledgeable as he explored me. He would learn the language of my body as quickly as he did the computer coding.

His finger is inside me now, and I gasp into the shower spray, one hand on the wall, my back arching. I have to bite my lip to keep from crying out his name. Maybe it's wrong to fantasize about him like this when he's just in the other room, but that only makes me pull my fingers out and roll them around my clit harder, imagining it's him.

You feel so good, he'd say, kissing along my throat. *I dream about being inside you.*

I've never had anyone inside me before. I've never trusted anyone that much. He's so experienced he must have been with tons of women. I trust him to use that experience well to pleasure me. I trust him. I *trust* him.

My sex clenches around my fingers.

That is so good, he hisses. *I want to slide inside you and make you mine.*

"Yes," I gasp into the water.

You saved me, and now I'll save you back. He's so hard. I imagine what he would feel like against my sex and insert another finger. Three fingers inside me, and I know it would be nothing like his cock but still.

You feel so good on my cock. I'm going to fuck you now, and you will belong to me forever. Me alone.

I can't help crying out as I imagine him in the shower with me, pressing me back against the wall and sliding into me. I'm wet for him. My fingers slide in and out of myself as I imagine him taking me.

What if he came in here right now? He's so close. Just a room away. I could make this dream real. If I shouted for him loudly enough, would he hear? Something in me is sure he would.

The thought terrifies me as much as it exhilarates me.

His hard body pressed up against me. His harder cock stiff, entering my ready, juicing sex. His lips on my lips. Or my neck. Or my nipples. I shudder as I pull my hand away from the wall to twist one of my nipples as I imagine his wild eyes looking into mine and—

I bite down hard on my lip as I come harder than I ever have in my life.

Chapter Fifteen

LAYDEN
Present Day

Jesus Christ, she's doing it again.

Here I am, trying to focus on tracking down Ammit when I smell that smell that used to torture me some nights when I lived here all those years ago.

She went to wash the scent of our alley sex off her. But it's stronger than ever, wafting out from underneath her door in between the scents of her sweet shampoo and body wash.

Just like back then.

I've just gotten the hunger back under control, but I immediately go hard again.

She's touching herself in the shower.

I remember the first time it happened. It was the second night I stayed here after she first showed me this lab. I can't remember all we said that night. She'd just gotten back from doing something Vlad had sent her to do, and she seemed upset. Then she disappeared into her room, and ten minutes later, a scent wafted out with the shower steam from underneath her door...

The scent was so primal. So *her*. Every time it latched on to the monster in my belly, it made me want to tear the door down and mate her. I never would have, of course.

Smelling Phoenix's scent then and now, though... I can't focus on the computer screen.

That first time, I barely knew what was going on. My cock hadn't been hard in... well, hundreds of years at that point. And suddenly, there I was, stiffening in my pants.

That night, I undid the buttons of my pants and pulled out my member, staring down in confusion at the foreign, long-forgotten hunger of my flesh even as my hand clenched around it. I'd relieved myself before occasionally, but it never felt like it did as I grabbed hold of myself and inhaled her scent.

Unwittingly, I do the same thing now as her scent comes to me, and I relive that first time my fingers closed around my cock. The hungry monster in my belly leaps in excitement.

Is she thinking about what happened in the alley? Or does she just need another release?

I never knew why she did it or what she thought about during. Maybe it was just a habit she had every time she showered, from long before she knew me?

I just know my mind floods with her as my fingers clench tighter on my cock as it swells. I pull upward and roll my hand around the tip. She was so fucking beautiful tonight as she gave herself to me. I always suspected sex with her would be amazing, but it turns out I never could have even imagined—

My spine goes tight, and my balls clench, my ass lifting off the seat. I grit my teeth. No, I don't want to lose it yet. This greedy space of voracious pleasure before release, lost in the fantasy space of reliving what we did in the alley while her scent is in the air— I want to live here as long as fucking possible.

So I drag my hand back down to my balls and try to remember what it felt like to be inside her. Yes, I was out of my mind with lust, taking her like that in the alley, which I assume was Ammit's doing. But it was only giving into the fantasies I'd played out a thousand times in my head. It was just the restraint of my disciplined brain that snapped. Was it the same for Phoenix?

Is she having one of those fantasies right now in that shower across the hall?

I imagine her imagining me.

I think about her, wishing I would stomp into her room and shove open her shower door. I imagine her begging me to come inside.

Like she begged me in the alley.

Fuck me. And when I push inside her. Fuck me *harder.*

I'd push her against the wall but wouldn't give her what she wanted. I'd take it slow. I drag my hand down my cock with excruciating slowness. I'd make her beg me for it. I'd tease her clit with my thumb while I entered her slowly. Torturously slowly. Then I'd drag her ass-cheeks apart to open her all the way to me, and she'd lift her leg around my hip.

Please. Please, Layden. Make me yours. You're all I've ever wanted in this fucking world.

Then she'd run out of patience, reach down for my cock, and drag me inside her, squeezing my balls for good measure for making her wait.

I squeeze them, imagining her hands on me and groan. Distantly, and only because of my enhanced hearing, I hear the faintest of cries.

In the shower, she's coming.

I jack myself harder, needing this moment of togetherness with her. Even if she'll never know about it. Even if it's twisted. My hand is nothing like her pussy or her mouth, but it's a small meal for a starving man.

I close my eyes and try to remember the feeling of her mouth on me when she was at my feet earlier, begging for my cum. Finally, *finally* abandoning herself to me in every way.

Desperately, I grab a napkin from a box on the desk beside the computer and roughly jack myself into it as one last burst of her scent perfumes the air.

Fuck.

I'm breathing hard as I crumble the napkin and toss it in the bin underneath the desk.

The first time this happened, I remember feeling the euphoric sense of momentary repletion. But I was also so confused I'd shoved my dick back in my pants quickly, worried she'd come back in and find me and know what I'd done. Of course she didn't. She went to bed just like she said she would. The next day, I tried to pretend I hadn't been imagining her naked and wet and trembling beneath my touch.

Now, after tidying myself and zipping my pants back up, I turn back to the computer and try to shake off the memories of the past, what happened earlier, and my constant wondering if, every time she showered and I was overwhelmed with that scent, she was thinking of me or if it was just a habit to de-stress, as mechanical as scratching an itch. Everyone talked about self-care these days. I was all for her taking care of herself. Truly, it was none of my business. She didn't need to know I was the monster hovering at the edge of her life, feeding off her scent.

I start clicking through camera feeds near the river, but my mind's not really in it. There's nothing on any of the feeds anyway. Occasionally some homeless folks are near the river, but no blonde women skulking around. Ammit might have put a hoodie on if she's smart, so I try to watch for those, too.

Maybe she's holed up somewhere for the night? Did she figure out we blocked off the exits to the city? All the cops will have her description and photo by now.

I jump when Phoenix's door slams open against the wall with as much violence as she did when she closed it. She swings into the computer lab with as much force, freshly showered, her hair wet and only the vaguest scent of what she was doing in the shower still clinging to her.

"What have we got?" she asks, sitting down in the chair beside me and not looking my way.

I try not to stare, putting my attention back on the computer screen. I swallow before saying, "Nothing yet. I'm watching the river, but we can't be sure how far she went up or down the bank. Or if she's holing up somewhere for the night."

Phoenix just wakes up another console besides the one I'm working at. "Well, we won't stop until we find her. Vlad has more surveillance on this city than fleas on a stray dog's ass. She's got to show up somewhere."

I nod. "Colorful as always."

She smirks but doesn't take her eyes away from the screen.

"I missed you," I say into the quiet room, eyes on my own screen. "And this. I've missed this." I don't elaborate. But I can tell she gets what I mean when, a long time later, I hear her sigh and get a quiet, "Me, too," back.

Chapter Sixteen

Sabra came over first thing the next day, and Layden was just as quick at picking up the principles of mage-craft as he was at computer languages.

We're standing in a large circle Sabra has chalked in the center of the courtyard, explaining the arcane symbols she's writing on the ground.

"The interlocking circles represent the different planes we're attempting to breach. If this curse was placed by a dybbuk—"

"What's a dybbuk?" Layden asks.

Sabra looks surprised he doesn't know. "A person possessed by a spirit from another plane. So if your curse was placed by a dybbuk, it will have an inter-plane dimension that we'll need to crack. Do you remember anything from when they laid the curse?"

Layden's excellent at keeping a straight face as he lies. "No. It happened when I was very young." I told him I didn't want to tell Sabra more than was necessary. "I don't remember anything. But I can do this... I don't know how I know how to do it, but I can."

He lays down some glowing runes beside her arcane symbols.

Sabra's eyes go wide. "Oh my gods, that's amazing!" She claps with excitement. "Phoenix, are you seeing this?"

I nod. Oh, I'm seeing it all right.

"I've never seen symbols like this before," she says, eyes glowing as she bends down to look at the shining runes. She looks back up at Layden. "What do they do?"

His forehead scrunches. "I'm not sure how I know, but they're interpretations of your arcane symbols, just in another language."

Sabra all but squeals. "It has to be from the plane the dybbuk who cursed you came from. This is a clue! And it should help us get it off you or at least manage it because wow..." She closes her eyes as she hovers her hands over his glowing runes. "Man, I can feel the power humming off these babies."

When she looks back up at Layden, she's beaming. "We're going to make magic together."

Oh dear. I've only seen Sabra like this a few times before. And it's always when she's cracked some new magical secret or attained some new level. I always wanted to close myself up in the lab and play computer games, but apart from normal teenage girl shit, Sabra was always chasing the next magical high.

I get it. It was her escape. Her mom was locked away in a mental institution that Vlad held the keys to, so she was essentially living in a prison, and all she had was me. Yeah. I was about as friendly as a jar of snakes most days, so she had to find her own way. And she did through magic. Vlad was happy to give her all her family's books and grimoires about magic and lore. He'd used them for centuries and no doubt expected to use Sabra just like he had her mother before her, her mother before her, and so on.

Vlad stopped allowing her to visit her mother last month, only finally admitting it was because she'd died after we both started boycotting our duties. Sabra fell into a deep depression before I suggested running away. Depression gave way to a spark of anger, then finally fury. It gave me hope for her. I hoped our leaving might be the start of the rest of her life, free of the connection to Vlad and the misery and death he'd brought to her family.

I thought for sure she'd never come back. But looking at her now, you'd never know it.

She seems light and bouncy as she and Layden lay out more symbols and runes, working their way around the circle. I haven't seen her like this in years. It's not just now. At the cabin and on the car ride home, she was like this, too. Happy and lively, like the last nine years since her mom was first locked up never happened. Is it just an act because Layden's here?

I'm startled out of my thoughts by her voice calling to me from the center of the circle. "Come on, Phoenix, let's try it."

When I look up, I see that the three circles they've drawn are lit up with runes and humming with power that even I can feel.

I'm careful to step between the runes as I join Sabra and Layden in the smallest of the concentric circles at the very core. It's a tight squeeze, but we all manage it. I'm very conscious of the press of Layden's chest against my back, especially considering the fantasizing I did about him last night in the shower. I'm glad I'm facing away from him because I can feel my cheeks heating up.

Sabra holds up a knife carved from stone, and I lift my palm toward her. I'm familiar with this part, but I hear Layden's sharp, surprised inhale as she slices the knife across my skin.

"Right on that symbol there," Sabra says, pointing to a symbol she's chalked in front of me, overlaid with one of Layden's glowing runes.

"Why does she have to be part of this?" Layden asks. I hear the concern for me in his question.

"She's a blood goddess," Sabra says as if it's obvious, and I try not to wince. I haven't told Layden everything, and it feels like she's outing me. "Her blood amplifies any spell we weave and calls to the other planes since—"

I jab her in the ribs, and she looks at me, seeming surprised at my glare. But she does stop talking. Thank fuck.

"Since?" Layden queries.

"Since her blood and Vlad's line are so powerful," Sabra covers smoothly. "Her blood is the jet fuel to our spell."

I can feel Layden's eyes boring a hole in the back of my head but ignore it as I clench my hand over the rune Sabra indicated so that blood drips down from it. I know there need to be at least three drops. Magic comes in threes and sevens. Don't ask me why. I'm just the blood bank here.

As I stand back up, the circles begin to spin around us.

"It's working!" Sabra says excitedly.

"Did you think it wouldn't?" I ask.

"What happens now?" Layden asks.

Sabra grins. "We wait and see."

"Wait and see *what?*" Layden asks. An excellent question.

The spinning circles start humming, and the ground under our feet starts to rumble. I've been in conjuring circles with Sabra before, and this doesn't usually happen.

"Sabra—" I start warily.

"Just wait and see!" Sabra repeats, her eyes glowing with excitement.

I reach back and grab hold of Layden's shirt. "What the hell are we waiting to see?"

The ground rumbles even more, and beyond the circle, I see Vlad and several of my uncles pour out of the compound. Sabra starts laughing with delight.

"What the fuck, Sab?" I say, my hands gripping onto Layden's torso. His arms wrap around my waist, holding me tight as blinding white light leaps upward from the ground where his runes were placed.

And then, just like that, it all disappears. The circles stop spinning, and the light dissipates in the blink of an eye, the ground returning to normal as if it wasn't just shaking underneath our feet like an earthquake.

Sabra starts jumping up and down. "Did you *see* that?"

"We all saw that, Sabra," I say furiously, letting go of Layden and trying to step up to her as she dances around the circle. Only problem is, Layden hasn't let me go. His arms are still firmly locked around my waist.

"Are you all right?" he whispers in my ear.

I turn around in his arms, my belly flipping over at how near his face is to mine. How near his lips are and the concern in his eyes by the time I'm facing him.

"Y-y-yes," I stutter out. "You can let me go now."

Reluctantly, his eyes search mine for another long

moment, and then his arms slide away from around my waist. I struggle not to reach for him the moment I lose contact. But then I remember I'm pissed at Sabra and spin on her where she stands, still looking absolutely delighted with herself.

"What the *hell*, Sab?"

"Oh, it was marvelous, did you see?"

"Yeah, Sabra, I saw. And so did Vlad and everyone else in the compound. It felt like you were about to blast us to kingdom come. What was that?"

"He's supercharged," she says, eyes so bright. "His runes finetuned my arcane symbols to breach the in-between. We'll be able to discover and make contact with so many new realms together; I can feel it!"

"Are you high?" I grab her and shake her a little.

She seems to come back down to earth, but not much, the grin still stretching her face so wide. "I'm not going to let you ruin this for me, Phoenix," she says fiercely. "Not this time."

I let go of her and step back. "What does that mean? What even *was* this? I thought we were trying to fix Layden's curse."

"We were!" She seems a little more grounded as she looks back at me.

"Then what happened?"

"We made contact with the other side!" She can't help herself. She starts bouncing up and down again. "Real contact!"

"The other side?" Layden asks.

Sabra waves a hand. "One of the other sides, anyway. Your runes are powerful."

"Wait," Layden says. "Are you saying you made contact with where I—" He breaks off. "With where the person who cursed me came from? And what does *contact* mean?"

"Contact means access. And access means powerful magic."

"How?" I ask, frustrated with how vague she's being.

"It's hard to explain to a non-mage." She shakes her head.

"Try," I demand, glowering at her. "Considering you're using my blood to power your engine and his runes as navigation."

Sabra just barrels ahead. "And once we get there, we can gaze into what's on the other plane. Even dip into their resources and gain special knowledge." She smiles at Layden. "Like how to break your curse."

"How?" Layden asks, sounding just as confused as me.

"By asking," Sabra says as if it's the most obvious thing in the world.

I feel my eyebrows hit my hairline. "Asking? As in, asking the spirits who exist in that plane? Holy shit, Sab, have you gone insane?"

All her happy vibes disappear at my question, and I immediately want to eat my words.

"I'm sorry, Sab, I didn't mean to say it that way."

"I'm not crazy," she bites out.

I wince. "I know you're not. It's just... What you're talking about sounds really dangerous. All the spellwork and circles we've done in the past... I thought we always agreed we'd never take it as far as talking to spirits from other realms."

She glares at me. "As if you're one to talk."

Ouch. Shots fired. Still, I'm not ready to back down on this.

"You know what happened to your mom."

"I'm not going to accidentally get myself possessed. We've learned so much more since then. *She* taught me better. She taught me how to be safe."

I just stare at her. *Then why did she end up in the insane asylum?* I want to ask but don't. Yes, Vlad had her locked away there, but Sabra visited her every week. She saw what her mother's attempts to push the limits of the arcane had done to her. She barely even recognized Sabra most weeks.

"Look, if this isn't safe, we don't have to try again," Layden says, hands up as if wanting to temper the sudden tension between Sabra and me. "After all, there's the Internet. I can be happy here."

"It's fine," Sabra says at the same time I say, "Maybe that's a good idea."

Sabra glares at me. "Why would you say that? You can't just keep him here as a toy. People aren't supposed to be trapped here for you to play with because you're lonely and bored."

My mouth drops open. Is that why she thought Vlad kept her here with me all those years? Then I look to the ground. *Was* it why Vlad kept her here? I always assumed it was because of her magic. Because he enslaved everyone in her family. But he'd never made any of the others live in his compound. They'd had lives outside.

It was only Sabra he kept locked under his roof. Controlled and never allowed to know anything else besides these walls. Never allowed to have any other friends besides me.

Sabra looks at Layden. "We'll try again. Let me do some studying, but I think I might have an idea of what was off with my calculations. I need to look at some star charts and go back to Mom's grimoires."

It starts to rain, big fat drops washing away all the chalk-work Sabra did. I reach out and pull her into a hug. "We haven't really talked since I got back. Maybe we can go out for coffee soon."

She nods as she pulls away, some of the bounce coming back into her voice. "I'd like that."

My tight chest loosens a little.

"Okay, I'm getting really hungry." Sabra looks apologetically at Layden. He immediately backs away from her.

"I'm so sorry."

"It's fine. Just time to call it for the day," Sabra says. "I'll call you soon when I know more."

"Of course, whatever you need, please don't make yourself uncomfortable on my account," Layden backs away even further. "I appreciate you trying to help me. I can't express how much. I didn't know strangers could want to help one another until I met Phoenix."

Sabra looks at him, then at me, then glances back and forth at us again. "Uh-huh," is all she says, then smiles and turns away. "Bye," she calls over her shoulder with a perky wave before bouncing away toward where she's parked in the large garage in the left corner of the compound.

"I like her," Layden says.

It's stupid to feel jealous at his simple statement. But I can't help feeling the sting of Sabra's words, too. Is that what I'm doing? Keeping him here so I can fantasize about him and have him nearby because of how safe he makes me feel? Like I would a comforting blanket or a toy?

Are you going to be a selfish little girl?

I always have been, though, haven't I? Freeing my parents from me was the one unselfish act of my life.

Layden might be so much older than me, but he's brand new to this modern world. He seems not to know how drop-dead gorgeous he is. If he wasn't literally a curse on any woman he spent more than an hour with, they'd all be drooling over him.

Of course he'd like someone sunshiny and bright like Sabra more than a gloomy person like me.

It only matters if she manages to free him from his curse. I'm ashamed that the thought makes me feel like stabbing my best friend.

Chapter Seventeen

LAYDEN
Present Day

Phoenix and I scrub the surveillance all night long but don't find a thing. So I set up some bots to keep searching for Ammit's face on all the video feeds we have in the city, something I probably should have done earlier, but it felt too good sitting beside Phoenix in the dark computer lab doing it manually. It was easy to agree with her that we might see something that the bots could miss.

Still, by three a.m., she was all but falling asleep at her console, so I told her we should get some sleep.

"Come on, let's go to sleep. I've already got the bots ready to take over for us."

She huffs out a quiet laugh as she scrubs her eyes. "Of course you do." But at least she nods and stands up. "Have the alert sent to my phone, too, if they find anything?"

"Already done."

She nods again and starts heading across the hall toward her bedroom.

"Should I head down to..." I leave off uncomfortably, jutting a thumb down the hall toward the room where I used to sleep when I stayed here ten years ago.

She stops and looks over her shoulder at me, then back down the hall toward the rest of the compound. "Oh, right. Shit." But then she just waves a hand. "There're no cameras in this part of the compound. We shouldn't have to put on a performance for Grandfather tonight."

"Goodnight, then."

"Goodnight."

She lingers only a moment before disappearing into her bedroom.

Not that I can sleep much after everything that's happened. Still, I never needed much sleep. I can go for days with none at all and be no worse for wear, but Phoenix is still human. Or, well, mostly human.

I head two doors down to the room that used to be mine. It, too, has been redecorated. I look around after I flip on the light. It's not as bright, either, now done in tasteful beiges. While she didn't go for the dreary blacks of the rest of the compound, it's still as if all the color has been leeched out of her world.

What happened over the last ten years? Now that we're in this odd place in between who we once were and who I still hope and dream we can become, I have even less idea of what's possible.

And maybe all that hoping is making me blind to who Phoenix actually is *now*. It's not fair to her. I sigh as I lay in bed, another sleepless hour gone. Especially since I'm not sure how to make it right.

I stay in bed staring at the ceiling until the morning

hour, which I only know by watching my phone. There haven't been any alerts, but it's probably a good idea to let my brothers in on the situation at hand. So I call up Abaddon.

It takes many rings before it's finally picked up.

"Here," Hannah's face appears on the screen before she hands it off to Abaddon. "You just push the green button when it rings like that."

Abaddon looks gruff and angry as he glares down at the screen. "I don't see why he couldn't walk himself over here if he wanted to talk."

"He's on his honeymoon!" calls Hannah from off-screen. "And you need to learn how to use the phone!"

"Lovely to see you, too, brother," I comment dryly.

"What is it? I'm eating breakfast."

Behind his head, I see Raven flying around. She seems to be making circles on the ceiling over the breakfast table, a favorite activity of hers.

"I only saw her last week, but I swear Raven's gotten bigger."

"She's a growing little menace," Abaddon says, but I can hear the pride in his surly voice.

"Anyway, I just wanted to let you in on the situation."

"That's new," he mutters.

I ignore him, only half rolling my eyes. "It seems like we might have torn a little hole in the continuum between the planes when we let the Devourer through last month."

"What?" he barks.

Here it comes. The blame and then telling me how terrible I am at everything I do. I sigh. "Look, we only know of one spirit who made it through right now. Ammit, a succubus goddess who kills men after she seduces them. We've got leads on her and are tracking her as we speak. But there might be more who slipped through."

Abaddon rubs his lion-like chin with his clawed hand. "But you've got the one under control. This Am—whatever her name is?"

"Ammit. Yes. Phoenix and I have it under control. We're tracking her and will take her down."

He narrows his eyes at me. "You have a plan?"

"Of course we have a plan," I lie. We'll make a plan when it comes to it.

"One that won't open up a rip in more realms?"

"Yes," I snap. There's no one like my big brother to make me feel like a dunce. "You don't have to worry. I hope you and the family are settling in. I just wanted to keep you in the loop."

He nods, the line still in his forehead as if he's not sure if he has faith in me. But finally, he says, "All right, then. I'll trust you with this."

It's stupid how his words make something clench and then unfurl in my chest. Not having a father worth the name, my oldest brother has always been... well, I always stupidly looked up to him. It was one of the reasons it hurt so badly when he stood there and watched our father slice off my wings without doing a damn thing.

I only learned after I reunited with my brothers that when they thought my father murdered me, Abaddon then killed our father in a rage. Or thought he did.

We all learned a hard lesson that our kind can't be killed when both I and our Creator-Father returned, very much *not* dead. I sent dear old Dad back to the Great Hall, where I hope the angels have shackled him in a deep, dark dungeon somewhere.

On-screen, Raven flies down and lands on her father's

shoulders, grabbing his horns as if to ride him. Except she's much bigger now than she was only a month ago, so Abaddon is thrown forward by her weight and momentum, tipping into the phone as Raven's black wings flutter, and she giggles wildly as if he's a bucking bronco.

"I'll talk to you later," I say, smiling into the mass of wings blocking out the screen.

"You need any help, just let us know, baby brother," is the last thing I hear him say before the line cuts off.

Wow. Kids. A month ago, I would have balked even at the idea. Way too much responsibility for me, I would've said.

And I get why Phoenix isn't eager to give Vlad what he wants, but if this marriage were real and she was at all open... The thought of Raven, growing bigger by the day and my other brother Kharon's daughter Luna... They're both a handful, especially given their angel-monster heritage.

The weeks before the wedding, Kharon and his wife did everything they could to keep baby Luna calm. Kharon is the Horseman of Death who carries humans to the deathly plane after they die, but it turns out that's not the only realm he can travel to. Not that he knew about it until the Devourer visited on the day Luna was born, and we learned she'd inherited his ability. Now Kharon's practicing his own jumps to different realms so he knows he can and is ready to chase her in case she disappears someday.

Crazy to think that what Sabra always spent so much energy and mage-work trying to do with her circles, my baby niece can do as easily as breathing.

I step out of my room to head toward the computer lab. I didn't get any pings on my phone saying the bots found anything, but I can't stand sitting around doing nothing anymore. Speaking of Sabra... I told Abaddon we had Ammit handled, but what exactly do Phoenix and I plan to do even if we catch her? We need Sabra if we're going to send her back to where she came from. My baby niece isn't exactly up to the job, and Kharon still can't control where he jumps to.

But Sabra. Back in the day, Sabra and I finally learned how to connect spirit energy back to the plane a spirit came from. It took a lot of trial and error, but we discovered a system that involved all three of us: Phoenix, Sabra, and me. Together, we provide the fuel, framework, and fine-tuning, respectively. Without one of us, it all falls apart.

We need Sabra.

I pull open the door to the lab, only to find Phoenix already sitting at the console.

Which, really, shouldn't surprise me.

"Find anything?" I ask.

"No," she says, not looking away from the screen. "Ammit's not in Sectors One, Two, Six, or Five, so she's not headed north or east. That leaves just Three and Four."

Phoenix pulls up a map of the city, and I nod, sitting down beside her. "The bots are working outwards in. But you might have been right about Ammit hunkering down somewhere. Still, she had to have gotten off the riverbanks at some point. Some camera had to have caught something."

"Or they will as soon as she pops her head up," I say. "Coffee?"

Phoenix nods distractedly, clicking through the data from the night before. I head over to the espresso maker in the corner.

"You still like it the same way?"

For the first time all morning, she looks over at me. "You remember?"

"I remember everything." Our eyes lock for a long moment before she tears them away to look back at the screen.

"Yeah, I take it the same."

I allow myself a brief smile as I prep the portafilter and tamp down the espresso powder, brewing four long shots into a mug and then adding steaming water.

"What are we going to do when we find Ammit?" I ask. "Have you called Sabra?"

She's quiet for a moment before she finally answers. "No, I haven't called Sabra."

I pull another few shots for a second Americano and bring both of our coffees over to the console, handing hers to her.

She takes the cup and inhales, her eyes falling closed. I don't even pretend not to watch. Coffee was always one of the few pleasures Phoenix ever allowed herself in her disciplined, driven life. It's always been a joy to watch her pause and enjoy a cup.

She slowly takes a sip and lets out a little satisfied noise.

Then she opens her eyes and looks at me as if coming back to the moment and real life after her brief vacation. A frown settles on her mouth. She finally answers the unspoken question hanging in the room. "No, I haven't called Sabra. Because I don't want to just send this spirit back where it came from."

I feel my eyebrows bunch in confusion, but she continues quickly enough: "I want to kill it."

I sit up in my chair, almost spilling coffee all over myself. "What? Why?" More importantly, "*How?*"

"Think about it," she says, setting her coffee down on the table beside her keyboard. "Opening portals to other planes was what started this mess in the first place. If we keep doing it, who knows what else could go wrong?"

"Last time, there were extenuating circumstances," I point out. "Your grandfather interfered—"

"That's exactly what I mean," she interrupts. "There's always going to be something. There are too many variables. Too many unknowns and the powers we're dealing with here... Ammit is a relatively small spirit and one we should be able to take care of with ease, which is why I think we need to eliminate her on sight rather than trying some inter-planar return operation. We just need to destroy her like your brother did with the Devourers. That's the only solution to any spirits who manage to break into this plane."

I can only blink at her. "You really mean that?"

"This world is no place for them. You've seen what Ammit does. She's a power this world doesn't know. Her only language is destruction. Spirits can't just come to this place and wreak havoc on unsuspecting humans who have no defense against them."

I stand up and turn my back to her. Her words are like knives.

I thought just like she did once when I tried to send my brothers back to the Great Hall where the angels live. It's where the Spark of Life inside us comes from, yes, but it also meant separating them from their wives and mothers of their children. All I saw was our destructive natures, not the change and growth and good we were capable of.

"Layden," she says. "Wait, you don't think I mean *you*?"

I feel her hand on my back and can't help stepping away. Even the lure of her touch isn't enough to hold me. Shame is stronger than hunger.

"Don't be ridiculous," she says. "I didn't mean you. You're one of the best people I know."

166

I turn to face her, incredulous. "I'm exactly what you just said. My Creator-Father and his kind broke their way onto this plane ages ago, and you know he set me and my brothers to be plagues upon humankind for *millennia*. I inflicted my hunger on millions. I starved them to death. Trust me," I speak through gritted teeth. "It's a horrible way to die."

"But you changed!"

I stare at the wall. "We still deserve to be destroyed for all the things we did." I certainly don't deserve happiness. That my brothers have managed to steal a happy ending for themselves in spite of the way we began is miracle enough. It's just greediness to think that I could do it, too.

"No," Phoenix says adamantly. "Not *you*." She turns away from me. "But some of us deserve to be destroyed for the harm we do."

Us? "What do you mean, *us*?"

"I'm not who you think I am."

"Phoenix?" I'm so confused by how this has suddenly turned. Phoenix is perfect. Is she saying she thinks she is—

She spins and glares at me. "I lied to you."

"What?" What is she even talking about? "How? When?"

"Every day you've known me. *I'm* a lie!"

I try to reach for her, but she snatches her arm away before I can touch her.

"Then tell me now."

"You thought I was nineteen when you met me, but I was much, much older."

I frown, not understanding. "Okaaay," I say, but she shakes her head.

"I'm ancient. More ancient than you. But most of my life was spent in a dark, dark place." She shudders, and again, I want to reach for her. "There was only darkness and no light, and it was so cold. I didn't know how cold and freezing it was, only that each moment was a misery until I finally glimpsed light and warmth."

Her eyes close, and her features twist in a mask of horror. "They say that hell is a hot, fiery place, but I know it's cold. Frozen with no light. So, *so* dark." She's shuddering so hard now, and all I want to do is take her in my arms. She's in so much pain, I can't stand it. But again, when I try to hold out a comforting hand, she yanks back.

"Do you understand what I'm saying to you?"

"No." I shake my head. "Not at all."

"I *was* a spirit!" Phoenix says, flinging her arms out. "I *am* one. I come from another realm. I glimpsed this realm when some mage or other was fucking around like Sabra does with her circles, trying to make contact with planes beyond this one. It wasn't even a mage, just a woman with mage blood who kept crying out in powerful desperation to whatever spirit might help her. I latched on to her and answered. I gave her instructions on how to save herself, but it came at a terrible cost. Because I was desperate, too. So hungry I would have done anything to get into this world." She flings an arm out again. "Just like those spirits breaking through now."

"Wait," I hold a hand up, so confused. "What are you saying? You lied about Vlad taking you from your mother and father? You're not related to Vlad at all? Is he another spirit, too?"

"No, no," she shakes her head impatiently. "I used him. I used all my ancestors." She looks at me, her eyes wild as if she's desperate for me to understand. "I felt the warmth coming from here when I was in the other realm. And I felt their pumping blood with its potential and all the life here. I

168

didn't know much, but I knew the blood... the blood was the key. It was the way in. It drew me like a moth to a flame.

"That first human with mage blood that made contact with me was the real Vlad Dracul's wife. She called out into the darkness of the spirit realm, begging for help, and I answered. I made a bargain with her. A blood oath just like Vlad used to imprison Sabra's mother and your family and countless others. It started with *me.* I made a blood oath with her—to save her life in exchange for the baby boy in her belly once he became a man. A son named after his father. Vlad. The first vampire."

Phoenix's voice is a dry, horrified whisper as she continues. "But I didn't bargain only for him. It was for his son, too. And his son, and his son, and his son. They would drink the blood of humans for generations, feeding me until I had enough power to finally, finally get myself born into this world twenty-nine years ago."

Holy *shit*. So that's where vampires come from.

I have so many questions.

But right then, a loud beeping alert comes from the computer behind Phoenix. We both turn to look, and then Phoenix leaps for the mouse to click on the alert. "There she is! We finally found Ammit."

"Where?"

Phoenix clicks through to get to the feed that caught Ammit's image and clicks play. Then she swears. "I've got to call John Paul."

"John Paul?" I ask, confused, then remember that's Professor Dickhead's first name. "Ammit's at the university?"

Phoenix stabs at the buttons on her phone in a panic. "Headed straight toward the building where he's got class in a little bit. Maybe he was trying to hunt her down himself and somehow managed to make contact with her? Or she heard about his research? It can't be a coincidence that she's there, can it? Dammit, pickup!"

The phone's on speakerphone, and I hear it go to voicemail.

She grabs me by the hand, fear in her eyes. "We've got to get there now. We've got to help him."

I nod, and together, we sprint for the garage at the opposite end of the compound. Me and my goddess wife, who bargained and lied and stole her way into this world through a path paved in blood.

Chapter Eighteen

PHEONIX
10 Years Ago

Layden, Sabra, and I stand at the center of another circle, trying for the I-don't-know-how-many time to make something happen.

We've been trying once every other day or so, always with the same outcome. Vibrations occur as the concentric circles begin to spin in opposite directions, light beams up from Layden's runes, and occasionally, an earthquake shakes underfoot.

Vlad banished us to a field far beyond the compound after our fifth try put a crack in the center stone of the courtyard.

So today, Sabra's chalked a circle in the middle of an old asphalt road between fallow fields. It's a street that leads to nowhere because Vlad bought out the contractor before he could start to build a planned neighborhood there.

"I think I really got it this time," Sabra says excitedly as the circles start to spin.

"You said that last time." I roll my eyes.

"I mean it. I found something in Mom's old notes. She was only using the barest of circle magic once when she made contact with the other side using a rare arcane equation. She'd scratched it out in the grimoire, but I finally figured it out."

I turn to look at Sabra, which is difficult considering the tiny circle the three of us are standing in. "If she scratched it out, maybe that was because she thought it was dangerous."

Layden's eyes ping back and forth between the two of us as Sabra faces off with me.

"Or really powerful," Sabra says, eyes shining with reflected light as the runes Layden laid on top of Sabra's work begin to leap and arc all around us.

"Shit," I say, glancing at Layden. Maybe if we call this off now, we can stop anything bad from happening.

But right then, a white mist suddenly gathers over our heads, and a beam of light shines down from above.

Layden's whole body goes ramrod straight, and his head tilts back at an unnatural angle as he looks up.

"Layden!" I start to reach for him, but Sabra holds me back, wrapping her arms around me.

"Don't!" she cries. "Look, it's happening!"

"What?" I struggle to get out of her grasp, but she just clenches tighter.

"Stop it," she says. "And don't step out of the circle."

Does she mean stepping out of the circle could do something even worse to Layden? I stop wrestling with her as we tip dangerously toward the outer rim of the central circle, near the whipping ring that's spinning faster than ever around us.

And I really get a good look at Layden. Not only is his whole body stiff, head staring up at the mist, but there's a white film now covering his eyes.

"Oh my god! What's happening to him?"

"It's okay," Sabra says. "He's just making contact with the other side."

I glare at her, our faces only inches apart since she's still got me in a bear hug. "What the fuck does that mean? Why is it only happening to him?"

"His runes were always directing us toward the realm his curse was from. This just means we finally found it."

"You don't know that for sure," I bark. "You're just guessing. All of this is just an experiment. I never should have let you—"

"What?" she asks, finally releasing me. "You never should have let me, what?" She shakes her head furiously. "When are you going to get that this is *my* life and *my* gift. Not everything is about you. I know that's hard to get through your thick head, but I know what I'm doing. And I'm good at it. It's not your job to protect me or *let* me do anything. You're not my freaking mother."

Is she really going to stand here arguing with me when Layden is catatonic like this? "It's not about either of us," I cry. "Look at him!"

Sabra does, not seeming worried at all, then she looks back at me. "I'm giving him what he asked for. He's making contact with the realm his curse came from. I'm helping him find a cure."

"He looks like a zombie. How is that helping him? Have you seen this happen before?"

Sabra stands steadfastly. "I trust the process."

I look back at Layden, feeling helpless. His face is lifeless. Is the glaze over his eyes getting thicker, or was it always that white? Can I really trust Sabra to know what she's doing? She's been obsessed with her mother's grimoires the past few weeks, but I've seen some of them before, especially the later ones. They look like nothing more than the crazed scribblings of a mad woman trying to hold onto her sanity. Entire notebooks were full of arcane symbols, sometimes drawn in spirals to the edges of the pages. Interspersed with drawings of monsters dripping with blood.

"Oh my god, you're in love with him, aren't you?" Sabra says.

I whip my head around to look back at her. "What? No."

"You are," she says, eyes wide. "You love him."

"Stop it. You don't know what you're talking about."

She just shakes her head. "If this works, then he'll be able to leave here, and you can't stand that. You'll be alone again."

I blink, the cruelty of her words hitting me deep in the chest. "Do you hate me so much? I never meant for you to be... trapped with me. I thought we were friends. It was Vlad that kept you and your mother imprisoned here—"

"We both know that's bullshit!" she screams with her whole chest. "It was you all along who did this to my family. You created Vlad! It's always been about what *you* wanted and what *you* needed. You're fed by him, and he preyed on us. You did *nothing* to stop it."

"What could I do?" I throw my hands out, only to be knocked back painfully by the spinning ring around us.

"Something. Anything! You're a powerful spirit from a nether realm, but you pretend to be a weak little girl."

"I was born as a baby into a human body! I was just a kid when I met you."

She rolls her eyes in disdain. "You're a god in a human suit. You were never a child. You just pretended and let yourself forget who you really are. I needed help. My *mom* needed help, and you stood by and did nothing. You trapped us all!"

Tears sting my eyes. "I tried to get you out."

"It was too late." The bitterness in her words is biting. But she's right. Her mother died, and I did nothing to stop it or to help. I didn't think I *could* help.

But was that true?

I didn't really try. I felt as trapped by my grandfather as she was. That was the story I told myself, anyway.

Is she right? In reality, was I the one trapping myself?

I open my mouth to say something, to defend myself or beg for forgiveness—I'm not sure which—when suddenly, the light beaming down from above cuts off, and Layden's body shudders. His head lowers, and his whole body blurs in and out of focus as the spinning rings around us slow down.

"What's happening?" I shout.

"Just wait!"

Layden continues to shimmer, and when the circles around us slow and finally stop orbiting, he's covered in fine gold dust.

Sabra starts bouncing up and down, a hand across my chest as if holding me back. "Don't move," she whispers. "Don't touch him."

My emotions are all over the map after the fight with her and my fear about everything happening to Layden, but he's finally blinking awake, and his body looks solid again.

"Layden! Are you okay? What happened?"

He looks around like he's not sure where he is and then shakes his head, some of the gold dust sifting off.

"Wait, no!" Sabra says. "Don't move!"

Layden nods, more gold dust sifting down.

"I said, don't move," Sabra barks, hurrying across the lines of the now still circle that has apparently become regular ground again.

Layden just looks at me, still blinking like he's reorienting himself. All I want to do is throw my arms around him. I'm so glad he's okay. Which makes my chest clench in all sorts of ways. God, is Sabra right? Am I in love with him?

Our eyes stay locked, neither of us saying anything until Sabra rushes back with a bag. She pulls out several little sample bottles, shoving a couple in her pockets and lifting one to Layden's face along with a tiny brush.

Like an archeologist, she brushes the gold dust from his forehead and cheeks into the sample bottle.

"Can I talk now?" Layden asks, and I'm so fucking relieved to hear his voice.

"Yes," Sabra says, forehead scrunched in concentration, "But otherwise don't move. Stay as still as you can. We don't want to lose a single particle."

"What happened?" I ask again. It takes everything in me not to reach for him. "Are you okay?" I'm pissed that Sabra is more concerned with gathering particles than making sure he's alright.

"Yes, I am okay," he says, blinking. "I think."

"Tell us everything," Sabra demands as she gathers the gold dust from his shoulders.

He takes a breath, eyes widening a little in wonder. "One second, I was here, and then it was like I was lifted out of my body and tumbling over and over and over in space. At first it was dark, and then it was light. So, so bright. And beautiful."

His eyes land on me again. "I wish you could have seen it."

I smile, feeling awash in relief. I guess I was worried for nothing. Sabra was right; she did know what she was doing.

"Did it feel like a physical realm?" Sabra asks. "Was there land or beings who moved in a physical space?"

Layden nods. "Yes. Both."

"Beings?" Sabra squeaks. "You contacted spirits?"

Layden nods. "Just one."

"Did you ask about your curse?"

Layden's eyes drift to the side, again full of wonder. "I talked with a being of light. They had a physical body, I think, but they were so bright I could hardly make them out with my eyes. I was sort of drifting at that point. Still in my body but out of it at the same time. We... spoke."

"What did you say?" Sabra presses. "What did *it* say?"

"Sabra," I chide. Layden looks pretty out of it, and all she can do is demand information. "Maybe he needs to sit down and rest a while. He doesn't need an interrogation right now."

Sabra looks affronted but continues furiously moving around Layden's body, moving onto a second little bottle after she fills and caps the first with cork.

"I'm not even sure I could tell you all that was said," Layden relays. "But I think I'm free of the curse."

"What?" Sabra and I ask at the same time.

"How?" she asks.

Layden looks down. "I drank from a stream while I was there." He lifts his eyes back up, and there's a strength and confidence there I haven't seen in him before. "I'm cured."

"An elixir from the realm the curse came from." Sabra nods. "Of course. Things like that have been written about." A line appears between her eyebrows as she finishes filling another bottle and holds the first up, full of sparkling, other-worldly material. Her eyes gleam. "I wonder what kind of potions we can make with *this*."

I frown. Sabra seems satisfied, but I know Layden, and it seems like he's holding something back. Then again, I was the one saying we shouldn't interrogate him, so I don't press.

It's starting to get dark out, and five full sample bottles later, Sabra's finally willing to let Layden out of the circle.

"Take off your shirt," Sabra says. "I'll soak it and save the water for potions. I don't want to lose any of it."

I roll my eyes, but Layden accommodates her willingly, pulling his shirt off over his head. I avert my eyes, but not before getting an eyeful of his wide, muscled chest, abs, and the sharp V that cuts down to—

Yeah, um. That's when I finally jerk my eyes away from him.

"Whoa. What's wrong with your back? I thought I felt something weird poking up through your shirt."

"Jesus, Sabra!"

I look back only to find Layden turning quickly so his back is hidden. But his face is down like he's ashamed. Not that Sabra notices. She just keeps giving orders. "Jeans, too."

Layden starts unzipping his jeans, and I have to spin away again as my cheeks go thermal nuclear.

This makes me think about what Sabra said about me being a god in a human suit. A sinking feeling fills my stomach. It's a very convincing human suit. It reacts and feels and is constantly yanked back and forth by its physical needs and driving emotions.

Most times, I forget there was a world before. Because Sabra's right. I *try* to forget the before.

"Come on, let's get back. I want to start testing the properties of this," Sabra says. She starts walking determinedly to the car. I follow, not looking behind me since I know Layden's just in his boxers and shoes.

"Do you feel hungry?" Layden asks Sabra.

She stops in front of me, then turns back, beaming at him. Obviously, she has no compunction about looking at him in his unclothed state. "No. And we've been out here for hours. Usually, my stomach would have started cramping a long time ago."

I blink at the ramifications. "Congratulations," I say to Layden. "You did it. I'm so happy for you."

I say it with feeling because I want to mean it. I hope I mean it. But after the confrontation in the circle with Sabra, all I feel is mixed emotions. Stupid human suit.

"Yeah," Layden says. "We did it. Thank you. Both of you. I couldn't have done it without you."

We all clamber into Sabra's car, Sabra and I in the front and Layden in the back. I lift my passenger's side visor mirror to look at him, adjusting it so I only see his face. "I'm so proud of you," I tell him, and he smiles wide.

He reaches a hand up and squeezes my shoulder. I feel the touch all the way to my toes.

"So," Sabra asks as we pull out of the parking lot and onto the road. "What will you do now? The world's your oyster. You can go anywhere you want. Do anything."

I frown, and Layden's gaze connects with mine again in the mirror.

"I don't know," he says. "I'm not in any hurry."

I look down and readjust in my seat, pulling my shoulder away from his touch. He withdraws his hand.

You trapped us all. Sabra's words echo in my head. Is that what I do?

And always Vlad's voice. *Are you a selfish little girl?*

I see myself like a spider in that other dark, frigid realm.

Waiting and spinning, patient for so long, selfishly drawing human after human into my web and feeding on their life force.

Oh, I got myself into the human realm eventually, all right, as they fed on others, an unending hunger. But only so I could keep trapping victims in my net and using them for my own gain. By then, it was all I knew.

I look back at Layden, smiling in his new freedom.

Once, Sabra and I were best friends. More than that, we were like sisters. And now she hates me.

Would Layden start to hate me eventually, too, if I asked him to stay?

Chapter Nineteen

LAYDEN
Present Day

"We need a plan," I say to Phoenix as we run for the garage. "What's to stop what happened last time from happening again if we manage to catch her?"

Dammit, I should have spent last night planning for when Ammit popped her head up instead of... well, what I was doing. Now we have to come up with something on the fly.

Phoenix's stride falters a little, but she keeps going, pulling out her phone. "Vlad, we found Ammit. I need a driver and to borrow your car." She rolls her eyes. "Look, do you want this problem solved or not? I need it now if we have a chance of catching her." She nods into the phone. "Good, have Lucian meet us at the garage."

We finally get to the door leading to the underground level of the garage.

"So what are we doing?"

"I have an idea." She bites her lip nervously. "But it's a little out there."

"I'm game. Whatever."

She nods at one of Vlad's minions, who slides into the driver's seat of a sleek black limo with blackout windows. I open the back door for her, she slides in, and I climb in on the long bench beside her.

"What's the idea?" I ask. "Spill?"

"To the university," she instructs the driver. "No interruptions." Then she pushes a button, and blackout glass slides up between the front and backseat.

"It's soundproof," she says. "He won't be able to hear anything."

I nod. "Okay, so what's the plan? Should we call Sabra—?"

Phoenix just waves her hand. "There's no time for that. We only have thirty minutes until we get there, and we'll barely have enough time as it is."

"For what?"

She breathes out hard and looks me in the eye. "To get out all our sexual tension so she doesn't have anything to weaponize against us."

"Oh." I swallow. The beast in my belly roars in approval. "And how do we—"

Her eyes are still on mine, and then she pulls off her shirt and climbs into my lap.

"Oh," I say, nodding. Her breasts hang full right in front of me, all but bursting from her bra. Beast happy. Very happy. "Oh."

Then she leans forward, stopping right before kissing

me. "Is this okay?" she asks, sounding suddenly shy. Moments before she was so in charge, a general executing a plan. But now, on top of me as my arms slide around her, she's all woman.

I lift a hand to her face, my thumb caressing down her cheek and then teasing inside her mouth. She sucks in a breath, lips closing on my thumb. Her whole body trembles on my lap. "I mean, we have to do what we have to do," I say.

I lift up to kiss her, but she pulls back right as my lips are a whisper away from hers.

"We could just. . ." She bites her bottom lip, and her cheeks go pink in a way I've noticed they do on the rare occasions she feels embarrassed. "Take care of ourselves individually."

My heart thumping, I nod even as I note how hungrily she's staring back at my lips. She's hungry for *me*. And there's no Ammit here now. My cock goes so hard beneath her I see her eyes widen as she feels it.

"We could," I agree. "But that might not be enough. We might need to do the real thing to," I shift my hips while staring straight into her eyes, "fully satisfy the itch or else Ammit could still..."

She nods, her hips bucking against my stiff cock that she obviously feels beneath her. "You're right," she hisses. "Better safe than sorry."

Her fingers drive through my hair, and then she's kissing me furiously. Like it's something she's barely been able to stop herself from doing all this time we've been together.

And holy shit, to have her mouth on mine again. Wanting me. Not because some succubus was making her want it but because it's just *her*—

I release my hold on the beast. She grinds her body

against me several more times, her breasts arching. She still has a bra on.

I reach around to unsnap it while I devour her mouth. Her breasts fall free right in front of my face. I dive my face between them, and my cock grows even stiffer. She rides me and groans. "God, you make me so wet."

Grabbing her ass, I lift and spin her in the open space of the limo, then place her back down on the wide seat. Together, we peel her jeans and underwear off at the same time, then mine. The anticipation now that she's so near, her scent all but in my nostrils, wet for me—

"Now," she says, breathing hard. Her eyes are a little wild as she looks up, pinging around everywhere except to make eye contact with me. "I'm ready."

She reaches between us for my cock, but I pull away before she can grab it. She frowns. "Layden. We don't have time. We have to—"

"For once, let somebody else be in charge." I kiss her, luxuriating in the feel of my bare skin against hers. She's so, so soft. "It'll take at least thirty minutes to get to the university with morning traffic."

My cock knows where to go. I'll let her get away with no eye contact, but only for now because I know this is a lot all at once. The bulbous head of my cock nudges against her wet sex, and she groans, opening her legs wider to me.

Her eyelids flutter as I suck on the bow of her top lip and crouch above her as I thrust. She moans and arches up against me.

She's so soft beneath me, for once receiving instead of demanding. Submitting to me. And I plan on taking everything I can get in this moment.

I pinch her nipples as I pull out and thrust in again. Fuck, so good. *So, so good.* The pleasure fills me even as I stuff her full. Her moan turns to a high-pitched whine. I pinch harder as her wet pussy clenches around my cock.

"You're so fucking tight on me," I break away from her mouth to whisper in her ear, then bite at her earlobe. "Do you dream about this when you're alone in bed?"

And then, I dare more. I dare everything because at last, I'm inside her when it's both really us.

I'm inside my *wife*. "Do you dream about this when you're in the shower? Do you think about what it would be like to be fucked by your husband? Because this is how I always imagined us. From the first time when it was just you and me in that cabin all those years ago. I would chop the wood, and you would go hunt down some terrifying beast. Then, I'd lick its blood off you before bearing you down to the forest floor to fuck you just as wild as you wanted to be fucked."

She squeals, and her hands clench in my hair, fingernails digging in. With my every thrust, her hips rise to meet me.

"Do your finger yourself and know it will never be enough because it's not my thick cock?" I thrust in again, and her legs wrap around my hips in a vice grip. Her hips jerk up against me furiously, riding me from underneath as I fuck her. Showing me exactly how right I am.

"Now you're going to show me just how pretty you are when you come for me. *So, come*," I demand.

And she does, fingernails scratching down my back as her hips jerk up and down on my cock. I keep thrusting, watching her face as it scrunches and her pussy clenches so fucking tight around me.

I feel the tension in my spine threatening to burst, but I hold it back. Not yet. Not fucking yet.

She continues spasming around my cock, high-pitched squeals coming out of her mouth.

I grab her waist and readjust us so that I'm sitting on the seat, and she's on my lap, facing me again like we were when she started riding me. Except we're both naked now, and she's impaled on my cock.

She's a little limp on me, but I bite at her neck. "That was one."

My thumb drops to her clit where I start rubbing circles, and her head pops up, eyes wide. I lick at the place I was just biting, and her breath hitches. I see her belly clench and unclench as I keep stroking her wet, swollen clit, round and then down against where my hard cock is seated so deep inside her.

She groans, eyes rolling back in her head.

I lift her by her hips and drop her on my cock, up and down, and she rolls her shoulders before putting one hand against the back of the seat behind my head so she can start riding me hard.

"That's it," I say, breathing hard myself now. "Give me another."

She nods, eyes squeezed shut. I pinch her clit with one hand and her nipple with my other.

She howls out another release. I guess we're gonna test just how soundproof that glass is because I don't relent one bit.

"I'm gonna let you rest a little bit now," I say, lifting her again and manhandling her until her knees are on the soft carpet of the limo floor and she's bent at the waist, face down on the backseat. I'm grateful for the spacious floor of the limo as I climb on the carpet behind her.

She widens her legs for me, half crawling on the bench seat so I've got a good angle to fuck her.

"Good girl." She moans and wiggles her ass at me.

I don't even know where all the words out of my mouth are coming from, but god, it feels so good. So natural. I'm just following every greedy impulse I have in this moment. Impulses I didn't even know I had.

So when I feel the instinct to slap her ass, I do it. She moans and jiggles her ass some more. I see her wetness leaking down her inner thigh. God, I want to lick it up. So I do.

I lean over and pull her ass cheeks apart so I've got better access to her pussy, and I start to suckle her there. *Fuck*. I'm finally tasting the source of that scent that's tormented me for years.

My hard-on pulses painfully in the air as I bend her over even more so I can bury my face in her. I all but gnaw on her, my mouth closing hard on her pussy, tonguing at the blooming bulge of her clit.

Her ass and hips shake against my face as she howls her orgasm into the back seat. "Layden! Layden!" She cries my name as she keeps shaking, her pussy quivering in my mouth. I don't let up, driving her up again, sucking her so hard just like I know she needs it.

"Lay—" she squeals. And then it's just a high-pitched shriek. Higher and higher and higher until it becomes a noise only an animal could hear. She spasms and freezes, then spasms again until she's shuddering in wild contractions against my face. Mashing her pussy against my mouth. Riding my face and demanding more.

She comes down from one orgasm only to head right back up the rollercoaster to another high. And then another.

A sudden beeping in the car has her banging the car seat and trying to twist away from me, but I keep tonguing her, wanting to give her just a little more. She takes it, shuddering so her pussy spasms wildly against my face before she finally drags herself away from me, reaching over the edge of the seat for her jeans. She pulls her phone out of it, her whole body shaking and covered in a sheen of sweat. She gasps as she thumbs at something on the phone that makes the beeping stop.

"What?" I ask, breathless myself.

Her eyes, dark and satiated, meet mine. "Ten-minute warning. We're almost there. Your turn."

"Oh. I, uh—" All the confidence I just had suddenly shrinks back to normal, Layden size. It feels like me and Phoenix in the car again. Yes, a naked, sex-drenched me and Phoenix, but still—

The look in her eye tells me she's no longer in a submissive mood. She shoves the hair that's come out of her tie back with one hand, a dangerous look on her face as she smiles. "I'm going to milk you now. Because you fucking me like that wasn't the only thing I fantasized about in the shower."

I feel my eyebrows hit my hairline. "Oh?" I manage to get out. So she did fantasize about me? It's the first true admission I've ever gotten from her that she thought of me sexually, if not romantically.

"Bend over the bench," she demands.

"Phoenix, I don't know if—"

"There's no time. You've gotta trust me," is all she says as she shoves me face down, ass out on the bench.

"I do," I say, looking over my shoulder.

"Good." She reaches down and puts several fingers inside herself, eyes locked on mine. Then she reaches between my legs and grabs my cock.

"Tell me what else you've fantasized about doing to me," she demands, her strong hands closing around my cock. I'm stiff in her hold, but I really go rock hard when she adds, "*Husband.*"

"Because all those times I fingered myself in the shower like I'm doing now, I thought about what it might feel like to have you on your knees just like this. And then I'd take my fingers wet with my own slick and put them right up here to see if I could make you lose that iron control you hold onto so tightly all the time."

I all but leap when I feel her fingers between the cheeks of my ass, rubbing at my anus. "W-what are you doing?"

"You said you'd trust me." She bends over my back, and I feel her breasts and warmth against me. "I've wanted to give you a release. You're so tight all the time."

Her fingers keep playing at my anus. "Give in so I can show you how good it can feel to let go."

She kisses down my spine, and her grip on my shaft gets tighter. She's fisting my cock as she drags her hand up and down.

Her tiny, wet finger slips into my ass. I hiss out in shock and clench around her.

"Ah ah ah," she says, kissing down to my tailbone. "There's no time for that. You have to let me in, big boy. Relax. Let it happen. Trust me."

Fuck.

I've never trusted anybody in my life. Once upon a time, I trusted Phoenix, and she destroyed me. Can I give her back my faith? Of course I can. I'd leap off any cliff for her. Even if there's just concrete at the bottom instead of water. I don't fucking care. For her, I leap.

I relax, and she slips another finger in. Then she starts massaging me there. Inside my anus. Not very deeply in. But hard and insistently.

Pleasure bursts hard immediately at my spine. Almost

painfully hard. My beast opens its maw to roar with a craving for a new pleasure. A pleasure so deep and intense and so, so close. Tangibly close. I want it. I need it. I need her to give it to me. I feel my face contort with the coming pleasure.

"That's right, husband. Come for me." She squeezes the tip of my cock and then drags her fist down to my balls.

"Faster," I groan. "Harder."

She strokes me faster. And harder. Then she leans down and bites the cheek of my ass while she presses that spot inside me.

"Oh fuck!"

I come, and I come *hard*. Harder than ever in my life. My spine fucking cracks, I come so violently, spewing cum all over the carpet.

When I'm done, I sag against the seat. Shit. I don't even want to think about the cleaning fees for this.

"Good, good," Phoenix murmurs. She pulls me away from the wet spot to the other side of the limo and the opposite bench there. "That was one."

"What?" I lift my head to look at her in shock. "That's all there is."

She just lays down in the middle of the bench seat, so gorgeous and naked and alluring. My shaft immediately perks back up. "Come on, there's only a minute or two left." She sticks her tongue out and licks indecently at the air. "Climb up here and feed me your cock."

My dick immediately leaps at her words. She's clearly got an agenda, and I'm not one to argue. Careful not to crush any part of her, I climb over her, my cock hanging down between us. She grabs it and immediately starts licking at the tip.

Oh fuck. If I thought her hand on me felt amazing, and

her pussy, her little seeking tongue is... My eyes roll back in my head. I spread my knees on either side of her head and bend over, perfectly positioned to drop my face down to the dark curls between the V of her legs.

She hisses in a breath around my shaft before pulling it deeper into her mouth. I start to lick hungrily at her clit. It's still swollen at the top of her pink lips, and I tease the tip of my tongue back and forth against it. She shudders beneath me.

And then I feel her fingertips at my ass again. Double fuck.

I haze in and out of concentration, my nose buried in her scent as I suckle her while those daring little fingers find that spot on my prostate again. My monster alternately roars and purrs in pleasure it never even knew to fantasize about—

I suck in a deep inhale of her, my hands pulling her wide open for my mouth as I thrust my tongue inside her honeyed channel—

My back goes stiff, and I feel my balls tighten. Holy shit. I can't believe there's any cum still inside me. But I feel the pleasure rising, and I want it again. I want it so bad. It feels dangerous to be this hungry. To crave anything this much. I thrust in and out of her mouth, trying to temper my motions so I don't hurt her.

Her hips jerk just violently against my face, though, and soon she's screaming out her orgasm. Which makes her throat vibrate wetly around my cock while she presses down on that spot inside me...

I barely manage to cover my teeth with my lips before I bite down on her clit as it hits again, cum spurting down her throat. She swallows, pulls back for a breath of air, then suckles down another swell of cum with my next thrust. And another. And another.

How? How the fuck am I still coming? But she's relentless until finally, she's all but gumming my still-stiff cock as she drags her fingers in and out of my ass. I thrust until there's not a drop left in the tank or anywhere in the backup chambers.

Gasping, I fall to the floor, and she laughs, legs still shaking as she lays on the bench. "Well, if that doesn't do it, I don't know what will."

She sits up weakly, spasms still occasionally shaking her legs every other second. "Come on. We're here."

Chapter Twenty

PHEONIX
10 Years Ago

I slam the door on the car and glare at Lucian, my driver. "I don't want anyone hearing a *word* of what happened tonight."

He just stares back at me with his sunken eyes beneath his too-broad, pale forehead. Always the same with my uncles. "I report faithfully to my Master," he says in heavily Slavic-accented English.

I try to hold my shit together. "Obviously, I know you're going to cry to Daddy. I mean, I don't want word getting to anyone else in the compound. This is not going to become the latest gossip while you all get together in the basement and fuck your blood bags or whatever it is you do down there."

"Ugly language for such a pretty little girl." He reaches forward, and I jerk back before he can touch my hair with his too-long, yellowed nails. He and my other uncles have been trying to touch my hair since I arrived here as a little girl. Fucking creepy. I cut it all off when I was fourteen to make a statement: Leave me the fuck alone.

I glare at him. "I'm a little girl about as much as you're a man. We're both monsters. Don't make me make you crawl on your knees again to prove it."

He hisses at me, exposing his fangs.

I stand still, cross my arms over my chest, and wave a hand pretentiously at a large yawn. Seen it all a thousand times before, buddy.

But then I stand tall again. "I'm serious. If I hear one word of this around the compound, you'll wish all I was making you do was crawl."

"What?" he demands. "What can you do?"

I smile at him. "You'll just have to wait. And wonder." I make a *pow* motion and walk away from him. Better to be thought of as a scary monster than a pretty little girl.

Most times, I didn't think I was either, but on nights like tonight...

Then, of course, Layden is *on* me from the second I get near the door of my room. He's waiting for me outside my door and follows me as soon as I push inside. We're always in and out of each other's rooms since there's nothing else to do down here, so it's not strange—just not at all what I need right now.

"Hey!" he says, full of all his bubbly good guy energy. "What have you been doing? Where have you been? I've missed you."

I look at the clock on the stove as I drop my keys on the counter, then glare at him in exasperation. "It's only been like four hours."

He steps back a little, looking puzzled. "Yes, but you're are usually around in the afternoons."

Shit. I scrub a hand down my face. What are we even still doing? It's been a week since the circle where his curse was lifted. And more and more each day, I'm starting to think Sabra was right. About everything.

"Did you look any more today about getting a job?"

"Yeah!" he said, still all but bubbling over with enthusiasm. "And I was thinking. This compound and all the surveillance work you do for your grandfather. That's gotta be a job for more than one person, right? I'll stay here. And help." He grins so big I can see he really does see it as a perfect solution. Especially when his expression softens. "And I could stay with you."

I start to back away from him. After the night I've had, this is too much. *Too much! Too much, too much, too much.*

Averting my eyes from Layden's bright, simmering-with-life gray ones, I murmur, "I've got to go wash my hands," and leave the room.

But Layden has never met a boundary in his life, or if he has, he was asleep too long in the forest to remember them, so he follows me to the little bathroom off the living room.

I start to close the door, and he says, "I thought you said you just needed to wash your hands."

"Goddammit, Layden, it's like you're a needy little puppy that's not housebroken yet! Just give me some fucking space!" I slam the door in his face. And then immediately feel like a piece of shit.

I look at myself in the mirror.

You are a piece of shit. You killed a man tonight.

The reflection shows what Lucian saw. Pretty, petite. Long black hair. Pointed chin. Big, full cheeks. Full lips.

Tonight was supposed to be just a routine visit with a

statesman. I've met with him before. There's new legislation that's come up, and Vlad needed votes to go a certain way.

But as soon as I got in the room with the man, he started trying to maul me, telling me how much he loved me, how devoted to me he was, and how I was all he could think about. He wanted to leave his wife and kids for me. I shoved him away, but he wouldn't stop. He'd do anything I wanted, he said.

Which is when I should have mentioned the voting Vlad wanted from him.

Instead, I screamed at him that I wanted him as far away from me as possible. I can't stand them when they get like that, all but suffocating me.

I turn on the tap, bending over to splash my face with water a few times before standing back up and looking into my eyes again. Water drips down my face and the front of my hair. I get these frightening flashes as if the liquid were blood. The blood I longed for so long in the dark.

"You sure got what you wished for," I whisper.

"Phoenix?" Layden knocks on the door.

I close my eyes, except when I do, all I can see is the statesman saying, "Of course, Mistress!" and spinning exactly where he was standing in his third-story office building where we were alone after hours. And then he sprinted full speed toward the window of his office, splitting his head open on the glass and plummeting to his death three stories below.

Chapter Twenty-One

LAYDEN
Present Day

Oh shit. For the past half hour, I've completely forgotten about the world outside. Ammit. Right. We're supposed to go confront Ammit now. That's the point of all this. We weren't just finally giving into our desires or consummating our marriage, or as close to it as I was likely ever going to get.

I take a deep breath and try to focus, but my mind feels completely blank. Like I just blasted every thought I had out from my balls through my shaft and down her throat. For once in my goddamn life, I don't feel an ounce of hunger.

I just feel... happy.

Phoenix licks her lips as she reaches for her jeans and shimmies back into them.

"Layden," she snaps, looking at her phone. "Hurry. We

could already be too late. I texted John Paul that there was a threat and he needed to stay in his office, but I'm not sure if he got it or not. He hasn't responded."

I nod, grabbing my own jeans as Phoenix finishes tugging her shirt over her head and reaches for the door.

"Wait," I say, but she's already out. I grab my shirt and follow her, zipping up my jeans and pulling my shirt on as I run after her. Shit. *Get your head back in the game.*

She's moving far faster than normal—she's usually careful not to show any of her superhuman characteristics when we're around anyone else who might be able to see. Now that she's finally told me everything, I wonder what else she might have hidden from me. I'm able to keep up with her only because I never claimed to be human myself. I might not have my wings anymore, but I can still run far faster than anyone from this realm has a right to.

No one's watching us, though. The limo double parked in an alley close to the building housing the Ancient Religions department so we don't have to cross much of campus before we're there.

"Something's wrong," I state the obvious as we see students spilling out of the building, some of them screaming. It snaps me back into the present, at least.

Especially when Phoenix starts to cry, "No, no, no!" She tries to shove past the people exiting to get to the double doors, but it's a mob.

I move in front of her since I have wider shoulders and push through like a battering ram until we have a path to the door. There's a bottleneck of students trying to get out. I yank several people through, and when more fill up the gap, shove into them and hold them back until Phoenix can follow behind me.

They shout at us, but I ignore them, letting go of the

flood only once I feel Phoenix at my back. Together, we thread our way through the panicked, pressing mob.

It doesn't take us far to figure out what has them fleeing. We're in the building with the large round atrium and research displays behind glass in the center apex of the building. There was a model display of an early religious temple behind the glass when we visited last time.

Now, there's a dead body.

Not just any dead body, either. Blood is everywhere, and the body is severed into pieces, arranged outwards symmetrically in a circle from the chest, exactly like the crime scene we saw in the dorm room. I don't feel like I have to even look to know that the heart is gone.

Phoenix is right. We're too late.

She runs right up to the atrium, a gasp of horror coming from her throat as her hands slap the glass. But then she backs up, a hand over her mouth. "It's not him. It's not John Paul."

Her head swings to me. "Do you think he's still in his office? Maybe he's already gone?" She looks toward the fleeing students.

I nod. "He had to have heard the commotion, right?"

"His class is at nine-fifteen." She looks down at her phone. "We still have five minutes. He might not have heard all this because sometimes he works with sound-dampening headphones all the way up until his lectures start. He says it helps him get into the right headspace."

"Where's his office?" I ask.

"Come on," Phoenix says over her shoulder, already taking off for the stairs at the edge of the large, circular space. The crowd behind us is finally thinning as students get through the doors. They must have all gotten out of their eight o'clock classes and found the gruesome murder scene. Someone wanted this to be public.

Anyone who could hear would have followed the mass exodus. Which explains why it's so empty when Phoenix and I get to the second floor. It looks like people got the message and left in a hurry; chairs are askew, computers have been left on, and doors to offices are left open.

But there's a light coming from under one door that's still closed at the end of the hallway. Phoenix hurries toward it. She doesn't knock, just yanks it open.

Right in time to find Professor Rossi on his knees before Ammit.

He looks up at Phoenix. "Help!" he cries.

Ammit turns at the same time, eyes going wide when she sees the two of us. She lifts a hand, and I feel it hit immediately—the churn of lust for Phoenix in my guts.

But, this time, it's bearable. My cock goes stiff, and I'm distracted by my need for Phoenix, but I'm still satiated by everything we did in the limo on the ride over. I can still actually *think* and remember what we're here for.

I see the surprise on Ammit's face as Phoenix lifts *her* hand toward Ammit, and she suddenly stops, not moving a muscle. Her whole body becomes paralyzed, and I realize Phoenix is doing her freezing-someone-by-their-blood thing.

"We've got to get her out," I say quickly. "There's already been enough of a scene here."

The police will be crawling the building any moment. Everyone downstairs had to have called after they ran out. Yes, Vlad might own the department, but it's going to get messy if his granddaughter is discovered on the scene when they get here. Especially if she tries to do whatever it is she wants to do to Ammit...

Two magical murders in one place might be hard for even Vlad to keep contained.

Phoenix nods grudgingly. "We'll have to deal with her elsewhere."

"What are you doing?" The Professor grabs for his phone. "It's her! Ammit! She's the murderer. We need to call the police! She was about to kill me!"

"You—" Ammit starts to say, but Phoenix closes her fingers, shutting Ammit's mouth so nothing but angry noises come out.

I snatch the phone out of the Professor's hands. "What are you doing?" He looks furiously at me, but I ignore him.

We don't have time for civilian bullshit right now. If Phoenix is feeling anything like I am, Ammit's still trying to throw everything but the kitchen sink at us. Phoenix might be barely holding on to her control, and I don't want numb-nuts over here distracting her focus.

"Walk," Phoenix orders Ammit, who looks furious but begins to do exactly as Phoenix commands, marching out of the office and down the stairs.

"Will someone tell me what's going on here?" the Professor asks, following us as we head down the stairs, Ammit at the lead, Phoenix right behind her.

"Not now, John Paul," Phoenix barks, and I can tell by the strain in her voice that I'm right; she is fighting Ammit's influence hard.

When we get to the bottom of the stairs by the atrium, John Paul's eyes widen as he stares at the gruesome scene. "Mother of God!" He crosses himself and turns away, looking like he's going to throw up as we pass by.

The whole building has emptied, and our car isn't far. If we can just get Ammit out of the city, then Phoenix will be able to deal with her in the way that she needs to. Or we can call Sabra to help us if Phoenix has changed her mind. Maybe I can talk her into it on the way.

"Go home," I tell John Paul as we approach the doors we came through. "We've got this now."

"Oh, I don't think you do," John Paul says from behind me.

I roll my eyes, but before we take another step, one of the double doors opens, and a familiar face appears.

"Sabra," Phoenix says in confusion. "What are you doing here?" She glances over her shoulder at me. "Did you text her?"

I shake my head because what the hell? Not only is Sabra standing there, but Vlad is behind her. Police sirens sound in the distance. That was fast. The college kids called the police, and they already notified Vlad? But if he's here already, that meant he had to have left the compound right after Phoenix and I did.

"I'm here to help," Sabra says, pushing her way into the building. Vlad follows her in, and before the door shuts completely, I see his black-suited vampire minions spread out in a perimeter around the outside of the front of the building.

"What are you talking about?" Phoenix says, confused. "We already have a plan. Look, I'm sorry I didn't call you—"

Something's wrong. But just as the feeling of wrongness tingles down my spine and I reach out to grab Phoenix's hand, yelling, "They aren't here to help!" a magical golden sizzle lights up around the floor of the circular atrium we're still standing in.

"What?" Phoenix asks, still sounding so confused. She tries to take a step toward Sabra, but it's like she's run straight into a glass window. She bounces backward.

"What the fuck, Sab?" she asks.

Oh fuck. I don't know why Sabra has betrayed us, but I suddenly have a horrible feeling that I know why this murder happened in the atrium, and it isn't because it's a public display. It's because the atrium is a giant circle. And of all the mages I've ever met, none of them are better at circle magic than Sabra.

"I'm just doing what has to be done," Sabra says, sounding nothing like her normal bubbly self. She doesn't sound sorry either, that's for certain. She just sounds... blank.

"She's loyal to *me*," Vlad says, taking Sabra's arm like one might a lover's and walking right up to the outside of the circle we're now bound in.

Phoenix's mouth drops open. "You?" And then her eyes widen and she gasps low. "You *didn't*." Her voice is low and horrified.

Vlad just shrugs and runs his hands over Sabra's hair. She turns her face toward his touch as if she's a pet and he's her—Her master.

Oh fuck. He made Phoenix's best friend his blood slave.

"When?" Phoenix demands. "How long ago?"

"Since right before the two of you ran away at nineteen, and you brought this wonderful opportunity to us." He shoots a villainous smile at me.

Then he looks down at Sabra, who's all but hanging on his arm. "Of course, she turned around and came immediately back when I called out to her. She can do nothing else but worship me and serve my every whim. As did her mother before her and hers before her."

"You son of a bitch!" Phoenix screams at him, running at the invisible wall again. I grab her to hold her back from hurting herself.

"I had no idea when you brought the boy back to us ten

203

years ago just how deeply he was connected to the ultimate power I've sought for so long." Vlad's twisted smile comes back to me. "We could have saved all this time, lad, if you'd just told me who your father was."

"My father's dead to me, you dickwad. And he's long gone anyway. So fuck off." I shoot runes at the floor to try to break whatever circle spell Sabra's laid, but they disappear as soon as they touch the marble.

Vlad laughs and claps his hands. "That's what makes all this so delightful. And to think, if you'd just done as I said and produced the offspring I asked for, none of this might have been necessary. But look, now we're here, and I love to be present for a family reunion."

What the fuck?

I look around, only realizing now that it's not just Phoenix, Ammit, and I who are caught in this circle.

John Paul holds out his arms and smiles a familiarly sinister smile at me.

Then his body and features morph until the creature from my nightmares is standing in front of me, handsome, black wings flaring out ten feet wide on both sides of his back.

"Son," he says. "It's been too long."

What in the ACTUAL FUCK?

Phoenix's professor has been my *father* all along?

Chapter Twenty-Two

PHEONIX
10 Years Ago

I shove through the bathroom door, the image of the politician bursting through the glass to his death still on repeat in my head.

"Hey, are you okay?" Layden asks, puppy dog eyes concerned.

I glare at him. "Why are you still here?"

He looks at me, confused. "What do you mean?"

"Cut the shit. You're free." I fling out a hand. "So go be free. You can go anywhere. Be anyone you want."

"I like who I am," he says. "And I don't want to be anywhere but here."

He steps forward, and I step back. He stops, frowning, but doesn't stop talking. "Phoenix, I feel like I really have gotten to know you over these past few months. You've become closer to me than any other person I've ever known in my life. I don't want to go anywhere else because I—"

I throw up a hand to try to stop him from saying it, but it doesn't work.

"—I love you."

I cringe and back away even further. "Don't! Don't say that."

"Why not? I do. I love you."

Every word out of his mouth feels like it's flaying me. All of them saying that they love me. Men. Women. Obsessed, following me, endless confessions of *I love you, I love you.* I hate those words. That guy earlier tonight loved me enough to throw himself out a window! No, I didn't care about him. I'm a monster, after all. But I do care about— I mean, if *Layden* got hurt because of some stupid obsession—

I back up. "I never wanted that!" I yell.

He blinks at me, too naïve to hide his hurt. "But I thought we..."

"You thought we, what?" I'm driving him even further away. But it's what I have to do. For him. For me. It hurts but feels good at the same time. I deserve to hurt.

"You thought we were falling in love?" I make my tone as scathing as possible, and he's the one taking a step back now.

"Why would I ever fall in love with someone like you? You see how I live." I wave my arms around me. "I'm used to *power.* I took pity on you."

I barely know what I'm saying; I just know I see the growing devastation in his eyes, and it's good. It's far better to wound him now than whatever might happen to him later from being around me. He'll get hurt by me or by Vlad. I'm poison. So, like the viper I am, I keep striking out at him.

"What good is an angel without wings? You're ugly. You're weak."

"No," he says, swallowing hard. "I was the only one brave enough to stand up to our father—"

"And how'd that go?" I ask mercilessly. "Your brothers buried you alive afterward, and you let them get *away* with it. Seems like they actually know how to make their way in this world." I shake my head at him and make the pity heavy in my voice. "You're just so naïve."

I turn and start walking away from him, even though it means I'm walking out of my own room. I don't know where I'm going. I just have to get away from him and the pain I see on his handsome face. The pain I've inflicted on him.

But he just runs to get ahead of me, turning to get in my face.

The puppy dog look is gone. Instead, his features are hard in a way that makes my heart break. "Fine," he says. "I'm too naïve? I'll go get experience. I'll give my brothers what they deserve. Will that make you happy?"

"Fuck what makes me happy!" I yell. I grab the vase of flowers from the foyer and fling it against the wall. "Do you hear how fucking useless you are? You sound just like all my fawning admirers. I adore you, Mistress, I'll do whatever you say, Mistress. I can't even tell if my fucking compulsion *has* started working on you or if you're just this fucking *pathetic*!"

I see the full weight of my words hit him in the chest. Worse than any blow.

"You don't want another fawning admirer?" he says through his teeth. "Fine. I'm gone."

Then he spins and walks away, out of the compound, and he doesn't come back. Proving yet again he was never under my compulsion at all.

Which is exactly why I have to let him go. Nothing's holding him here now. Not yet. Sabra might feel like she's been trapped here and hates me, but I'll never let that happen to him.

Knowing I've saved him from me and my family doesn't stop the tears from coming. I lean against the wall and slide down as I start to cry. Quietly at first, swiping the tears away quickly and trying to deny I'm even sad. It's not a big deal. He was only here for two months and two months is nothing considering how long I've existed.

But soon, I'm hiccupping from crying so hard, and then it's outright sobbing. Ugly, ugly sobbing that leaves me holding my stomach in the fetal position because I'm crying so hard.

I wish I could call Sabra like back when we were teenagers and gossiping about the boys we liked. Back when the boys we liked were just faces on the screen of our at-home theater projector in the upstairs wing.

But it's all different now. I sob into my hands. The things I said to Layden. My stomach cramps, hurting over how mean I was. What I said about his brothers. And his... his father. I cover my face with my hands. Because this isn't just a crush. And I know the ache of losing someone never really goes away... when you... when you *love* them.

Chapter Twenty-Three

"We sent you back to the realm of the angels!" I stagger away from my father. Phoenix runs to my side, facing off with me against him.

My father laughs in my face. "Which I must thank you for. The angelic hosts were not happy to see my thieving face and did not welcome me back with open arms. But I pretended repentance and ate of their manna and drank of their heavenly ambrosia, refilling my angelic powers to their fullest like they had never been since I was first spawned many ages ago. And I planned, oh how I planned."

My stomach sinks with every word.

"It was easy to jump back to this world using the same well of realms I came through the first time. I just had to wait for them to let down their guard and not watch me every moment. Then, once I was back here, I sought to take over this world and become its ruler as I did in the ages of old. Except this time, I would rule it fully. Not just an empire for an age or a century or two but the entire *world* forever."

"It was you behind the angelic runes that took over government systems last month and launched those nukes," Phoenix says breathlessly. "You weren't going to rule the world. You were going to destroy it!"

"And remake it in my image," my father says, grinning madly. "With every being left bowing down in worship to *me*. For all time."

Of course it was him. I should have known at the time. I'd just hoped that when we sent him home through the rune circle I'd created, it meant we'd be done with him once and for all. But Phoenix is right. The only way to deal with a rogue spirit is to *kill it*. I don't care if my brothers tried once before by burning my father's body to ash.

Unbeknownst to them, he regrew from an ember. But it took him years to regain his shape and strength. We'll have to just keep burning him eternally. I don't care how. He can't be allowed to live. He's a creature of destruction.

"But when you so creatively foiled that plot by creating a crack in the continuum of spirits, well," my father chuckles. "I realized I'd been thinking too small. Why rule one world when I could rule *many*? This world is the nexus point of access that is drawing in more powerful spirits than I could only dream of. I no longer have to create an army. The army will come to me."

He holds out a hand toward Ammit.

"I won't be part of your army, you bastard! I never wanted any part of this."

Wait, what? I forgot she was even here. I look toward her now as she backs away from all of us, past the gory scene in the atrium, to the other edge of the invisible circle on the floor.

"Is that why you lured me here?" she asks, looking at my father.

Lured her? Phoenix and I exchange a confused glance.

"Oh, come, my dear," my father says. "Don't be dramatic. You hungered for this realm just like the others do."

"I was happy where I was," Ammit cries.

"You were an outcast," my father's voice bites out. "In a realm of spirits in constant consummation and orgasmic bliss, you were *alone*. You cried out, and I answered. I gave you a body. I paid for your passage into this world in *blood*." He gestures at the atrium, and she winces away in horror. "You should be the first bowing at my feet in worship of your god."

"Never!" she shouts.

"Wait," Phoenix says confused. "Are you even Ammit? Was it you who killed those people?" She gestures at the sliced-up body in the atrium.

"What?" the woman looks horrified. "No! I'm not a murderer. They did that to bring me into this world." She points to my father and then to Sabra and Vlad.

Phoenix swings around, and I see the devastation on her face. She stumbles back a step. "Why?" She can barely gasp the question.

"Please," Vlad sneers. "You think I was fooled by that little performance you pulled on your wedding night? I need you to produce me heirs. That was the deal he and I made." He gestures toward my father. "He came to me after the stunt with the Devourers and offered me a partnership. We were about to become in-laws, after all." Vlad's eyes gleam with avarice and greed.

"You're a fool if you think he considers you a partner," I say. "You're nothing more than a pawn to him. An insect."

I know my father better than anyone. He "partnered" with many powerful emperors, kings, and rulers over the years, only to crush and betray them the moment it amused him.

Vlad's pissed, I can tell, but Phoenix interrupts before he can say anything.

"Fine, you're both big and bad and evil; I get it," she says, holding up her arms. "You're going to raise a great, evil army together. What does any of this have to do with why you've trapped us in this circle here with a dead body and the spirit you already pulled over? Just so you could keep us contained while you did your big, Machiavellian reveal? Okay, great, you've done it. Now let us out."

Both Vlad and my father laugh.

It's not a good sound.

"You think we would waste such a magical conduit?" my father says, gesturing toward the body. "Oh no, no, no, son. I have such plans for you"—he comes over to me and grabs my shoulder in a crushing grip—"and your new bride."

I shove him away from me and stand in front of Phoenix, blocking him from her. "You won't touch her."

"You're right," my father says, walking right out of the circle without any trouble at all. "I won't."

I grab Phoenix's hand and try to follow him but run into the invisible wall just like she did when she tried.

"Don't," she says, pulling me back.

"You'll never get what you want!" I yell at my father. At all of them.

But he just chuckles and walks right up to me on the opposite side of the invisible barrier. Behind him, Vlad brings Sabra close, dips her head back, and sinks his teeth into her neck.

"No!" Phoenix yells, running up beside me.

Sabra's eyes go vacant, and when Vlad lets her up moments later, she looks so pale and zombie-ish that I can't believe neither Phoenix nor I caught on to what was happening with her a long time ago. She's always worn a lot of makeup the entire time I've known her, but I thought it was just her style.

"The question," my father asks me, "is what *you* want."

Sabra stands in front of Phoenix and lays a hand on the floor at our feet, the tips of her fingers just making contact with the circle she somehow laid there before we ever arrived. Did my father help her make it invisible? His runes were always golden instead of silver, if I remember.

It was a trap. This whole thing was a set-up for us to catch the murder at the center of a super-charged sacrifice as a power source so they could— What? So they could *what*?

"What do you *really* want, deep down inside your soul?" my father asks. "Do you want your wings back?"

I look at him, furious. What is he even talking about?

"And you?" He looks at Phoenix. "From what your grandfather tells me, you've always wanted to be anything but what you are. You want a *normal life*. Isn't that right?"

My head swings toward Phoenix, and I see the shocked truth of it on her face. Her gaze drops to the floor as if guilty at being caught out, especially by my father. And Vlad, if he's the one who knew it too.

My chest clenches for her. I reach out for her hand and squeeze. Of course she wanted a normal life. She couldn't even tell me the truth about herself for years. She was embarrassed... or guilty, it suddenly dawns on me. She feels guilty about what she did, back when she was a spirit who didn't fully understand what she was asking for when she made bargains with a human from this world.

She's kind-hearted in nature but didn't understand humanity until she was born as a baby to loving parents. Then she's had to live with the decisions she made before she was even *born*, only a shapeless spirit in some other place...

Of course, all she wants is to be normal.

"You," my father says, his cold eyes coming back to me. "Yes, you've wanted your wings back since the day I sliced them off and poured hell-metal down your back to keep them from regrowing. But more than that, you are a pitiful little being that craves love. Each of you hopeless creatures wants what they can never have, doomed to live out stories without a happy ending." My father *tut, tut, tuts.*

"Fuck you," I bark at him, my face flaming with anger for taunting us like this.

"Don't you see?" My father laughs. "Today is your lucky day. Today," he says, his voice lulling, "both of you little desperate beasts can have everything you want. Just look."

He points behind us. Golden runes light up beneath our feet, and Phoenix gasps.

"Layden, look!" Her voice sounds full of wonder.

I don't want to look. I know the moment I do, my father gets what he wants. She grabs my hand, and I want to yank her away. To warn her of the danger.

But her voice is so insistent and delighted when she cries, "Layden!"

In spite of myself, I turn.

The little house at the end of the cul-de-sac is perfect. It couldn't be more perfect.

It's sea-foam green with white shutters and a white picket fence. The grass is so, so green, and the sky so, so blue.

"Oh, Layden, I couldn't be happier," Phoenix says from beside me. I look over, and she's in her wedding dress, beaming up at me. "This is all I've ever wanted. Come inside."

I clench her hand to mine like a lifeline. Because *she* is all I've ever, ever wanted. I finally have all I've ever craved. I finally feel *full*.

I lift her into my arms, and she giggles with joy as she throws her arms around my neck. I've never heard her so light and happy and free.

Life starts here, at this moment, with her.

I carry my bride over the threshold of our new life.

The house inside is just as perfect, and not because it's some mansion. It's not. It's small. Cramped even, some might say.

"I love it," Phoenix says, looking around, then smiling back at me so big. "And I love *you*."

My chest expands at her words. Why does it feel like I've been waiting forever to hear them? "You do?"

"Of course I do, silly," she laughs, then nuzzles her forehead to mine. "I have since that first day I ran into you on that hiking trail and gave you first aid."

I nuzzle her back, so full of love even as my memory blanks a little, but then, piece by piece, the blanks are filled in. Oh yes, the day we met. I'd gotten into an... accident of some kind on the hiking trail deep in the woods. I frown as I try to make out the details, then forget as soon as Phoenix kisses me.

The details don't matter. I remember Phoenix coming

to my rescue. She took me back to her cabin while I recovered. Tended to me. Brought me back to life, it felt like.

I nuzzle my face against hers, whispering into her hair, "I couldn't admit to myself how long I've loved you."

She shakes her head. "We were so stupid for so long. We never should have let anything come between us and keep us apart."

I nod, and like magnets, we turn toward each other, kissing as hungrily as I've always dreamed. I pour all of my love into the kiss, and our tongues dance as she presses her mouth eagerly back against mine.

She tugs hers away only long enough to say, "Show me the bedroom?"

I carry her down the short hall to one of the two bedrooms of the small house. The carpet's a little worn, and it could use some new trim, but Phoenix just looks around as I carry her and sighs happily. "I *love* this house. It's so *normal*."

I laugh. "That's not exactly what most men want to hear their wives say when they try to buy them their dream house. We've been working for years to afford the down payment on the mortgage. I'm exhausted most nights after my job at the construction site, and you've been killing yourself to get tenure at the university."

Her bright gaze comes back to me. "I know, but now we have a mortgage! And the most perfect house. Isn't it wonderful?"

I chuckle deeply as we finally arrive at the bedroom. "It's wonderful finally being able to call you Mrs. Layden Eques." Lovingly, I lay her down on the bed.

The glint in her turns mischievous as she drags me down on top of her.

"All you've ever done is tease me," she growls. "Will you

finally give me everything? All of yourself? Mr. *Phoenix* Eques?"

Gently, and one by one, I tug the little pins out of her hair. From my position on top of her and propped up by my elbows, I can only reach some of them, but it's enough to run my fingers through the hair around her face as I gaze into her eyes. "You've always had all of me."

Her face sobers as she holds onto my waist beneath my tux jacket. "I know. I'm sorry I wasn't able to give you all of myself before. It's just been..." She frowns, her eyes going a little distant. "I was just so ashamed for so long. I'm not even sure *why* now..."

Her eyes come back to me and brighten. "But that's all over and done with. Now it's just you and me in this beautifully ordinary, perfect life we've created together." She beams at me.

She's so beautiful, it all but bursts my chest open.

"I want to make love to you," I whisper.

Her breath hitches, and her hips jump involuntarily against mine. "What are you waiting for? I've been wet for you since we crossed the threshold."

My cock has been stiff for a while now, but it all but leaps in my pants for her. "There's too much fabric between us," I groan.

She giggles and starts pulling up the miles of puffy fabric of her dress.

I reach down to help her and shove my own pants down. When we've freed ourselves and each other of our respective clothes, I move my hand to touch her.

As soon as my fingers make contact with her sex, I exhale. She's not lying. She's so wet my finger immediately becomes slick and slippery. She's not wearing any underwear.

"Fuck, woman."

"Why aren't you inside me yet?" I love her needy, impatient whine.

"I like to tease you."

I rub my middle finger around her silky opening and love the way she trembles, both when I circle her clit and dip my finger in, pressing down against the bottom wall near her ass.

"You like it dirty, don't you?"

"Yes," she gasps.

I smile. For all her talk of normal and ordinary, my woman still wants to keep it wild in some areas. And it's our wedding night. She's going to get everything she wants.

So I lift up from her.

"What are you—" she starts, then squeaks when I flip her over so she's facedown on the bed, a fluff of white tulle and her rosy little ass staring back at me. She's wearing a sexy as fuck white lace garter belt that attaches to her thighs... but I was right. There's nothing covering that sweet little pussy that's winking up at me from below her ass.

"You're a naughty girl, aren't you," I breathe out.

She goes further up on her knees, wiggling her ass at me. "What are you gonna do about it?" she asks, looking over her shoulder from where her face is smooshed against the pillow. She's got a challenge in her eyes that are dark with lust.

My cock goes stiff. "I'm going to turn this little ass pink until you squeal."

Her eyes glitter before she puts her head back down and sticks her ass out even further. Still, it's quite audible when I hear her say, "Yes, *sir*."

Fuck. I spank her right where the fullness of her ass

meets the top of her thigh. First one cheek and then the other.

Each time my palm makes contact, she twists and moans beneath me. So I do it again. And again.

Her back arches and her ass turns pink from my hand-prints. I don't know why it's such a fucking high to feel this powerful, usually-so-reserved woman submit and give herself over so completely. But for her to make herself so vulnerable to me, trusting me completely—

I spread her ass wide and bend down, tonguing my wife's dripping cunt. My cock grows so hard and long it hangs heavy against my thigh.

But I pull back, my mouth smeared with her cream, and grin when she begs. "Please, fuck me now. *Please.*"

I spank her again, in the center of her ass so the tips of my fingers smack her swollen pussy. She squirms in need, trying to press back against me.

I reach over to the bedside for what I put there in preparation, pulling open the drawer of the nightstand. Aha, just where I left it.

"What are you doing back there?" she asks, trying to look over her shoulder again.

I angle myself so she can't see, bending over as I drip lube over the object I've just drawn from the drawer.

Anal beads.

"You're going to take everything I give you, isn't that right?" I demand, my voice low.

"Yes, sir."

Fuck, I like that a hell of a lot when she says that. I spank her again before lifting the lube-drenched beads to her ass.

"What is that?" she asks, feeling me roll the smallest of the beads on the string against her puckered little opening.

"Relax and take it like a good girl."

I reach underneath her and stroke her clit. Bending down to get the best view of her ass, I draw her cheeks wide with my other hand and press the bead against her sweet little pinkish-brown opening. "Give in to me," I say low, dark. "It's easy. And I'll make it feel so, so good. Relax and take everything I have to give you."

I lean over and lick all around the bead at her anus, also pushing it in.

She gasps, and I feel her entire body contract and then finally *relax*. The littlest bead pops in. Her ass shoves against my face, and I smile, tonguing her ass harder as I push the next bead on the string into position.

I love the way I can feel her body react to every single thing I do. Even though she's faced away from me, I can feel how intimately connected we are. I keep rubbing her clit as I push the next bulb against her little opening. It's bigger than the last one.

I slip the finger rubbing her clit inside her pussy and massage against the bead I'm pushing in her anus with my tongue and, when it catches resistance, my chin.

"Let me in," I demand, my face nestled in the crevice of her ass. There's plenty of lube plus my spittle. She can take it.

The bulb sticks out of her ass like a little nub until finally, it pops through and again, her whole body reacts. With my finger in her pussy, I can feel the two bulbs inside her ass through the thin wall between them.

"So good. You're doing so good for me."

She whines out as we continue to the next, bigger bead. There are eight on the string, and each one is a struggle for her.

By the fifth, I'm done with taking it easy on her.

I bite her ass and crawl up over her back until I'm licking and nibbling her shoulder, my fingers still putting pressure on the biggest bead lodged at the opening of her anus.

"I can't take it," she whines, turning to look at me over her shoulder

"Oh, you'll take it," I say darkly. She sucks a deep breath in, then twists up to kiss me, biting at my tongue and lips. My little viper. Everything is a fight.

She pulls away and pushes her ass out against my hand. "*Make* me take it."

"That can be arranged," I say, pushing relentlessly against the large bulb. Her eyelids flutter, and her eyes roll back in her head as she twists underneath me.

"Fuuuuuuuuuuuuuck," she whispers, and then finally, I feel her body give way as she loosens and the bulb slips into her ass.

"Good girl," I growl, biting lightly at the back of her neck. Now that she's taken the largest bead, I'm ruthless with pushing the rest of the string inside her. Still, her body reacts with each one that enters her back channel until she's full up, a little black string hanging out of her ass the only clue that anything's there at all.

"Will you fuck me now?" she begs.

I grin. "Patience, little wifey."

She grins at the term, turning her face away as if I won't see it. God, I love playing with her. She's so fucking feisty. I undo the little button at the top of her dress and then slowly, ever so slowly, unzip the back of it.

She squirms beneath me, and every so often, I finger her clit while tugging on the string of beads to make sure she's still nice and ready for me.

Each little high-pitched moan tells me, yes, she's beyond

ready. Still, I love to draw it out. Keep both of us on edge. There's nothing like making love to your *wife* for the first time, and I'm relishing every fucking moment of this. Even if my cock is all but bursting with wanting her. It never hurt so good.

I kneel and then gently tug her up before lifting her wedding dress off over her head.

"Jesus Christ," I whisper. "You've never been more beautiful." I can't imagine anything more beautiful or sacred than my *wife* sitting before me in her white lace bra and garter belt, eager and begging me to fuck her.

She looks at me coyly. "How do you want me now?" she asks.

I climb off the bed, dragging a soft throw down from the bottom of the bed. I toss it so that it billows outwards on the floor, then kneel down on it. I pat my thighs. "I want you right here, honey."

She doesn't even pretend to think about it. She just immediately obeys and joins me on the floor.

I chuckle and point to my lap. "*Here.*"

She gulps as I take her hand and direct her how to sit— facing me, legs on either side of me so that when her sex comes down, it lands right on my jutting cock.

She stares into my eyes as I draw her wet pussy down onto me with my hands on her waist.

We both hiss in satisfaction as soon as my bulbous crown makes contact with her sex. Fuck, she's so wet, and while I've stretched out her ass, her pussy is still so fucking tight. Made even tighter, in fact, because of everything I crammed in her ass.

"Layden," she whispers, eyes brimming.

I nod. I know. I feel it, too, expanding my chest. "I love you."

She throws her arms around me as I gently enter her.

She shudders and clenches around me. I lean in and kiss her, our lips barely touching at first. Light, glancing kisses. The barest brush of my bottom lip against her top one. Then, a gentle suckle on her cupid's bow that becomes more urgent as she sinks all the way down on me, lifts up, and sinks down again.

"I love you so fucking much," I murmur, wrapping my arms around her and holding her so tight it's like I'm afraid she might disappear.

"I feel like I've loved you my whole life," she says. "I was so alone before I found you."

We make love passionately. Urgently. Her hips riding me as much as I'm thrusting desperately up into her hot, tight, wet—

"Layden!" she cries, and I can't hold it any longer as I feel her start to spasm and shudder around me.

Our arms hold even tighter to one another as she comes, and my spine seizes, my balls tighten, and then finally, *finally*, I pump into the hot clench of my wife's center as we climax together.

For several completely full moments, all of my life's desires have come to fruition. I am so perfectly satiated, so perfectly in love, so perfectly fulfilled—

"Now, was that so hard?"

I blink in confusion at the deep voice that comes from nowhere. I'm still holding Phoenix tight, buried inside her, as the room around us begins to dissolve.

"Layden!" Phoenix cries, and I hear the fear in her voice as the actual room around us becomes clearer. We're laying naked on a blanket on the floor, not a bed.

Horror hits as soon as I realize what's happened. My father—our fathers. . . They're watching on with satisfied grins on their faces. I move to cover Phoenix, a sick feeling settling in my stomach. They've gotten us to—

"Layden, my stomach!" Phoenix's shout is frantic, and when I look back at her, I see why. Her lower abdomen is distending like a balloon. Like she's—

"What's happening?" she screams.

She drops a hand to her expanding belly, frightened eyes coming to me.

"First comes love," my father sing-songs, "then comes marriage, then comes a baby in a baby carriage."

Chapter Twenty-Four

LAYDEN
Present Day

P hoenix looks bewildered and horrified as she clutches her quickly expanding stomach with two hands now. "I can feel something moving. Oh god, Layden—"

I reach out and clutch her hand, not knowing what else to do. We've seen accelerated pregnancies in my brothers and their wives before, but nothing like this. Then again, their wives were normal human women. We never knew what might happen if two spirit beings from other realms made it here and tried to procreate. Not to mention whatever magic our fathers have conjured in this circle by their evil, infernal sacrifice.

Phoenix's eyes squeeze shut, and her head tips back. "Oh god, Layden. I think the baby's coming."

My eyes fly wide. Baby? I look toward my father, but he's still just standing there, grinning in satisfaction like a cat that just got the cream. Son of a bitch!

"It's okay, we're okay," I tell Phoenix because I don't know what else to do at this point other than lie.

"Layden," she screams, her legs falling open.

Fuck, fuck! Am I about to deliver a baby? I move between her legs, and holy shit, I see a head crowning. A large head.

"Push," I say for lack of any other ideas. If the baby keeps growing, it might get too big for her to push out. "Push now!"

Phoenix screams, and her hands clench in the blanket as she starts to push. Blood pounds in my ears as I reach forward to catch my child only minutes after procreating them. This is a mind-fuck if ever there was one.

The head comes out, face down. I don't know if that's a good or bad thing. I just know I can see the hair on the kid's head actively growing from peach fuzz to a downy brown. "Push!" I order, reaching out so I can catch the shoulders after Phoenix screams and bears down again.

The kid almost slips out, but I catch him. Him. "It's a boy!" I cry, tears in my throat as I look down at my son, perfect little black wings nestled against his back.

"Layden," Phoenix reaches down and grabs my shoulder. "Layden!"

"What?" I look up at her and lift the baby to her chest. She takes him, then starts shaking her head.

"There's another one."

Oh fuck. I look around us. Both Vlad and my father hold out their hands to take my newborn son from me, but I hold him in my arm, gook and all.

"Okay," I say, trying to hold all my freaking out on the inside. "Okay! Now we know what to do."

Phoenix screams louder than I've ever heard anybody scream as our second son is born into this world, covered in blood and goo and also so completely perfect.

My first son has started crying. Loudly. I lay the second on Phoenix's chest and am about to move up to her side so I can sit behind her back while she cuddles both our newborns who are still growing, now fat cherubic babies. Children. I have children. I can hardly believe it, but there's no time to really take in all the emotions I'm feeling. Especially when Phoenix's eyes fly up to mine, tears squeezing out.

"Oh god, Layden, it's not over."

Fucking fuckity fuck my whole fucking life—

Her face contorts in pain, and she clutches our one crying sons to her breasts as I drop down again between her legs, where, indeed, a third head is crowning.

"I can't," Phoenix cries. "I can't do it."

"Yes, you can," I say with determination, even though I'm terrified because the two babies that are out have already grown so much. "Push now. Don't wait. You've got this. You're a badass goddess who can give birth to this last baby because there's nothing in the world you can't do. I believe in you. I love you. You're the most amazing person I've ever met and—"

Her animalistic scream breaks off my stream of encouragement. I reach down and catch our daughter, who, unlike her brothers, has snow-white wings.

Phoenix collapses back after passing the placenta, and I pull out the pocketknife I always keep on my belt to cut each child's cord. Our firstborn has continued to grow and looks like he's a toddler at this point. I use the pocketknife to cut swaths from the blanket where it's still clean to wrap around each child's shoulder like a long, hanging toga with room for expansion, especially considering how fast they're growing.

I'm about to turn to Phoenix and ask what she wants to name them when my father suddenly strides forward and produces a glowing halo from the pocket of his cargo pants. Before either Phoenix or I can react, he snatches our first son from Phoenix's breast and snaps the glowing ring around his throat. "You are named Asmodeus." My son immediately stops crying and gets a distant, faraway look in his eyes.

"Go stand outside the circle," my father orders. I stand up, holding my little girl. I lunge for my firstborn as he obeys, walking on chubby little legs toward the outside of the circle. But I slip in the afterbirth and barely catch myself before dropping my slippery daughter. He makes it out of the circle to stand beside his other grandfather, Vlad.

"This one will do nicely," Vlad says, smiling down at the little boy, who's growing taller by the second. His brother and sister are also continuing to grow, but at the moment, I can't care about that because my father is walking toward where Vlad stands.

"You are happy with our bargain then?" my father asks.

Vlad nods. "If I continue to get the firstborn of every yield, our deal shall continue."

My father also nods his head, but by the glint in his eye, I can foresee what is about to happen next even if Vlad can't. No, oh shit—Vlad feeding is necessary for Phoenix to be healthy because of their twisted blood bond thing.

"Vlad, don't, he's going to double-cross y—"

But before I can even finish my sentence, my father has

produced a glowing blade, again seemingly from his pocket even though there was no natural way it would have fit there, and swings it in a killing blow, lopping off Vlad Dracul the Second's head.

"No!" Phoenix cries. I'm not sure if it's because she's losing the source of her energy and health or because, in spite of his betrayals and the fact that he never gave her a reason to deserve it, Phoenix loved the old man.

My firstborn stands silently, looking on as Vlad's head spins on the floor not far away from him. He now looks to be a kindergarten-aged child. Our second-born clings to Phoenix's neck but is similarly growing, so much that I can see it's hard for her to continue holding him like that. But still, she clutches him to her as dearly as I hold our growing daughter in my arms.

My father turns back to us.

"We'll find you," I say with all the hatred in my heart. I have no secret chamber of love for the being in front of me. If I could see him burn in the fires of hell right this minute, I'd send him with a one-way ticket there myself. "There's no place you can take my child that I won't find you."

"Oh, don't be silly," Father says. "Why would I leave you behind when this worked out so well? I'd be a fool to leave the production factory behind, now wouldn't I? No, the two of you are coming with me."

"You going to snap gold bands around our necks, too?"

My father looks genuinely remorseful. "Would that I could. But the halos are only truly effective on newborns who have developed no will of their own yet. And I trust you and your lovely wife will give me a fresh supply of those."

"That's never going to happen," I growl, but he disappears from in front of me. Poof, one second, he's there, and then he's gone.

"It already has," he whispers in my ear, suddenly reappearing beside me and snapping another halo around my growing daughter as he snatches her out of my arms. "She shall be named Lilith."

Chapter Twenty-Five

"No," I say, my voice calm and cold. My entire life, I have denied what I am. But now, in the face of this monster, I need to become everything I've been afraid of. I need to remember who I was... *before*.

I will no longer be afraid of who I am. I am the one who searched with endless hunger for better than I had. I am the one who didn't give up until I got what I wanted. I pushed beyond the boundaries of spirit and hunted until I found the warmth I craved. Until I found flesh and blood. I was young then. I can forgive myself for all I didn't know.

Because everything that I was then has brought me here to where I am. It brought me to Layden. And now, life has given me three more gifts. In my arms, my second-born has grown almost to pre-pubescent age.

I look the angel hunting me in the eye. "You will not have my children."

I will remember who I am if that is what it takes to protect what is mine. I will remember the darkness. I will remember my strength. I will remember all the sacrifices made to become flesh, born wailing into this world as my own children just were.

With my son in my arms, I lift off the ground. Not standing or even flying. I float up. The laws of gravity have no hold on me. I am beyond. I am not of this world, and its rules cannot hold me. My son begins to flap his wings, and he flies, hovering beside me.

"That is good, son," I say to him, though I'm not sure if he can understand me. So, I speak in his mind through our blood bond: *That is good. Stay away from that man.* Mentally, I project the picture of his grandfather into his head, along with a bad feeling. My son and I rise higher.

My father-in-law only laughs, white wings suddenly appearing behind him. He lifts off the ground, easily flying to face off with me.

Below, Layden forms glowing runes in his hand and hurls them at his father. His father casts them aside with a careless swipe of his hand.

I try to feel for the blood in his father's body. But there's something... off about what's inside him. There's liquid circulating, but it's not blood. Not the kind I can manipulate anyway. I can't stop the flow of blood to his head or yank him apart from the insides out like I want to.

But what if...

Quickly, I glance toward the door. I'm still flooded with power even though Vlad is dead. His death didn't immediately sap me of power. So either I'm still running on the juice of what he last fed on, or... or he's been lying to me this whole time. He was never the sole source of my power.

I call to the rest of my family, pulling on the threads of the blood bond between us I've never dared to fully embrace. But gods of every realm, now I *yank*.

All my uncles come spilling in through the door, dark suit after dark suit. They immediately begin yelling when they see Vlad dead on the floor. But I don't let them stop there. They're able to come into the circle like I thought they would. I had the feeling it's the kind of spell that lets anyone in but only certain people out.

I intend to finish this here.

I tell my second-born son, now a teenager, through our blood bond, to fly in the other direction. Then I launch myself at my father-in-law, bearing him back toward the floor where all my vampire uncles wait. He looks momentarily surprised, then smiles at me in the instant before he disappears right before my reaching uncles can snatch him to the ground.

Dammit, I know exactly where he's going. I turn around and launch myself through the air back toward where my second-born is flying near the very apex of the atrium. I can see the terror on his young teenage face as my father-in-law reaches out with a glowing halo for his neck. My new son doesn't know much about this world, but he knows to be afraid of his grandfather. I hate that this is his introduction to life, but there's no getting around it.

He dodges when the old man lunges for him, ducking underneath his arm and diving down. But my father-in-law grabs the tip of his wing and spins him back around. My son cries out in pain. The fury that burns through me at the sound—

I scream as I slam into my father-in-law, knocking him

away from my son. He spins end over end back until he suddenly *poofs*. He's disappeared again. I move so that I'm hovering in front of my son, my eyes bouncing everywhere, searching the air for where my father-in-law might appear again.

Below, I notice some bright blue light. Layden is creating more runes. I'm not sure why. His father seems invincible.

But he's only a spirit from another realm. Just like I am. If anyone can end him, it's going to be me. Sheer power versus power.

I grit my teeth, ready for his next attempt on my son.

But he doesn't appear in the air with us. To my surprise, he pops up outside the circle beside my firstborn and my daughter. My heart suddenly clenches in my chest. Is he going to run away with just the two of them, leaving the rest of us bound in this circle?

Then he looks back up my way and grins, and I know that no, he would see that as defeat. He wants all three of my children and me as well so I can produce an army for him.

From seemingly nowhere, he produces a golden sword, just like the one he killed Vlad with. No natural sword could have done that. It's why Vlad walked around fearless in this world. I can't feel anything except glad about his death right now. He betrayed me one too many times. He thought he was indestructible. All my uncles think the same.

But now my father-in-law hands the vampire killing sword to my firstborn son, who stands at the stature of a mature, broad-shouldered teenage boy. He produces another glowing sword and gives it to my daughter, who looks of similar age. Then he bends down and whispers something in each of their ears.

I want to kill him for how he is manipulating them. It's so like what Vlad did to me all my life; I want to skewer him and roast his heart in front of his eyes while it still beats.

I don't allow my building rage to make me do anything rash, though. I watch the expressions on their young faces never change as they charge inside the circle with their glowing angelic swords raised. My breath hitches. Are they going to attack their father? I get ready to fly to his defense.

But they don't attack Layden. They begin swinging and slicing at my uncles.

Son of a bitch. I meet my father-in-law's eyes and growl. He's figured out what I've only been guessing at. If Vlad alone wasn't the source of my power, maybe it's all of them. Or maybe the magic of who feeds me simply passed down to the next eldest vampire. Which, in that case, is Radu. Who my daughter beheads right before my eyes.

My children have shocking dexterity with the weapons. As if they are masters who trained for years, not children born half an hour ago. I zero in on my father-in-law again. He's controlling them to such a degree they're *his* puppets. I shudder. It's even *worse* than what Vlad did to me.

How can I get to him? I fly at the edge of the circle, my elbows out. Maybe if I have enough will and enough speed, I can—

I bounce backward ruthlessly, my elbows busted from the effort.

My father-in-law laughs. Below me, my uncles are a mass, some fighting and others trying to flee what is quickly becoming a massacre. It turns out I've called them to their doom. All they have is speed and fangs on their side, none of which help in this scenario because it turns out my children are just as fast. They speed around one another so fast that I can barely clock them.

Meanwhile, the light of Layden's runes continues to grow brighter. What is he even doing?

When I properly glance his way, I see that *Sabra,* of all people, beside him. When Vlad died... I guess she was freed of her blood slavery to him? But what can they do against an angel like Layden's father?

My question is answered before I barely finish thinking it because when Layden next throws his runes toward his father, his father tries to wave a hand and brush them off like before. Except this time, they seem to be sticky. The more he bats at them, the more the blue-white runes attach to him until they're completely surrounding his body. And once they've enveloped him, Layden's able to start pulling him back inside the circle.

"Now," I scream, and all the remaining vampires attack him as soon as his legs are within the circle. Layden runs toward them, runes still extending from his hands as our children begin to hack away at my uncles from behind. It's cruel, but I don't stop the vampires from what they're doing. They ruthlessly sink their fangs into my father-in-law's legs, hanging on like rats at a feast.

When Layden gets to them, our eldest spins, brandishing the shining sword at his own father. He's still completely dead-eyed, with no trace of emotion on his face.

Layden doesn't try to reason with him. With one hand connected to the runes, yanking his father further into the circle, he tosses out another hand of runes toward our son. Our son lowers his stance, ready for an attack. But the runes aren't meant to attack. They simply yank the glowing sword out of our son's hand and pull it toward Layden, who catches it nimbly.

Meanwhile, I'm feeling the energy that's being fed to me by my uncles. They're feeding off whatever that power is that's beyond blood in my father-in-law, and now it's singing through *my* veins.

I attack with all my pent-up fury, letting out a scream so loud and high-pitched that it breaks the glass of the atrium's center display surrounding the sacrificed body. Glass explodes outwards.

I fly down and grasp my father-in-law, where he squirms, surrounded by blue light that is obviously keeping him from disappearing. I can tell he's trying, but runes have banded around his arms and legs, holding him tight.

Now to send him to the darkness.

I grab him by his neck and drag him over until he's at the very center of the sacrificial circle inside the atrium where the body is. I understand what all of this was for now.

They made this circle to call forth more spirits from the cold so they could be embodied in my children. The succubus we thought was Ammit and spirits like her who cross over to this realm by means of a sacrifice will only ever be shadows hiding in the shell of a human body. Possessing a human who already has a life in this world is usually the only way for a spirit to gain entry into flesh.

Unless one is incarnated at the moment of conception, otherworldly spirit uniting with human flesh before there are any other souls to occupy it. I bought my way in slowly, generation by generation of blood drinkers, until I got myself incarnated.

My father-in-law and Vlad decided to speed up the process with this unholy circle magic, my womb, and Layden's seed. I won't know what sort of spirits my children are or where the proclivities from their realms might lead until we get to know them more. But they are *mine,* and they can learn to choose the person they want to be, just like I did. Or just like I'm learning to do.

I slam my father-in-law down on top of the already sacrificed body. Apparently, part of this new person I'm embracing doesn't back down from gore as long as it's in protection of the ones I love.

"What do you think you're doing?" my father-in-law laughs up at me. "You can do nothing to me other than bind me for a while." He looks up at Layden as he approaches. "You think this will hold me? I'm invincible! Indestructible. I've been here since right after the first garden, and I'll be here to see the winking out of the last star!"

Layden holds up the sword he took from our son and lops off his father's head.

Unlike Vlad, though, my father-in-law just keeps laughing as his head rolls to the side. His face grins up at us. I snatch it up and set it in place near the other head. This is a creature who grew back from a mere ember in ashes. We have to do this right so that not a single piece of him is left out. "Get his legs and arms, too. Section them up just like the body beneath him."

Just as I'm about to carve his heart out of the center of his chest, Sabra yells, "Behind you! Phoenix!"

I swing around just in time to see my daughter, a young woman now, running full speed at me with her sword raised. Her toga barely skims her thighs at this point, not that she appears to care in her dead-eyed state.

I roll backward right as Layden lifts his sword to block her strike. She's knocked back by the strength of his block. Layden doesn't waste a moment. He brings the sword back down on his father, severing his right leg and then his left.

Our daughter raises her sword right as our firstborn

comes in from the right like a linebacker, tackling Layden away from the severed pieces of my father-in-law.

Which is when all mayhem officially breaks loose.

Our second-born flies down, as fully grown as his brother, and rips him off of Layden. Then, the two brothers start to wrestle viciously on the ground. I hate to see my sons fighting, but neither of them has swords, so I'm hoping the damage they can do to one another is limited. I turn back toward the pieces of my father-in-law and our daughter, who's crouched in a protective stance over what's left of him. She's squaring off with Layden, both of them with swords raised.

I glare at my father-in-law, who watches on with glee even as he lies in severed pieces. It's time to end this.

I call my remaining vampires to me, and only seven hobble toward me out of the twenty who initially rushed the circle. Together, we circle my father-in-law on the floor. As one, we all grab whatever piece of him that remains intact and begin to yank him apart. It's far more grisly than the sword would have been. If he feels pain as he's dismembered, he doesn't show it. We don't stop until we're all covered in blood and my father-in-law is in as many pieces as the sacrificed human below him.

Behind us, sparks fly from the golden swords as Layden fights our daughter.

"Sabra!" I call.

She runs up to me. We look into each other's eyes, a thousand things we both want to say but have no time for brimming there. "Let's do this," she says.

We lean down as one, her hand on his head and my hand on his chest, as she begins to chant.

I could already feel the power flowing through me, but as her words call forth the channel between the spirit realms, I feel it surge. It reminds me of old times in a weird way. I'm still the battery. I'm just super-charged this time.

Which is good because I want to send this motherfucker into a hole so deep and far away he'll never be able to find his way out again.

"It's opening," Sabra whispers, and I hear the fear in her voice. I'll never ask anything like this of her again. She's been enslaved by my family for her entire life in ways I never imagined. I hope after this, she can live free and do anything she wants with her life. Away from this darkness so she can heal from the trauma we've inflicted on her.

But now, it's time to focus. I focus all the power roaring through my veins and an energy I've never felt before. If ever I felt godlike, it's now. I see the haziness between flesh and spirit. As Sabra continues chanting, that line becomes even more ephemeral.

"Hear me, foolish whelp," my father-in-law snarls, for once not laughing, "Wherever you send me, I'll just come back. I'll never stop coming for you. For your family. For *my* family. This world is *mine*. Wherever you send me, I'll only conquer it. No realm can hold me. All will bow!"

I reach down with my blood-soaked hand and turn his severed head toward me so I can look him in the eye.

"No, *Gol'gonaar*," I say his true name calmly, "you will be the one who bows."

For the first time I see true fear register on his face. Right in time, too, as I press down on his chest, my hand sinking through until my fingers grasp and clench around his beating heart.

"I name Gol'gonaar," I pronounce, "and claim his spirit in sacrifice."

I squeeze his heart in my fist and crush it. Then, the

flesh in my hand disappears as the space between realms opens up.

My vision schisms like a kaleidoscope. Power pulses behind my eyeballs, and I give in completely. I am only spirit again and the most powerful in the room. This weakened spirit I hold in my hands will go where I take him. Where I *drag* him.

He only thought he was the strongest because he picked on those who were weaker before. Like a bully in a playground.

But I cannot waste time, even though here in this space, time feels like nothing at all. Time is just a silly construct humans made up to file away their lives. First this, then that. But there is no forward or backward here.

There's only now. Always *now*.

And *now*, I will send the devil to the darkest, coldest, most remote hell I see in the kaleidoscope of realms. There are no other beings to conquer there. It is a void, and there are no pathways back. It is a lonely place for souls who deserve no better.

I press down with my will, and Gol'gonaar's spirit is siphoned through what I can only liken to a cheese grater to the portal I desire him to go to. I hear a brief scream of disbelief, but that's all. The being who has tormented my husband and his family is finally *gone*.

Chapter Twenty-Six

I sit on my bed, staring around my pink room and thinking about Layden. Missing him feels like all I do lately. I think I'll miss him forever. I shouldn't have sent him away like that. I'm wracked by grief and guilt one second and then sure I did the right thing the next.

I miss him *so* badly. I grab my phone and check it for texts, but of course, there are none.

I didn't think missing someone could hurt this much. I miss my parents, yeah, but that missing just feels like a dull ache. I was a kid back then and didn't understand what was happening. This is fresh and hurts in my lungs. And my stomach.

I look at the clock. 9:12 at night. Almost time for another long night of tossing and turning, unable to sleep. I slump down on the bed and pull a blanket over me.

I miss the stupid moments, like when we'd stay up late in the computer lab and he got so excited learning about some new programming trick. He was always so enthusiastic to show off to me. Like a kid, but at the same time, there was never mistaking him for anything but a man.

I ache for him in places that remind me I'm a woman. Not that it will ever matter now that I'm doomed to be alone.

I pull the covers up over my head and close my eyes. They say it's better to have loved and lost than never to have loved at all, right? Maybe I should be feeling lucky to have ever had him in my life. Because we had so many good times together.

Like the night we stayed up late talking last week and he told me what really happened the day Sabra actually managed to send his spirit back to his realm. When he talked with the angels.

He hadn't told us the whole truth that day when he got back. He saved it and shared it only with me. Because he trusted me. He trusted me, and then I hurt him so badly. I try to push those thoughts away and focus just on the memories; those are all I'll ever have of him. An ache stabs at my stomach even as I remember.

"It was a beautiful place. More beautiful than I can even describe," he said, his eyes getting a faraway look of wonder. Layden was usually incredibly handsome, but in that moment, as we sat on his bed together, he looked practically beatific. Like an angel carved from marble himself.

"What was it like talking to an angel?" I asked.

"She was so bright I had to shield my eyes. And I was also sort of floating because I was out of my body. She knew me. She called me a creature of the thief and asked if I was a thief too."

"The thief. You mean your father?"

He nodded. "They knew my father well. I could barely answer her. I kept stuttering because she was so overwhelming. The whole place was..." He drifted off, his eyes still lost in the distance before coming back to me. "It was just the most beautiful place I'd ever seen. So full of light."

I felt a pang in my heart then, because I knew that was the kind of place he belonged. And here I was, dragging him down into my darkness. "I'm so sorry your father ever took you away from there."

Layden shook his head. "I was born on earth. He's a thief because he stole the spark of life to create my brothers and me in a forge here. But to know that any part of me came from there..." A soft smile lit his face. "After feeling so monstrous my whole life..."

"No part of you is monstrous," I interrupted with feeling. And I knew then that I couldn't keep him here even if I couldn't admit it out loud. It would be wrong. No matter how I felt about him as we both sat there together on his bed, our thighs so torturously close to touching.

"Eventually, as we talked, she said she'd looked into my soul and decided I wasn't like my father after all. She said I was young." He smiled. "And she said my brothers and I were always welcome home, unlike Gol'gonaar, who had used up his chances. I never even knew my father had a name before then. He just always told us he was Creator-Father."

"Because it gave him more power over you," I said. "And if you'd known *his* true name, it would have given you power over him." Sabra had taught me that. With the right spell and knowledge of a true name, you could have complete control of a spirit. "He always wanted you to feel as helpless as possible so he could control you." It was a feeling I understood well. I might know Vlad's name, but only because he wanted us to know he was the direct descendant of a merciless, bloody king.

A ping sounds from my phone, and I throw off my covers to scramble for it. Could it be Layden? In spite of all the horrible things I said to him, is he texting anyway? Maybe he's just letting me know where he is. That he's safe.

I grab my phone and click to see the text.

My heart immediately sinks. I have a new message, all right, but it's not from Layden. It's from Vlad. Speak of the devil.

The text is just an address and a name with a short message. VLAD: GET COMPLIANCE ON UPCOMING SALE OF PTR PETROL.

Fury lights in my chest from the pain of all that I have given up because of Vlad's control over me. I might not be able to escape completely, but I can't stand things continuing this way. Sabra changed the deal she had with my grandfather to make it more bearable for herself. So can I.

I jump out of bed and stomp the entire way to Vlad's wing. I'm done being his pawn. It's time to stand up to him. I might be bound to him, but I'm done being his beck-and-call bitch. I might have lost Layden, and I'll never truly be free, but I'm still going to be in charge of my own life as much as possible from here on out.

Chapter Twenty-Seven

LAYDEN
Present Day

My daughter drops her sword and looks behind me. Carefully, I back away from her and do the same. My father is... gone. There's no trace of his body. Not even enough for an ember.

I rush to Phoenix's side. I heard her use his name, but I'm not sure what it all means. She turns to me, and her eyes are glowing. I don't pull back. "Phoenix?"

She blinks, and when she next looks at me, it's my Phoenix back at last. She shakes her head and tries to stand, but her legs shake. She's covered in blood, both from the birth and the fight with my father. Sabra comes quickly and throws the rest of the blanket around her shoulders.

When I look up, my daughter is standing there, halo still around her throat, watching on with a face that's not quite blank but slightly confused.

246

"Help me up," Phoenix says to Sabra and me. I quickly take one side, and Sabra takes the other. We lift Phoenix to her feet, though I hardly let her bear any weight at all after everything she's gone through.

She walks over to our daughter and puts her hand around the halo. Phoenix's eyes flare, glowing again as she snaps the halo, and our daughter stumbles back, hands going to her neck. If I thought she looked confused a moment ago, it's nothing to now as she looks around at all the blood and dead vampire bodies all over the floor. Sabra goes to her while I help Phoenix walk to our firstborn, where she does the same to his collared halo.

"Bring the car around," Phoenix says, and one of the surviving vampires snaps to attention with a quick nod, limping out of the building.

I'm about to ask Phoenix what she's going to tell the police, then remember it won't matter. Now that Vlad is gone, she can finally compel them on her own behalf. She can take over Vlad's kingdom for herself if she likes, or, more likely, if she's even half the woman I remember, she can finally leave it behind forever, once and for all. She's finally, truly, free.

* * *

After we send the vampires back to Vlad's compound, me and my new ready-made family show up at Abaddon's door. Abaddon quickly ushers us inside, not knowing what to make of us. Hannah, however, is delighted to see us all and immediately starts fussing over everyone. First things first, she sends us off to shower. There are six bathrooms and five showers in the estate that my three brothers and their wives are renting, so that's enough for my family to get washed all at once.

Although apparently my children take a little longer since they don't quite know what to do. Advanced sword-play they'd been proficient at, but only as my father's puppets. Human showers? Not so much. Hannah, Abaddon, and Kharon help them figure it out while Phoenix and I get washed up.

They lend us clothes, too. As soon as Phoenix is out of the shower, she wants to see our children. Abaddon brings them in as I urge Phoenix to sit on the comfortable bed.

They all stand so tall and silent, eyes big as they look around. Our second-born watches the other two suspiciously. They've finally stopped growing, thank the gods, and look to be about the human age of twenty-five, like I do.

"Do you know where you are?" Phoenix asks.

They all look at her as soon as she speaks, but none of them speak back. Then she frowns slightly like she's concentrating. Not long after, our kids shake their heads.

"Um, what just happened?" I ask.

"I talked to them inside their minds," Phoenix says, like that's a totally normal thing to do. "Well, not like *talking* talking. More like images. Feelings. They don't know human speech yet."

She frowns again, and our children look like they're listening intensely. I can't stop looking at them. Even the sight of them makes me ache in a place so deep down, a place so full of love I didn't even know I was capable of. They're beautiful, their features an amazing mix of their mother's and mine. Their strong wings are perfect and full. I'll never be able to fly with them, but their mother and uncles can.

"What are you saying?" I ask Phoenix.

"We're trying to establish their names. I'm trying to tell them they get new names, not what your father named them, but they're being stubborn about it."

"Lilith," my daughter says out loud, hand hitting her chest lightly.

My firstborn nods and does the same. "Asmodeus."

I look at Phoenix and shake my head. No. They will not keep the names my father gave them. She just shrugs.

"They are the first names they were given in this world."

"Those are *not* their true names."

"We may not have a say about that."

I let out a frustrated breath, then look toward my second-born. "Can we at least name him?" I look toward Phoenix. She nods and smiles gently. "What do you want your son to be called?" she asks.

He seems to know we're talking about him and looks at me. He's so young. His eyes are so trusting. I wonder if my eyes were like that when I came out of the forge. My father still had no difficulties crushing me cruelly. Me and all my brothers. It makes my chest squeeze in a vise looking at my son now. I could never do that to them.

"Asher," I say, looking toward Phoenix. "His name is Asher."

She grins. "Perfect." She holds out her arms for all her children. Asher goes first. He was with her in the fight, so maybe it's natural for him to trust her. He climbs in bed and lays on Phoenix's left side against her shoulder.

Lilith bites her lip and seems hesitant but eventually takes Asmodeus's hand and tugs him closer to the bed. He looks downright cross at the idea. After some more gentle nudging from his sister, he goes.

Once at her mother's side, Lilith has no trouble

climbing in bed and snuggling up against her side opposite Asher, wrapping her arm around Phoenix's waist. Gods, that's good to see.

Asmodeus takes a stiff perch at the bottom of the bed.

Phoenix grins at all of them, and her eyes are sheened over with tears. I move to her side, making sure to keep to her left, closest to Asher, so I don't scare them all away like a flock of terrified birds. Asher reaches out and takes my hand, looking up into my eyes. "Father," he says, and I have to swallow hard.

I look at Phoenix. "Did you push the word into his mind?"

She just lays her head back on the pillow, obviously exhausted but still with that serene smile on her face. "He wanted to know who you were, so I told him."

I look down on my new, perfect little family and know I would fight any army, take down any predator, and slay any monster that ever threatens them. They are mine, and I will give the world for them. I will protect them with my life, down to my last ember.

*   *   *

Later that day, after a well-needed nap for Phoenix, we all sit around a huge outdoor table that barely seats us all in the center courtyard of the villa. Abaddon pulled out a padded armchair for Phoenix. It's turned into a gorgeous, sunshiny day as we gather.

Me and my brothers with our families. The Four Horsemen of the Apocalypse. If only the world could see us now. Kharon, the Horseman of Death, is making zooming airplane noises as he spoons food into his baby daughter

Luna's mouth. Ksenia, his wife and a former deadly assassin, smiles as she watches on.

Meanwhile, Abaddon's daughter, Raven, flies with her little black wings curiously in a circle around Lilith's head. "Who are you? You're pretty. You smell new."

Lilith just blinks at her.

"Raven!" Hannah says. "Don't be rude."

Raven flits off to inspect her other new cousins.

"When did she start talking?" Phoenix asks Hannah with excitement.

"Just the other day!" Hannah smiles proudly as she sets yet another platter of food down on the table. She must have started cooking with some of the others right when we got here and didn't stop until now. They've laid out an absolute feast. There's everything: scrambled eggs, bacon, sausages, pancakes, a rack of ribs, steaks, cheesy broccoli and salad, fresh baked bread, and cinnamon rolls. That had to be from Remus and Romulus's consort, Lauren. She loves to bake.

Phoenix starts filling plates for our sons and daughter.

Asher stares down at the full plate she sets in front of him, then looks inquiringly at his mother. Phoenix must do that silent communication thing with him.

"You can't do that all the time," I say, "or they'll never learn to speak."

Phoenix rolls her eyes at me, and something inside me relaxes. We might have these new grown-up kids, but underneath, we're still *us*. I'll still drive her nuts all the time and she'll roll her eyes at me but then I'll see her secret smile.

"Fine," she says. "We'll do it your father's way. This is *food*. You *eat* it."

She mimes putting food from her own plate into her mouth and chewing it.

Asher picks up a piece of cheese-covered broccoli and puts it on his tongue, delicately putting it into his mouth. Almost immediately, his face lights up. Then he starts shoving food in his mouth like a madman with no manners at all. Raven giggles, tumbling end over end in the air.

Asmodeus is far more cautious than his brother. He delicately picks up a piece of bacon and nibbles suspiciously at the end of it. He can't hide the widening of his eyes, and though he eats quickly, he gives no expression of enjoying it.

Lilith, on the other hand, can't *stop* making noises. Like her brother Asher, everything she tries only seems to delight her more. She's jumping up and down in her chair and squealing with every bite of cinnamon roll.

I look at Phoenix darkly, suddenly realizing that fatherhood is not going to be easy. "We're going to have to keep her locked up until she's thirty. Or glamour her to look like a troll."

Abaddon laughs. "Welcome to fatherhood, brother."

"Glad it's not us," Remus and Romulus say at the same time. I still can't get used to my conjoined twin brothers occasionally being awake at the same time. Much less the two of them actually agreeing on anything.

"And it never has to be," their consort Lauren says, kissing Romulus and then leaning over his shoulder to the back of his head to give Remus a kiss. "I've always been more of an aunty than a mommy type of gal." She pulls back to look at the rest of us. "And apparently, I'm never going to be lacking for aunty duties if you all keep up at this pace."

"Don't even think about it," Phoenix calls pitifully from her armchair. "Never again!"

"Ahem," Abaddon not so subtly clears his throat. "Speaking of. How exactly did these three grown bundles of joy come to be so... *grown?* Does it have anything to do with why you were all drenched with blood?"

Ah. We hadn't exactly had a moment to talk since we'd gotten here. I'd considered Phoenix resting more important.

Remus reaches out and smacks Abaddon upside the head. "Ever heard of a little something called the birds and the bees? Obviously, their children just grew a little more quickly than yours."

"Well, yes," I say, looking to Phoenix, who's only nibbled at her food. For having given birth just this morning, she's been an absolute trooper to even try to come out for this big dinner. I need to get her back to our rooms as soon as possible. But I also need our brothers to understand some of the things I never told them.

"But we also had a little run-in with our Creator-Father this morning."

"What?" Abaddon leaps up from the table, throwing his napkin down. Romulus and Kharon look similarly shaken. "Where is he?"

"Gone," Phoenix says. "I destroyed his body and sent what's left of his spirit to a realm so dark and faraway, he can never return."

"You don't understand," Kharon says. "He's come back before. Several times—"

Phoenix stands up in spite of still being weak, fists down on the table. "You don't say? He's come back from the dead before?"

Asher immediately gets up and stands beside her, glaring at my brothers. Then she turns to Asher, putting a gentle hand on his arm. "It's fine, darling, I can handle this."

I know she can; it's the only reason *I* didn't leap to her defense. "Layden learned your father's true name many years ago," she says calmly, and I feel all my brothers quickly swing in my direction. Well, there's no one and nothing to hide behind now. So I stand up straight.

"I learned it when I visited the realm of the angels many years ago, treasuring that time in my heart."

"So why didn't you tell us?" Abaddon demands.

"What good is a secret name if you don't keep it secret?" I throw my hands up in the air.

"You and your secrets," Abaddon says, shaking his head.

"You should be glad for his secrets," Phoenix says. "They saved us all today. Your father assumed he had the upper hand on us the whole time and that arrogance was his undoing."

"Why didn't you call us to help you once you saw you were facing our father?" Abaddon asks me accusingly.

"Uh," Phoenix interrupts, now really unleashing her attitude on my sanctimonious older brother, "maybe because we were busy being naked and fucking like rabbits under the influence of a succubus and some mixture of Sabra's and your father's magic?"

Sabra holds up her hands and shrugs. "Guilty."

Abaddon's mouth falls open.

"Which is where the aforementioned birds and the bees talk comes into play," I deadpan from the sidelines.

"Then I was busy giving birth to my lovely children. Wave hello, sweetie," Phoenix says to Asher. She must have mentally instructed him what to do because Asher waves. "Of course, they were babies at first, but they quickly started getting bigger, which was, ya know, a little disconcerting."

"Then our evil father tried to claim them as his own, but my badass wife and I cut him into pieces with his own sword, and with his true name, she..." I look back at her, not really sure what happened next.

But Sabra pipes up. "The goddess used the evil circle of sacrifice I'd laid the day before and the power of his true name to irrevocably send him from his fleshly body and out of this world."

Phoenix nods. "I sent his spirit through a cheese grater, too, before I shoved it into the deepest, darkest spirit pit I could find." Then she sits back down, reaches for another piece of bacon, and starts munching happily.

"Badass!" Raven announces from where she hovers over the center of the table, a sausage between her fingers.

"Raven!" Hannah says. "Table manners!"

Abaddon has risen from his seat and approaches my wife. I frown, unsure of what's happening. But when he gets on his knees and bows at her feet, I relax.

"You have relieved us of a great burden, goddess. I give you my thanks." For once, the great Abaddon is humbled.

"Yeah, well," Phoenix says, only looking mildly uncomfortable. "You can repay us with babysitting."

Epilogue

"Can you believe it's been almost three months since we got married?" I ask, leaning back against Layden's chest as we lay out by the pool of the rental estate, looking up at the stars. His strong arms come around me. We're finally on our honeymoon. A real honeymoon this time since the marriage, against all odds, has become real for us.

Layden huffs out a laugh. "Feels like three *years*."

"Right?" I turn over my shoulder to look at him. Damn, he's so handsome. And mine. Finally, after the long road we had to travel to get here, he's finally all mine.

Ever since the triplets arrived, it feels like all we do is chase them around. Which you'd think would be less work since they're already full-grown. Nope. It's just three times

256

as hard because when they start wandering, they can really run *fast*.

We moved to America last month, along with all the brothers and their wives, to a wide-open property in Montana. There are mountains nearby, and I'm hoping the coming snows will make the brothers feel at home. The mountains should make for good flying for Abaddon and little Raven, and for our kids too when they decide to spread their wings.

We're mostly settled in, and the triplets have come a long way in their two months of life. They can talk now, so it's easier to understand what on earth is going on in those fascinating brains of theirs. I asked Lilith what she was thinking about the other day when she was staring at the sky in our new backyard, and she asked, "What does blue taste like?"

They're fast learners. Too fast, I worry sometimes.

But then again, they aren't exactly babies. I was right when I suspected they were spirits being implanted in my baby's bodies. They *are* my children. But they are also their own spirits and are starting to remember the worlds they came from before. At the same time, this world of flesh and matter is completely new and foreign to them.

They might as well be aliens. In a way, they are, but so am I, so I'm helping them adapt as best they can.

"Do you think your brothers can handle Asmodeus and Lilith while we're gone?" I ask, biting my bottom lip.

"Of course. No one can get past Abaddon. He's had to put up with Remus's tricks his whole life. Plus, Asher is there to help keep his brother in line."

I wince. "That's even worse. I hate how the two of them fight."

Layden just laughed at that. "All brothers fight. And the

fights the two of them have are nothing to the brawls my brothers and I used to get into. We'd destroy entire cities tearing the shit out of each other. You always pull them off each other before they even get in a good punch."

"You say that like you approve."

I feel him shrug underneath me. "Maybe it's better to let the aggression out than keep it bottled up. It worked for my brothers and me."

I roll my eyes. "Your father was a psychopath who forced you to fight each other. It's hardly the path I want for my boys."

His hands come to my shoulders and he begins massaging me. I can't help but melt against the relaxing touch. "Why don't we forget about the boys for once? These two weeks are supposed to be about *us*."

"Do you remember our wedding night?" I ask.

He laughs again, then groans. "Are you kidding? I'll never forget. Worst case of blue balls I ever had."

"What?" I flip around on the lounge so that I'm cradled underneath his arm, right up against his warm chest. It's only a little chilly out, but I love any excuse to snuggle. For as long as I've known Layden, I always cherished even the brush of our fingertips. Any little bit of touch I could get. It still feels extravagant to have the entire length of my body laid out beside his.

"You were turned on that night?"

"You're seriously asking me that? Of course I was. It was our wedding night. And you took off that sexy dress right in front of me and started making all those noises on the bed."

My cheeks heat, and I bury my face against his warm chest. Which is ridiculous because, obviously, we're a real husband and wife now and have done so much more than make pretend sex noises while jumping up and down on a bed. "I was so nervous that night."

"You were?" He sounds astonished. "But you came in so sure and confident. You just grabbed the headboard and started banging away like you knew exactly what to do. I was completely intimidated."

I pull my face back from his chest. "You were?" I shake my head. "I was just mortified that after I'd basically told you to fuck off the last time we'd really spent any time together that Vlad managed to pull not only you but your whole *family* into one of his schemes."

"I thought you were pissed off at me for contacting you when you'd basically told me to fuck off the last time."

"You know why, now, though, don't you?" I look up into his eyes. "You understand?"

He frowns a little. "I think... Maybe?" Then his eyes go a little distant. "I know I'd do anything to protect the kids. Say anything I had to if I thought it would keep them safe."

"And why is that?" I prod.

"What do you mean?" he scoffs. "I love the hell out of those little fuckers."

But then his eyes widen. "Wait. You loved me? Even back then?"

I nod, and his eyes go soft. "Phoenix. What the fuck?" His hands come to my cheeks, and he lowers his head for the softest, sweetest kiss.

Then his hand slides to the back of my head, where he fists my hair, gently tugging my head back. "You've loved me since then but made me wait all this time? All these *years*?"

I blink up into his dark, dangerous eyes and nod again.

His voice is deep and growly when he says, "Well. You've been a bad, bad girl, haven't you?"

I swallow, getting tingly in all sorts of places as I whisper, "Does that mean I deserve a punishment?"

"You know it does."

My breath hitches.

"I think you should run, little goddess," he rumbles. "Run, else you'll get punished."

I feel my eyes widen with thrill. We haven't been able to play any of these little games the way we really want to yet. Not since that day in the limo, and once last week when we barely got started before the boys burst in, arguing about something.

Luckily, I was able to explain away the leash as just some new jewelry their father had bought me that I was trying on. They're still too new to this world and involved in their own squabble to question more.

I roll off the pool lounger and start to sprint away, but before I can get very far, a lasso of blue-white runes lashes around my waist and stops me in place. I squeal and try to squirm out of it, grabbing onto the shining rope. It doesn't burn, but it's also not going anywhere.

Behind me, I feel the warmth of Layden's body as he comes up and tugs off my robe. It falls right off through the shining rope. I'm naked beneath it because we couldn't keep our hands off each other as soon as we got to the luxury mountain cabin tucked away where no one else could see us. It was only the basics, though. No games. Just enough to already have my sex primed so that I'm quickly throbbing again.

"Not fair," I hiss out. My nipples immediately pebble in the cool late fall air.

"I'll show you not fair," he says, and a rope of light splinters off from the other and wraps between my legs, undulating back and forth against my sex. The rope lets out stimulating little lightning pulses against my pussy.

"Layden!"

"Walk to the spa," he orders.

I do, but I'm panting and barely keeping upright. I'm glad the hot tub is already on, with rushing jets that bubble and steam the air.

"In."

Shakily, I climb the steps and lower myself in. I'm briefly worried about the electricity from Layden's rope but know he would never put me in danger. Indeed, when I sink down, the otherworldly blue light just glows from underneath the water. And continues pulsing against my clit.

One pulse hits so good my back arches, pushing my breasts outward. Layden seems to like that a lot. He runs his palm down the valley of my breasts while I'm incoherent with rising pleasure. But then he releases the pulse from below, and I fall back into the water, gasping for breath.

He shucks off his pants and climbs into the glowing water with me. My eyes widen at how hard and full he is. I swallow, then lick my lips as I look up at him.

I want to grab him and take him in my mouth. I want to take control back. It's my natural inclination. To put others under my compulsion and make them bend to *my* will.

Which is why it makes me whine with even more heightened pleasure when Layden sees that and shakes his finger in my face. "Ah ah ah," he says and fuck, he's never been more handsome. He sits down on the bench inside the spa. "Over my lap. Time to take your punishment like a good girl."

I nearly come.

But then he says, "And don't you dare come until I give you permission."

Tears prick at my eyes. I want to come. I want to beg him to let me come. Instead, I obey and bend over his lap, my ass sticking up and out of the water. It's indecent the way I feel his hard cock against my belly, but it thrills me to feel how much I turn him on. I'm not *completely* without control after all.

As if he can hear my thoughts, his rune lasso zaps my pussy, and I jump in his lap.

"Naughty girls don't get to come," he murmurs right in my ear, his lips caressing my lobe. Which is when I realize I was sort of humping his cock with my stomach, trying to entice him with any and all friction. I sigh, but then he zaps me again, and the water splashes with my leap.

He chuckles low and runs his palm over my ass. "Count, sweetheart, and make sure to call me *Sir* when you beg for the next one."

He slaps my ass then, and the nerve-deep satisfaction that runs from my pussy all the way to my toes is just *wrong*. So fucking wrong that it's right.

This is the good, naïve man that I found alone, depriving himself all those years in the woods.

"One. May I please have another, Sir?" I barely manage to croak out.

He thwacks my ass again. Harder, and it's so, so good I'm moaning now and don't bother to hide it.

"*Two.*"

"You didn't say Sir. Now we'll have to start all over again."

I sigh out with pleasure as he lands another, harder smack.

"One. Please give me another, Sir!"

He gives me several in succession, and I beg Sir for every one. Yes, that sweet, tender man I brought home who was so polite and eager to learn is the same one punishing my ass now—

"Ten! Please give me another, Sir!"

But he doesn't, not right away. He runs his palm down over my now sore ass cheeks, and I tremble on his lap. His cock is even stiffer beneath me.

"I should punish you for a long time for how you teased me. All those nights I heard you touching yourself in the shower. Tell me what you thought about, but don't you dare come."

He splashes his hand in the water as I feel my face grow hot from hovering over the water and from embarrassment. "You could hear that?"

"Of course I could. Didn't you want me to hear?"

His finger rubs my pussy under the water, buzzing the electric pulse of his runes like a sex toy against me.

"No! Both doors were closed. I never imagined you could—"

"I could smell you, too."

He inhales long and loudly. "The sweet, tormenting scent of you. Always just right out of reach. Torturing me every night while I lay there cock-stiff in bed."

My eyes all but roll back in my head. His runes pulse against my clit at the same time his thick finger starts to push against my anus. Oh god. I haven't felt him there since that day with the beads...

The runes sneak backward from my pussy right when I'm about to come, biting at the sensitive flesh of my asshole right as his finger presses there. I squeal and splash, and he lets me go.

I turn to look him in the eye, breathing hard.

"It's completely in your control if you get to come again tonight."

263

He holds out a hand and gestures for me to return to his lap.

I look down and the rune lasso has opened around my waist. I have to willingly step back into it.

Oh god. My trembling legs feel even weaker. Weak as I am strong. In control as I submit. *Safe.* Thrilled, I bite my lip as I step back into the bindings of glowing light.

Immediately, Ladyen has me flipped over his lap again.

First, there's his finger. And then, the warmth of his runes. His finger retreats, and he pulls my ass wide open with his hands, only for his runes to inch forward to replace his finger.

I crawl up him as he starts to fuck my ass with his rune light.

"That's right, baby, show me what you can take."

I cry out, overcome by sensation as the runes reach further and further inside me, pressing on so many places I can barely tell inside from out. And then Layden's fingers are there strumming on my clit while other fingers pinch my sore ass.

"Not yet," he says, bent over my back.

I whine as my orgasm creeps higher. "Please, Sir," I pant.

"Not yet."

I'm crying, tears racing down my cheeks by the time he flips me over and the runes slip out of my ass.

"That's my good, good girl," he croons. "Letting me let my monster out." He breathes in the night air and then heaves it out again, his chest like a huge bellows.

"Do you want your monster's cock? Because I've never been hungrier. So fucking hungry for you."

"Please," I beg in a shout. For once in my life, my mind

is blessedly blank except for this one pure desire. "All I want is you. Please fuck me, Sir."

On my back in the spa, Layden holds his hands out and runes spring from them. They lash around my wrists and then more around my ankles, pinning me to the edges of the spa. My ass is in the cauldron of bubbles, my naked breasts out in the chill air.

Layden steps between my legs, and runes begin to glow on his skin. And I mean *everywhere* on his skin. His cock lights up like an otherworldly dildo, and I feel the sizzling buzz of it the second he places it against my pussy.

"Layden," I cry out, tears still slipping down my face as runes arc from his cock back up my ass. His entire body shudders as he slowly thrusts inside me. He grabs my hips and bends over, eyes aflame with white-blue light.

"I love you," he says.

"I love you, too," I cry back. "Now *fuck me*."

He doesn't need to be told twice. His cock buzzes and thrusts and lights me up—literally—from the inside. I can see his glow through my pelvis, and oh my *god,* that feels incredible. Holy shit, this is what it's like to be fucked by an angel. My angel.

The pulse from his runes in my ass presses up against his cock buried deep inside as he thrusts again, and I gasp. My very, very fucked up angel.

"Can I please come?"

"You made me wait so many years," he growls.

I look up into the eyes of my dark angel. Still, always my Layden. I see the young, naïve, tortured man he was. And also the strong, confident lover and father he's become.

"But I'm here now," I whisper.

He dips his lips down to mine as he pulls out and teases the tip of his cock against my sex. His arms are around my waist, hands clutching my ass as he begins to fuck me in earnest, and he kisses me. Pulsating runes begin to throb at my clit as he does.

"Oh," I cry out against his kiss.

"Not yet," he says, tonguing and biting at my lower lip. My hands fist in their restraints.

"Oh!"

"Not yet."

"Oh, Layden. Please!"

"Not yet."

I can only mewl out noises.

"Yes. Now. You may come."

I howl as spasms of pleasure clench and release throughout my entire groin and ass, making me buck so hard in my restraints I'm shocked I don't break Layden's goddamned dick. But he manages to hold on for the ride, fucking me the whole way through as I spasm hard once, and then again, and then again—

The whole world goes white as—

"Lay—" I squeak "—*den!*"

And then I'm just convulsively shuddering while clenching around Layden's cock. I feel him clench my waist and thrust to the hilt inside me.

My wrists and ankles are suddenly let loose, and I'm in Layden's arms, shivering in spite of the warm water jetting all around us.

"Shhhhh," Layden holds me close to his body, cock still buried inside me though he's no longer glowing. "Shhhhh, you're alright."

I nod against his bare chest. "S-s-so, s-s-so good," I chatter.

He lifts me, and I wrap my legs around his waist as he carries me inside. There's already a fire burning in the fireplace. I don't remember him lighting it, but then, he always does seem to think of everything. He lays us down on the couch, and I sigh sadly when he slips out of me.

At first, I have the ludicrous thought that maybe we just made another baby! But no. We put a stop to all that. Maybe not permanently, but at least for now.

Sabra helped us with a contraceptive spell before she took off backpacking on a spiritual quest to *find herself*, as she put it. I told her she should stay, that I would help her work through whatever trauma my grandfather had inflicted, but she just shuddered at the word and said that no, she needed to go find her own way for a while. I let her go, knowing that while I would always consider her family, mine might be too painful a face to see for a long time. Maybe forever.

I have plenty of family now. I just hope the same for her one day.

I shake my head, little spasms still shooting through my legs from the incredibly intense orgasm Layden just gave me. "I'm so glad you came back to me." I roll my eyes. "Even after making you wait so many years."

"Are you kidding? I would have waited forever."

I throw my arms around him in a hug. "I love you so fucking much."

"I love *you* so fucking much," he says into my hair. "And I'll love you forever, my beautiful, beautiful *wife*. It feels so good to be able to call you that and know you feel it as much as I do."

I grin into his chest. "I can't wait for our forever to start now, husband."

* * *

Love Phoenix and Layden's love story? Find out how her parents came together and fell in love against all odds. River is always solving her troubled sister's problems and finds herself accidently caught in the clutches of a nest of vampires, a virgin sacrifice to their latest son. Alex wants nothing to do with his grandfather Vlad. He has no plans of taking the "bite" that will turn him into a monster like the rest of his family.

But on his twenty-fifth birthday, when the thirst for blood is almost insurmountable, his grandfather kidnaps a woman and tosses both of them down into the family dungeon. What's a reluctant, not yet-turned-vampire to do? Can his morality outweigh the overwhelming power of his bloodlust?

Get closure to the story of Phoenix, her parents, and the Monsters' Consorts Saga in *Vampire's Captive*, coming this Summer!

Missed any books in the Monsters' Consort series? Catch up now:

Abaddon & Hannah: Monster's Bride
Thing & Ksenia: Thing
Remus, Romulus & Lauren: Between Brothers

About the Author

STASIA BLACK is a USA Today Bestselling Author of dark contemporary romance and paranormal romance novels.

Stasia grew up in Texas, recently spent a freezing five-year stint in Minnesota, and now is happily planted in sunny California, which she will never, ever leave. She loves writing, reading, listening to podcasts, and going to concerts any time she can manage.

Stasia's drawn to romantic stories that don't take the easy way out. She wants to see beneath people's veneer and poke into their dark places, their twisted motives, and their deepest desires. Basically, she wants to create characters that make readers alternately laugh, cry ugly tears, want to toss their kindles across the room, and then declare they have a new FBB (forever book boyfriend).

* * *

Join Stasia's Facebook Group for Readers for access to deleted scenes, to chat with me and other fans and also get access to exclusive giveaways:

Stasia's Facebook Reader Group

* * *

Want to read an EXCLUSIVE, FREE novella, Indecent: a Taboo Proposal, that is available ONLY to my newsletter subscribers, along with news about upcoming releases, sales, exclusive giveaways, and more?

Get **Indecent: a Taboo Proposal**

When Mia's boyfriend takes her out to her favorite restaurant on their six-year anniversary, she's expecting one kind of proposal. What she didn't expect was her boyfriend's longtime rival, Vaughn McBride, to show up and make a completely different sort of offer: all her boyfriend's debts will be wiped clear. The price?

One night with her.

* * *

Connect with me on social media!

Website: **stasiablack.com**

tiktok.com/@stasiablackauthor

facebook.com/StasiaBlackAuthor

x.com/stasiawritesmut

instagram.com/stasiablackauthor

amazon.com/Stasia-Black/e/B01MY5PIUH

bookbub.com/authors/stasia-black

goodreads.com/stasiablack

Also by Stasia Black

The Virgin Next Door

Reece

Jeremiah